AFTER SETH

Caron Garrod

Copyright © Caron Garrod 2020

ISBN: 979-8-63993-296-0

For my mum, Ann Lefley,

Thank you for everything.

And also for Kate - because I miss you, you daft old bat xxx

PROLOGUE

2010, Suniton Cemetery

The car had arrived almost silently. The rear door opened and a woman burst out, shattering the silence across the bleak hilltop. She called out as she crossed the ground towards the two mourners, striding past the headstones without glancing while she crammed a hat down on her head, fought with her scarf, tried in vain to put up an umbrella. She gave up and tossed it onto the ground at their feet as the women turned to greet her. The small white dog that had trailed her with the handle of its lead in its mouth settled down beside it, gazing at her.

"Good girl, Fitch. Bloody umbrella. Bloody trains. Bloody hell. Why am I always the one who's late? No, don't answer that. Sorry I missed the service. Did I miss any fun?" No-one spoke. She peered down into the open grave beside them. "So he really is dead, then? Did anyone give him a poke with a sharp object? Just to make sure?"

The smaller of her companions let out a sob, while the taller suppressed a smile. "Ssh, Tobes is around somewhere."

"I should bloody hope so. I only came because he asked me." She fished around in the oversized handbag, strung satchel-like across her body. "God, I need a fag. And for God's sake, Imogen, stop snivelling." She pulled out a pack of blue Gitanes, shook the pack and took out three cigarettes. She lit them one by one, passing them to the other two women. "The strongest, smelliest I could think of." She grinned, inhaled deeply on her own cigarette and threw her head back to exhale the smoke into the darkening sky, obviously relishing the feel of the rain on her face, closing her eyes. "Rain." She smiled again and turned to gaze at the other two. "That answers the question, doesn't it? Thunder, lightning or in rain? Although maybe thunder would have been more appropriate. It isn't thundering, is it?" The other two women shook their heads.

She regarded the burning cigarette in front of her. "Okay, ladies. Do you remember how he hated smoking because of the way it made his hair smell? And gave everyone else a hard time because they made him stink? How do you think he'll feel about spending eternity reeking of French cigarettes?" She tossed the butt onto the lid of the coffin below her.

Imogen glared at her but then dropped her cigarette in behind the first.

The other woman caught the arm of the latecomer and turned to face her. "Can you see Tobes anywhere? Or anyone?"

"No, honey. You're clear."

"Good." She tossed in her own cigarette, then put her head back and hawked up a huge spitball which she aimed with perfection onto the brass nameplate below her. "You can go down with that on your face too, you bastard," she growled. "And you can't wipe it off like I had to all those times." She barked out a laugh and glared defiantly at the other two. "I'm tempted to get down there and piss on him too."

"You go, Roz," said the newcomer. "Don't let us stop you. I'll even hold your coat."

"Eleanor, don't." Imogen was tiny and looked even more so inside a coat with a broad fur collar and matching Russian style fur hat. She raised a leather-gloved hand, like a policeman stopping traffic. Tipping the hat back, she turned to face the other two. "I said don't. Don't encourage her. Surely it's enough that he's dead?"

"No, I don't think so." Eleanor stared down at Imogen. "Okay, he's dead. But that just means that he deprived me of the pleasure of killing him, the bastard."

The dog, who until now had been settled quietly on the ground at Eleanor's feet, suddenly jumped up against her.

Roz laid a hand on Eleanor's arm and nodded towards a couple of women approaching from the access road which ran around the cemetery. "Who's that?"

Before either of the others could answer, the taller of the newcomers spoke. "That's an interesting thing to say, 'deprived you of the pleasure of killing him'. Would you care to elaborate?" She was as tall as Eleanor and looked to be in her early to mid-fifties.

"I think not." Eleanor raised her chin defiantly. "And certainly not before we're formally introduced."

"Of course, how rude of me. I am Detective Inspector Beatrice Nixon and I believe you must be Eleanor Chandler." Eleanor shrugged. "And you are Rosalind Peterson?" she said to Roz, who nodded. "Which would make you Imogen Barnes-Colon." Imogen gave a barely perceptible nod.

Detective Inspector Nixon indicated the younger woman beside her. "This is my colleague, Detective Sergeant Alex Wood. I have been asked to reinvestigate the death of Seth Peterson, following information received that he may in fact have been murdered."

The silence that followed the Police officer's announcement was broken only by the sound of the rain drumming on the coffin below them, and by Imogen sobbing softly.

The first person to speak was Eleanor. "Did she just say what I think she just said?" Her eyes swept over the group. "Did she just say murder?" Her companions nodded slowly.

"Yes I did, Ms Chandler. And I will need to speak to each and every one of you."

Eleanor was again rooting in her bag and made no response. DI Nixon repeated herself, but louder this time. Still, Eleanor ignored her.

Roz said quietly, "You can shout at her all you like, Inspector. She can't hear you. And if she can't see you when you speak she has no idea that you are talking."

Eleanor found the cigarette case she had been searching for, took out a rollup, lit it and stared intently at DI Nixon. "In what way, murdered? Jesus, I don't even know how he died." She looked around for Roz. "Toby just said he'd died. I was negotiating a lock when he called, so I couldn't talk. He gave me today's details and I said I'd see him here. I assumed it was a heart attack or something."

"It was… something," murmured Roz.

"What? Look at me! What the hell has been going on? And where is Toby?"

"Calm down, Ellie. He's just coming now." Roz gestured behind Eleanor, who spun around.

"Hello Ellie." Toby Peterson was easily six feet tall but his hair added at least another couple of inches. It had the look of the windswept trees along the seafront, as if Toby had been standing with his back to the prevailing wind all his life.

"Toby! Could you get any skinnier? Come and give me a hug and tell me just what the bloody hell has been going on here. This detective says your father was murdered."

"Murdered? What the hell?" Toby released himself from the hug. "You can't be taking that seriously?" He leaned over and kissed Roz on the cheek. "You okay, Mum?" Roz nodded. He bent down to greet the dog and then glanced at Imogen, still sobbing, and nodded briefly. She didn't acknowledge him.

"Someone's taking it seriously and I've been asked to investigate."

7

"You shouldn't. They're just refusing to acknowledge what a complete shit he really was."

"Oh yes, and who's 'they'?"

"I believe 'they' would be the Concrete-haired Witch – otherwise known as Mrs Marjorie Evans – and my would-be stepmother, Audrey Coombes."

"I don't think you should be calling Granny Marjorie that," muttered Roz.

"Bollocks to that." Toby shuddered. "She gives me the creeps and she always has. Anyway, at a guess I would say it was 'they' who called in the rozzers. Am I right, Detective?"

"You know I couldn't tell you that." No-one spoke. "Well, I'll be in touch." DI Nixon glanced around the group, making a point of eye contact with Eleanor who turned and gazed into the distance. She nodded at her sergeant and they walked away.

Eleanor watched them go and then bent to make a fuss of the dog and pick up her umbrella. Straightening up, she addressed the group. "Pub, I think. I need a drink, several in fact. And I believe there some explaining to do."

*

Beatrice Nixon waited until she was out of earshot and halfway down the hill towards their car before she spoke. "So what do you think of that?"

Alex inhaled deeply, paused for a moment and then spoke slowly, "Well, obviously they're not mourning him too much. Tell me again how we got this case. If they've buried him, surely it was all done and dusted?"

"It was. I'm afraid, Alex, we've got this one because someone upstairs has been leaned on. I only have six weeks until retirement and so they can afford to let me waste my time going through the motions."

"So we're not going to put too much effort into it then?"

"We'll get them all in and talk to them, see if there's anything in it. If we think there is it will get passed on to one of the Murder Investigation Teams. Sorry."

"Don't worry about me, Guv. I'm moving to an MIT anyway, once you're gone. If it comes to anything, I'll probably move with it and I'll have useful background. If it doesn't, then it's all experience."

"Thanks. I know that six weeks of kicking your heels isn't much fun but I'll be glad to have you around. Right, back to the factory. We'll start getting them in tomorrow. You're driving."

In the pub Eleanor commandeered the table next to the log fire, settling Fitch at her feet. "Wow, this place hasn't changed at all," she said as Roz joined her. "Where's Imogen?"

"She said it was all too much for her and she couldn't bear the thought of us sitting around, slagging him off, so she's gone home." Roz rolled her eyes as she pulled up the chair opposite Eleanor's. "Still the drama queen, as you can see."

"I half expected a faint into the open grave. Bet she realised that neither of us would pull her out. And what the hell was that outfit all about? Like something out of Dr Zhivago."

"Who knows? At least she didn't bring Adrian with her."

"Crikey, are they still together? Hasn't he seen the light yet?"

"What can anyone say? He loves her."

"That's not love. Not quite sure what it is, but honey it ain't love. Tobes, my dear boy, you are an angel." Eleanor smiled as Toby came to the table bearing a tray with three glasses, a bottle of champagne, a jug of water and a bowl. Eleanor put the bowl down on the floor and poured some of the water into it for Fitch, while Roz poured the drinks.

Toby touched her arm as she straightened up. "Bernard said to say hi and he's missed you. He's put the second bottle on ice. He did ask if I thought two bottles would be enough." He grinned. "Not sure if that's because it's you two, or because it's Seth. And on that note…" He raised his glass. "To my father, good riddance."

"Good riddance," Roz and Eleanor repeated, raising their own glasses in turn.

"Okay, you two." Eleanor set down her drink and positioned her chair so that she could see each of their faces. "I'm listening. What the hell has been going on here?"

"Nobody knows. He was found dead at a Travelodge north of London and—" Toby started.

"What was he doing there?"

"He'd put a meeting with Marjorie in his diary, but she knew nothing about it. And why would she arrange to meet him so far from the office?"

"So I'm assuming he wasn't supposed to be there?" Eleanor glanced at Roz, who shook her head slowly.

"They ID'd him through some paperwork found with the body… Amongst other things," Toby said grimly.

"So what had happened? Was he there with anyone? Why does that detective think it was murder?"

"I don't know," Toby sighed. "There was no evidence of anyone else and, until now, the conclusion was death by misadventure."

"Misadventure?"

"Death by A-S-P-H-Y-X-I-O-P-H-I-L-I-A," Toby finger-spelled the word as he said it. "Do you know what that is?"

Eleanor stared at him. "I think I have an idea," she said. "But I can't believe it. Is it…?" She tailed off and frowned.

"Better known as autoerotic asphyxiation," Toby was deadpan as he said this. "He was found strangled, with cocaine and champagne beside him. Not to mention a load of hard-core porn magazines." He shook his head and closed his eyes.

"Oh my God, really?" Eleanor had been about to take a drink but paused with the glass halfway to her lips. She thought for a moment, her head on one side, and then put the glass down. "You know, I couldn't stand that bastard, and I thought nothing about him could surprise me but that has."

"According to the post-mortem he didn't appear to be a habitual practitioner," Toby said. "Although how they can tell, I don't know. It appears to have been a one-off and, as I said, the Police could find no evidence of anyone else at the scene, which is why they put it down to misadventure. Of course, Audrey refuses to believe that he could have done it himself. 'Some hussy must have lured him and forced him against his will.'" He mimicked a woman's voice. "She's obviously roped Marjorie into her theory and you know she has all kinds of contacts. I'll bet it's Marjorie who's pulled strings to get the case reopened." He shook his head.

"Who do they think would have done it?" Eleanor mused.

"Who do you think?" Toby responded with a grin.

"You're joking! Me?"

"You, Mum, Imogen." Toby shrugged. "It could be any other of the endless parade of women who he has shagged and then shafted over the years, but you're the ones he called The Coven."

"Bloody hell, this investigation could take years. Well, it wasn't me – unfortunately – and I wouldn't blame your mother if it was her, although I wouldn't think for one second that you would have done it, Roz." Eleanor laughed but then caught sight of her friend's face. "Are you okay, honey?" She regarded Roz with concern.

Roz had been staring gloomily into the fire but now she picked up her glass and downed its contents. "I'm fine, but sick of talking about him. Can we just get drunk now, please?"

"Sure thing, honey. Cheers."

* * *

ROZ

2010, Roz's House

Toby woke me the morning after Seth's funeral. "Mum, phone for you. It's that Detective Sergeant woman. Do you want me to tell her you'll call her back?"

I want you to tell her to fuck off. "Yeah, please."

He appeared in my doorway five minutes later with a cup of tea. "She wanted to know if you could go into the Police Station today. I told her no way, so she said can you be there ten o'clock tomorrow?"

"In the morning?" I groaned.

"Yes, Mum, in the morning. I don't think they suspect you enough to drag you in under the cover of darkness to interview you in the dead of night. Anyway, the guy who operates the thumbscrews only works nine-to-five." He placed the tea on my bedside table and sat down on my bed, sending Mungo scurrying for the door. "You're not worried about it, are you?"

"Of course not, it's all completely ridiculous. Just a monumental waste of everyone's time."

"I know," he sighed. "I thought it was pretty obvious what had happened. And even if someone did kill him, really, who cares? They deserve a medal, not locking up."

"Tobes…"

"I know, I know. He is – was – my father, but he wouldn't win any prizes for Father of the Year, would he? And I can't forgive him for the way he treated you, Mum. I thought yesterday would be the end of it, not the start of a whole new nightmare."

"Oh sweetie, it's not another nightmare. It'll be a short interview, that's all. I didn't do anything, so I've nothing to worry about, have I? Other than having to get up at the crack of sparrows fart to get to the Police Station for ten."

"I can drop you off on the way to College."

"Ah, thank you sweetie." I grinned. "You're so good to your decrepit old mother."

"Just think of it as my stint of caring in the community." He stood up and leaned forward, ruffled my hair and kissed me on the tip of my nose. Then, raising his voice and speaking slowly, "Now, drink your tea, dear, before it goes cold. Do you need any help finding your teeth or getting dressed?"

"Get out of here!" I grabbed a pillow and threw it at him, but he had already dodged through the door.

*

He tried to insist on coming in with me when we pulled up outside the Police Station the next day. "I'm allowed to worry about you, Mum," he said when I refused. "At least let me walk you inside."

"No, you're not. I'm the mother, worrying is my job. Yours is to go to college, study hard and become fabulously wealthy, then keep your mother in the champagne lifestyle that she's been missing all these years."

"Really, Mother, champagne? That's so 1980s. I've always thought that there's a secret Thatcherite lurking inside you, desperate to get out."

"How very dare you? Now, bugger off!"

*

Despite having got to the Police Station in plenty of time for our ten o'clock meeting, I was still sitting in the reception area an hour later when the woman who had been with Inspector Nixon yesterday finally came to meet me. She introduced herself again as Detective Sergeant Wood and led me through a myriad of corridors, into a small interview room where Inspector Nixon joined us a few moments later.

We took our seats, with them on the opposite side of the table from me. There was a little small talk, while DS Wood set up a tape recorder and then DI Nixon started. "Mrs Peterson, you are aware that you are under caution?"

I swallowed, hoping I didn't look as nervous as I felt. "Is that the not having to say anything stuff?"

"Yes. And you are quite sure that you don't want a solicitor present?"

"Do I need one?" *I hope to God I don't, I certainly can't afford one.*

DS Wood smiled. At least, I think it was supposed to be a smile. "You tell us, Mrs Peterson."

"I don't think I do. Depends whether you're planning to stitch me up or not." I giggled. "Ha, that was a joke by the way. Sorry, I can't help it, I talk too much when I'm nervous." *For Christ's sake, Roz, pull yourself together. This is not the time for one of your stream of consciousness rambles.*

DI Nixon regarded me with a cool gaze. "Why are you nervous, Roz? May I call you Roz?"

"I suppose." *Like I have any choice?* "Let's see… Why am I nervous? I'm in a Police Station where I can't smoke, can't drink, and you're talking to me about whether I killed my ex-husband. I can't think why that would make me nervous, can you?"

DS Wood not-quite smiled again. "Well, it would if you're guilty, I suppose."

"Of course I'm not. Why would I kill him?"

"You had plenty of motive," DI Nixon said.

"Did I? Once, maybe. But I don't see what motive I would have had now." *Other than I hated him now as much as I ever did. God, Roz, don't say that out loud.*

DS Wood's voice broke into my thoughts. "He was about to marry Mrs Coombes."

"And?" *That's no motive for murder, poor deluded cow.*

"And you still had feelings for him."

"Ha! You are joking?"

DI Nixon riffled through the file in front of her. "I think you did, Roz. His phone records show that you phoned him a lot, at least two or three times a week, up until a few months ago. Round about the time he announced his marriage."

"Because I could never get him to take his responsibilities seriously. I could never get him to pay what he owed for Toby, or to make proper arrangements for seeing his son. I didn't want to talk to him, he enjoyed making me have to grovel."

"But Toby's, what, eighteen? Couldn't he have dealt with the arrangements for seeing his father on his own?"

"He's just eighteen. And maybe he could have done if his father had ever returned his calls, or even just bothered to contact him himself. Tobes gave up on him."

"So why didn't you?"

"Because if I didn't, then it would come back to me in the end. He was his father, for crying out loud. And if he didn't see Tobes, he wouldn't give me any of the money he owed me."

DS Wood cleared her throat. "It's a court-appointed sum, surely? It makes no difference whether he sees his son or not."

"You'd think, wouldn't you? That's how it's supposed to work, but it's not how Seth worked. He'd taken the number of days he was supposed to see his son, divided that into the maintenance I had been awarded, and he would deduct it if he didn't see Toby, even when it was his fault. 104 days a year." *How could he reduce his son to an equation? He claimed to love him, but he knew exactly how much each minute he spent with our precious, wonderful boy was 'worth' to him.*

DI Nixon looked down again at her notes. "But then you stopped? After he announced his marriage."

"After Toby turned eighteen." *And the timing of the two events was not coincidental. He marries Audrey, becomes entitled to half of her everything, but no longer has to take care of Toby or me. He must have been so relieved that the old cow Marjorie has lasted as long as she has. We'd have no claim on the millions he's probably conned her into leaving him in her will.*

"So it wasn't that you realised you would never get him back and set about planning to murder him? While his son would still be his legal heir?"

"Christ almighty, is that what you think?"

DI Nixon sat back in her chair and stared at me. "Isn't that how it happened? We have access to all his papers and it appears he hadn't made a new will."

Shit. "I think I had better call a solicitor now, please."

DI Nixon nodded to DS Wood. "Okay, interview suspended at 11:29. We'll leave you here, Mrs Peterson, while we wait for a solicitor. Don't go anywhere."

Don't go anywhere. Does she think she's funny? I'm not even sure if I'm under arrest or not. Christ, it's cold in here. Do they keep these places cold on purpose? So that you'll confess just so you can go somewhere warm or get a cup of tea. Or a cigarette, I'm gasping. What is this all about? Who the hell knows? He seemed so harmless the first time I met him — can't believe it was twenty years ago — with those eyes. God, those eyes…

*

Isn't it funny how the big events of your life can disguise themselves as trivialities? One moment I was at my desk proofing the insert for the Lads in Leather CD, and the next I was trapped – like a rabbit in headlights – in a penetrating gaze from the deepest, darkest brown eyes I had ever seen. As they blinked, and went from full beam to dipped, I became aware that Stuart – my boss and my friend for many years – was introducing me to their owner.

"Roz, this is Seth Peterson from Peterson Management. Seth, Roz Hill – my right-hand woman. Without whom, all this…" He waved his hand airily, encompassing the offices of our independent record label and its staff. "… would crash and burn and we would all be sleeping on the streets."

"Hardly, Stu. I'm pretty sure you wouldn't miss me until the photocopier broke down, or you ran out of coffee for the coffee machine."

"Oh, fair Rosalind, how little you know. Roz looks after all our new signings," he explained to Seth. "Nurtures all the little darlings just like a mother hen, including giving them a well-aimed peck on the backside when they need it. Now, I'll leave you two to it. Play nice, Seth. Roz is very precious to me, okay?" Stu disappeared into his office.

"I've never heard of Peterson Management. You don't manage one of our acts?"

"We're a new company, but I'm an old friend of Stu. I have a couple of new acts I'm hoping you're going to sign. I guess that would mean you and I would be working together a lot? I'll look forward to that." Once again those headlights flipped up to full beam.

"Probably, if they're signed." *Oh, Seth Peterson, you know exactly what effect those eyes – and that smile – have on any female you turn them on. I think you and those eyes could prove to be quite dangerous.*

*

Is there anything more seductive than a man who hangs on your every word? Throughout the next couple of weeks or so, after that initial meeting, we had many more – Stu signed both his acts, even though they weren't great; it seemed men were not immune to his charms, either – and nearly always ended up finishing the discussions over dinner in some quiet pub or cosy restaurant somewhere. Before long, the business took second place to the personal. I would find that I had told him things about myself that no-one else knew: how I felt about my mother's death from cancer, my father's subsequent drink problem; how it felt to more or less bring up my sister alone afterwards and how I longed – but was equally afraid – to have a child of my own.

And he would tell me about his daughter, Donna, and the guilt he felt about her and her mother, Catherine. "I know I treated them both badly. I don't know how I could make it up to Donna, she's only four. I just wish I had the chance to do it all again." It was so refreshing to hear a man talk openly about his regrets and his feelings. "It's only been a couple of months and I still feel so raw. Thank God for my friend Dave, I'm still sleeping on his sofa. He's such a good mate, we've known each other since college."

We both knew where we were heading, but were taking the time to enjoy the journey. But the evening came when those velvet eyes regarded me from across the table even more intensely than they ever had before.

"Rosalind Hill, are you going to take me to bed, or not?"

*

If I'm completely honest, that first time was a disappointment. In fact, the first few times were. It was almost as if he felt no need to please a woman, having deigned to go to bed with her. I had to do something about it, not just for me but for the women who would no doubt follow me - he struck me as too self-centred to be the settling-down type. In the meantime, I enjoyed my role as teacher. I didn't let him out of my bed for the whole of that weekend and, wow, did I make the most of it.

I couldn't tell you when he moved in. There was no big decision or discussion. One day I just realised he hadn't gone home for a while. "I ought to start charging you rent," I joked while we were lying in bed.

He sat up and rolled over on top of me, pinning my arms to the pillows. "I pay you in kind," he growled, his eyes darker than ever above me. And then he smiled. And then he began moving inside me and the conversation was forgotten.

*

We'd been together for about six months and were firmly established as a couple. Seth was revelling in the social side of launching his acts, but I have never been into all that stuff and avoided the parties when I could. I still had a job to do, after all. I was at my desk doing just that one morning when Stu asked to see me in his office.

"Come in, Roz, and close the door." Stu had never gone against his own 'Open Door' policy before. I wondered what was coming next. "I've decided to let both Seth's acts go. I'm sorry."

Although it didn't affect me directly, I knew why he was apologising. "You want me to tell Seth?"

"No, I'll do it. But Roz…"

Yes?"

"Be careful. You've known Seth only when things are going well for him. I've known him for a long time."

"And…?"

"Sweetie, I love you. You know I do, and I would hate you to get hurt. You know where I am if you need me, right?"

I frowned. "Right. But I'm not sure what you're trying to say. Seth's a businessman. He'll be fine. Disappointed, but fine."

"Just remember what I said, okay?"

*

"That fucking stupid no-talent waster." As I walked through the door at home, Seth's words hit me with as much force as the phone hit the wall beside me.

"Hey–"

"Did you know about this? Did you know he was going to drop both of them? Did you put him up to it? Is this your way of dumping me?"

"No! He only told me this morning." I had never seen Seth lose it like this before.

"And you didn't think to warn me? Some fucking loyalty that is."

"How could I? Your phone's been engaged all afternoon. And don't question my loyalty. I've done everything I can to help you."

"Oh really?" He sneered. "So why have I been dropped then?"

"First of all, you haven't been dropped; your acts have. Because they're just not up to scratch. And the decision was nothing to do with me."

Seth strode across the room and grabbed my wrist, twisting it so that I had to turn towards him. His face was against mine, white, as if all the blood had drained from it. His eyes were almost black with temper. "Are you sure?"

"Of course I'm sure. And let go, you're hurting me. Christ, I've never seen you like this." My eyes were filling with tears from the pain.

He seemed to gather himself together and released his grip. His eyes began to soften. "Oh my God, Roz, I'm so sorry. It's just that I care for those guys, you know? And not only that…"

"What?"

18

"Never mind." He let go of my wrist and threw himself back onto the leather sofa we had bought just a couple of weeks ago. Well, I had bought. He had brought the wrong credit card out with him when we had gone shopping.

"Tell me."

"All my money was tied up in those two acts. I don't know what I'm going to do now." He put his head in his hands and groaned.

I sat down on the coffee table we had bought on the same shopping trip, so that our knees were touching. I took hold of both of his hands, wincing as I did so. "Find another label, or find another act. You can stay here, you know that. And I'll help you as much as I can. We'll get through this."

"You're amazing, you know? I guess that's why I love you."

He had never told me before that he loved me and as he stood, picked me up and carried me to bed only one thought was whirling through my mind. *He loves me.*

*

"Roz, have you seen the house prices in Brighton?"

"What?" I had only just walked in from work and Seth's question came out of the blue.

"Look, we could sell this place and buy a huge place down there. With no mortgage if we get the right place."

It was only a few weeks since the row. Neither of us had mentioned it since, but Seth hadn't taken rejection well. His first reaction had been to take it out on the two acts, who had promptly sacked him, and unemployment didn't suit him at all.

"But I love this flat. My mum left it to me, as you know, and I like Ladbroke Grove. And what about my job? I can walk there in ten minutes."

"You could go freelance. The music scene down there is bubbling. We could both work from home." He waved the Brighton property paper at me.

Where did he get that from? "And make babies?" I'd given up worrying about sounding desperate. I was desperate. I was twenty-seven and my ovaries weren't getting any younger.

"If you really want to, but wouldn't you rather have some fun first?"

"Yeah, I guess."

When he had an idea, he could be a force of nature. That weekend, we had Donna. We caught a train to Brighton and as soon as I walked out of the station, smelt the air and heard the seagulls, I was hooked. The three of us strolled hand-in-hand along the promenade, eating ice cream and watching the holidaymakers enjoying the sunshine. It was like a corny montage from some Rom Com film, but I was prepared to believe it.

*

The country may still have been reeling from the worst property slump ever, but the flat was only on the market for two or three weeks before some bank snapped it up as a corporate flat. My beautiful home, left to me by my mother, was going to be used for visiting Japanese bankers. I tried not to be upset, I tried to look on it as a positive move, but I was going to miss it.

But as soon as I walked into the apartment in Kings Gardens, I knew I had found the ideal replacement. I felt I had come home. I wandered around the spacious rooms and stood at the sitting room windows looking out over Brighton Lawns.

"Hey, I can have a study." Seth came up behind me and put his arms around my waist. "And have you seen the bath?"

"We can have a study." I felt the familiar stirring as he began kissing the back of my neck. "Until we need a nursery."

"We've got plenty of time for that." His lips were against my ear and his breath was hot. "Let's have some fun practising first. So shall I tell the agent we'll have it?"

"Mm-mm."

"And the best thing of all is no mortgage. We might even get some change from Norburn Street. We could put it into the business."

Business? What business?

*

I have always loved my work, but these days it was even more precious as a distraction from Seth's grumpiness at home, as his enforced unemployment continued. So I was totally absorbed when I answered the phone one afternoon at the end of September.

"Rosalind, my dear. It's Andrew Dillon."

I loved the sound of my solicitor's plummy baritone voice. Since I was a teenager it had meant security and safety. "Andrew, how are you? Is there a problem with the sale?"

"No, not with the sale. I do, however, have a small problem with the purchase. I had been proceeding with the sale of Norburn Street and the purchase of Kings Gardens on the assumption that you were going to be the sole owner."

"Yes, that's right."

"Ah, it's just that I have had a Mr Peterson on the phone this morning and he seems to be under the impression that he is going to be a joint owner of Kings Gardens. He became quite aggressive when I said that I was unaware of him."

"Oh dear."

"My dear, your mother left you the property in Norburn Street so that you would always have your independence. I don't know who this Mr Peterson is, but as an executor of your mother's will and a trustee of the fund, I can't allow you to sign over half of your only asset. Unless he's putting in half of the finance?"

"No, Andrew, he isn't." I sighed. "I'll talk to Seth tonight. And I'm sorry if he was rude to you."

Andrew chuckled. "I'm a lawyer, my dear, it comes with the territory. You take care of yourself and I'll be in touch when we are ready to exchange contracts."

"Thanks, Andrew, and give my love to Margaret."

I sighed again as I put down the phone. Stuart looked over at me and made a T shape with his fingers. "Yes, please, with extra sugar."

"Trouble?" In the corner of the office, Stu busied himself with kettle, mugs and tea bags.

"Not really, just Seth getting the wrong end of the stick."

"Is everything okay with you two? I thought you were all loved up, with the move and everything."

"We are. He's just finding unemployment a bit frustrating, and I can't blame him. I'd hate it, too. That's why I wouldn't leave you until he's got something going. No point in both of us succumbing to the sofa and Countdown."

"Is he behaving himself, though?" Stuart put the tea down on my desk and perched himself on the corner, looking down at me.

"What are you trying to say?" I busied myself tidying the papers that he had dislodged.

"Nothing, my sweet. I'm just taking an interest."

21

"Is there something I should know?" I forced myself to look him in the eye. This wasn't the first cryptic comment Stuart had made about Seth.

"No, my darling. But you know that Gavin and I both care about you? If you ever had any problems, I hope you'd come to us."

"There's no problem, okay?" I knew Seth had a temper, I'd seen quite a bit of it lately, but it was just the frustration of being out of work. As soon as we got to Brighton I knew things would be much calmer.

*

It was starting to be a familiar feeling that as I crossed Ladbroke Grove towards home in the evenings, my stomach began sinking a little. In fact, I had taken to dropping into the bar at a nearby hotel to buy myself a little 'cheerio' – as my granny used to call them: a couple of shots of vodka, just to take the edge off Seth's mood when I got home.

I'd told Stuart that there was no problem and I was sure that was the truth, but Seth wasn't taking unemployment very well. He seemed to resent me for still working, even though there was nothing to stop him looking for more acts to manage. It was as if he was in limbo and his life couldn't restart until we got to Brighton.

This evening, however, I didn't have to worry about Seth's mood. He wasn't in and there was no trace of him. Everything was gone: clothes, CDs, everything. I looked around for a note or some form of explanation but found nothing. Bewildered, I went through to the bedroom and sat on the edge of the bed. My address book was on the pillow, open at the entry for Andrew Dillon, and the bedroom phone was next to it, off the hook. I replaced the handset, collected a bottle of wine and a glass from the kitchen and went back to lay down on the bed and think through my options. I had drunk half the bottle before I even noticed, so I lay back and closed my eyes to try and slow myself down.

I was jolted out of some very disturbing dreams by the phone ringing. I grabbed it quickly. "Seth?"

"No, my darling, it's your rather confused boss here. Were you booked for a day off today?"

"What? No. Today? What? It's only…" I glanced at the window and realised that it was, indeed, daylight outside.

"Roz, darling, is everything all right?"

I dragged my attention back to the phone. "Yes, of course, sorry. I must have overslept. I'll be there in twenty minutes."

"Are you sure? Because if there's something wrong, I'm sure we can cover."

"Yes, I'm sure," I snapped. "For Christ's sake Stu, I just overslept. Okay?"

Stu had given me my first job when I had arrived in London, fresh-faced and full of dreams, from Norfolk. We had clicked instantly and had built up his business together. I had never not turned up without warning. Neither had I ever snapped at him and now I had done it twice in two days. I knew I was going to be facing an interrogation when I got to work.

He was full of concern when I finally made it into the office. "Do I have to beat it out of you? Or force-feed you chocolate until you tell me?" His head was on one side as he regarded me intently.

"God, no, not the chocolate! Anything but chocolate." I smiled. Stu knew I hated the stuff. "It's quite simple. Seth's gone away for a couple of days and I've become rubbish at sleeping alone. So I had a few drinks last night and forgot to set the alarm. Mystery solved." It was the best I had been able to come up with on the ten-minute walk into the office.

"Hmm." Stu was obviously unconvinced. "And Neil Armstrong really did land on the moon in a spacecraft made of tin foil and balsa wood."

"Yup, one small step for man and all that." I sat down at my desk, put on headphones and made a great show of selecting the studio tape of one of our new bands. I raised my eyebrows to Stu challenging him to continue questioning. He knew me well enough to know that the 'discussion' was over.

*

I suppose I had been sitting, thinking, for about an hour when Sergeant Woods came back into the room, making me jump.

"Roz, your solicitor's here. But he's not the duty solicitor – they never get here that quickly. He says he's—"

"Thank you, Detective Sergeant." A sharply dressed man, who I would guess to be in his 30s, strode into the room and placed his briefcase on the table. "I can take it from here. I'd like some time alone with my client, please. Now, I understand she is not under arrest and I can see that you haven't offered her any refreshment, so I will be taking her out to lunch and we will return in an hour to continue this interview. Is that all right with you Roz?"

I was sitting, mouth agape, trying to process this latest development. The beautifully cut suit, the silk tie, the incredibly shiny brogues and the radio four announcer's voice all put me in mind of Andrew Dillon, but this man was thirty years too young and anyway Andrew was 150 miles away in Norfolk. More to the point, he didn't know I was here. "Er, yes," I stammered. "That's fine." Anyone who could get me out of here to have a cigarette and a drink, particularly if they happened to be a handsome younger man, was fine with me.

"Right then, let's go. Detective Sergeant, perhaps you would be good enough to show us out?" He stepped behind my chair to pull it out for me then picked up his briefcase and went to the door and held it open.

Sergeant Wood appeared as astonished as I was. "Of course," she muttered. "It's this way."

As we hurried through the corridors behind her, I hissed, "Sorry, who exactly are you? Not that I'm ungrateful, but that suit makes me think you are not the kind of solicitor I can afford."

He chuckled. "Let's get out of here and I'll explain everything."

Once we were outside the Police Station I fished my cigarette case and lighter out of my pocket, took out one of the cigarettes I had carefully rolled that morning and lit it. I offered one to the solicitor who shook his head, but led me around the corner to a bench and indicated I should sit.

"No thanks," I said. "I seem to have been sitting for hours. I could actually do with a drink."

"Good plan. Let's find a pub, but before we do I should explain. I can do so as we walk." He held out his arm in a curiously old-fashioned gesture and, still somewhat bemused but with an instinctive feeling that I could trust this man, I took it and we

24

started walking arm-in-arm like two old friends. "I'm Ian Dillon, Andrew's son. Toby called his Aunt Cecilia in America, last night, after you told him you were going into this meeting on your own. She rang my father and he rang me. I specialise in criminal law and I have a practice in London, so I cleared my calendar for the day and caught a train straight down here—"

"Now you are definitely sounding too expensive for me. Let's cut through the park, there's a café in there that sells wine and it's on your way back to the railway station."

"Roz, if my father thought that I had left you to deal with this... ah... situation alone, he would disown me and rightly so. You don't need to worry about my fee. If it makes you feel any better, I'll count it as part of my pro bono charity work, okay?"

I was still feeling uncomfortable, but figured I needed all the help I could get if those detectives really were thinking that I could have killed Seth. "Okay."

In the café, over sandwiches and a glass of wine (for me) and an orange juice (for Ian), I gave him a brief outline of the situation. We agreed that I could tell my story as I wished, but that he would step in if he felt I was likely to give the detectives any grounds to suspect me.

I phoned Toby to reassure him and thank him for the intervention and also to ask him to ring Ce-Ce and let her know that I was okay.

Returning to the Police Station, Ian told the detectives that I was prepared to tell my story and that if they had any questions they could ask them as I went through. They seemed content to let me do this, after he explained that there was quite a lot of background I felt they needed to know.

*

That evening, after I had scrubbed the flat from top to bottom – my usual reaction to a stressful situation was to clean – I sat down with a bottle of wine I'd bought on my way home from work. The only phone number I had for anyone Seth knew was Dave, the friend whose sofa he had been sleeping on when I first met him.

"Hi Dave, it's Roz." I tried to sound breezy and unconcerned. "Seth's Roz? Seth's away at the moment and like an idiot I've lost the piece of paper with the contact details. I can't even remember where he's gone. I don't suppose he mentioned anything to you?"

"Me? No. I don't know him that well. He just crashed here a couple of times after a row with Catherine."

"Oh? Sorry, I thought you'd known him from College?"

"Yeah, that's right. But we only got in touch a short while back. I knew Catherine better at College. I don't suppose you've tried her?"

"Er, no."

"No? To be honest, I wouldn't be at all surprised if he was back there. They were always breaking up and getting back together at College."

"Okay, thanks."

The only other person who had known Seth a long time was Stuart, but I wasn't going to call him. I thought it unlikely that Seth had gone back to Catherine. It was some time since they left College, I didn't think that Dave's theory was worth anything. Okay, Donna was five now and they'd only been apart six or seven months, but he'd moved on and now he loved me. Right?

My thoughts were interrupted by the telephone ringing. I picked it up, trying not to get too hopeful.

"Roz, is that you?" Donna's voice sounded small but also echo-y.

"Donna, darling, how are you? Are you okay?"

"I'm fine, thank you. Why don't you love my daddy anymore?" *What the fuck?*

"I do still love him, darling. Why do you say that?"

"He says you don't love him anymore and now we can't move to Brighton with you and we won't be able to see you anymore." All of a sudden I realised what the echo was on the line. He was with her and he had the call on speakerphone.

"Sweetheart, Daddy's got a bit muddled and he's made a mistake. I can't find him at the moment, so if you see him please will you ask him to call me and then I can talk to him?"

"But he's—" The line went dead.

I couldn't believe that Seth would be so manipulative as to use his daughter like that. I was still fuming when the phone rang again.

"It's me."

"What the fucking hell was that all about? How could you drag that poor little girl into our row? Hell, it's not even a row. It's you, behaving like a spoiled brat because something isn't going your way. You haven't even given me a chance to explain."

"What's to explain? Love is supposed to be about trust and you don't trust me enough to put my name on the deeds of the new apartment."

"It's not like that. Please let me explain."

"I'll meet you at Capriccio's. Let's at least be civilised and talk about this over a meal."

*

I didn't feel much like eating, but Seth wouldn't have dreamed of missing a meal under any circumstances. While he tucked into two courses, I toyed with a salad, downed a couple of glasses of wine and explained.

"… And so it's not that I don't trust you, it's just that I can't give you half my property until I'm thirty, under the terms of my mother's will. Or until I'm married. I'm so sorry, I should have explained. I just didn't think." I drained my glass and tried to pour another, but the bottle was empty. Seth signalled to the waiter who brought another one.

"I thought you didn't love me enough to trust me." Seth's eyes had been dark black when we first sat down, but now they were softening.

"How could you think that? And how could you just walk out with no explanation?" Even to myself I sounded like a whining child, but I couldn't help it.

"There seemed to be no point in hanging around under the circumstances. But it was cruel and I shouldn't have frightened you like that."

"No. I love you so much and I thought you'd left me for ever." *Wait a minute, what are you doing? Roz Hill, you don't plead and you sure as hell don't cry.*

"I nearly did. But I'm back now and everything will be all right, as long as you always tell me what's going on."

"I will. Of course I will and I'm sorry."

"Finish up your drink, darling. And don't cry, I hate snivelling."

"Sorry." I sniffed.

"Come on, let's get you home."

"Thank you."

*

"Oh my God, Roz darling, it's wonderful." Stu stood at the sitting room window, just as I had done a few months ago, and gazed out over the Lawns. "You are a lucky girl."

"I know." I smiled. "Now, stop ogling the talent and help me get all of this sorted out."

"Talent?" Gavin appeared in the doorway, clutching a piano stool. "Show me."

"Nothing to compare with you, my dear." You could see the love written plainly on Stuart's face. "Where are you planning on putting that?"

"I'm looking for the corresponding piano?"

"There isn't one." I smiled at the look of confusion on Gavin's face. "I always meant to buy one, but haven't got around to it yet. I don't suppose the neighbours will thank me if I get one here."

"Call me stupid—"

"Hello stupid," Stuart and I chorused and then gave each other a high five.

"Children, please. It may sound like a stupid question, but where is the point in a piano stool without a piano?"

"It was my mother's. I have that, and I have Jack. Things that she loved and I can never part with."

"Jack?" Stuart asked.

"This ratty old thing." Seth was in the doorway and chucked the old teddy bear directly at Stu's head. "It must be riddled with germs; you should throw it out."

"No, I love him. And I've loved him longer than I've loved you, so think on." I laughed.

"He'll be easier to get rid of," Seth snarled, his eyes starting to darken.

I felt my stomach sink, but the mood was rescued by Gavin.

"Look, I've found the kettle. Now let's have a cup of tea before those removal men get here. How clever of you to find the most gorgeous removal men in London."

"Is that all you ever think about?" Seth didn't like Gavin and didn't bother to hide it.

"Sometimes, darling, I think about food. Now do you want sugar in your tea?"

*

By Sunday night, everything was in place and the four of us sat around our brand-new dining table, sharing an Indian takeaway and several beers.

Stuart raised his bottle. "To the divine Rosalind and her new home. May you both be happy and healthy here, beyond your wildest dreams."

"Thank you, Stuart. And Seth and I would like to thank you both for your friendship and support, wouldn't we darling?"

"Yeah, thanks." Seth had been in a strange mood all weekend. I had put it down to having Gavin around. "We really appreciate your help moving into our new home." He placed an emphasis on the 'we' and 'our'. Stuart caught my eye and raised an eyebrow.

"Well, thank you both," I said cheerily. "And here's to you both accompanying me on my very first commute tomorrow morning."

*

Seth barely stirred when the alarm went off at six the next morning. When I brought him a cup of tea just before I left at seven he raised his head slightly and mumbled his thanks before going back to sleep.

"I'll be back by eight tonight," I said and kissed him.

"Mmm." He rolled away from me and pulled the duvet tighter around himself.

Stuart, Gavin and I let ourselves out of the apartment and set off for the station.

"Christ, it's cold." Gavin was muffled up in a scarf.

"Well, duh, it's December." I laughed. "Only ten days until Christmas."

"You think you're going to do this every day?" Gavin shuddered.

"Of course she is." Stuart chimed in. "She's a professional. Now shift that gorgeous arse of yours, my darling, and let's get to the station."

*

"Happy Christmas, darling."

I opened my eyes to the smell of warm croissants. Seth was sitting on the bed with a tray laden down with goodies, including a bottle of champagne and a jug of orange juice. "Mmm, yummy, what have I done to deserve this?"

"You don't have to have done anything. Have some champagne." He poured out two glasses and handed one to me.

"Er, the orange juice?" I raised my eyebrows.

"That's just for show and, as for what you've done, I could think of one thing you can do…"

"Oh wait, I have to go and get my cap." I sat up and started to get out of bed.

"Let's not bother." He leaned towards me, his dark eyes shining. "How would you like a baby for Christmas?" He started kissing my neck.

"I thought you didn't want to yet." I couldn't believe that I was putting the brakes on, but… "And shouldn't we wait until you start earning some money?"

"Let's not worry about that. We have the balance from the sale and I'm bound to find some acts locally. I've spotted some potentials already."

"The money from the sale is supposed to go into savings, for emergencies. I still think maybe we should wait…"

"You aren't going to have a choice." With a grin, he climbed on top of me and proved his point.

That day was so lovely. It was just the two of us and we stayed in bed for the whole morning. Christmas lunch was a selection from one of the delis on Church Road, bought the day before, and afterwards we got dressed and went for a walk along the prom. We'd missed the Christmas Day swimmers but there were plenty of brave souls paddling.

I've always loved walking on Christmas Day, watching the families out and about with the children trying out new bikes or roller skates, or clutching their new toys. Seth was as excitable as any of them. He had bought himself a leather coat for Christmas and was in his element, strutting along the prom showing it off.

"That might be us next year." He nodded towards a young family with a toddler, barely able to walk, as they strolled very slowly hand-in-hand.

I should have been ecstatic that he had finally come around to my way of thinking but instead, deep inside me, I had a tiny feeling of foreboding. I couldn't explain it, not even to myself, so I brushed it away, resolving to bring up the discussion after Christmas was over. In the meantime, however, I would not be consigning my cap to the bathroom bin just yet.

*

I don't know if Seth had picked up on my reluctance, or if he had worked out my plan, but he carefully avoided any sort of discussion over the next week or so before I went back to work. I continued to use my cap whenever I could, but I would frequently be woken up by Seth entering me from behind and it would all be over before I could protest. I tried to talk to him about it. "That really creeps me out."

"Most women would find it sexy."

"Once or twice, yes, but not every day to the exclusion of anything else." I tried to sound as if I were making a joke. "I mean, when do I get my share?"

"I hadn't realised that you were keeping score."

"Don't be silly, it's just that now and then I'd like a little give-and-take. That's all."

Stuart had given me (and him) an extended Christmas break, so it was twelfth night before I was back in my office. I got in early and immediately phoned the local Family Planning Clinic. They came up trumps with an appointment in two days' time.

"I'd like to go on the Pill, please," I said to the young female doctor who was interviewing me. "As soon as possible."

"Is there any chance you might be pregnant now?"

"God, I hope not, but I guess so."

"We'll have to test you then, before we do anything else."

*

Of course it came out positive, as I had known it would. So why did I burst into tears when she told me? This, only a couple of months ago, was all I had thought I wanted in the world. But that was before Seth had begun scaring me with his apparently obsessive need to have a baby.

"Let's make an appointment for next week, when we can discuss your options." Dr McIlwain smiled sympathetically. "In the meantime, there's no need to worry. From what you said you can't be more than a few weeks gone. You have plenty of time."

But I knew I had no options and no time. I knew I wouldn't be able to keep it from Seth; he had a way of telling if I was hiding something from him. I called him from Victoria. "Hey, it's me."

"Hey babe, I'm glad you called. I'm going to be out tonight until late. There's a couple of bands playing locally I want to see."

"Oh, okay."

"What were you calling for?"

"Nothing, just to say hi. I'll see you later."

"You probably won't, I'll be in really late. You'll be in bed. I'll see you in the morning before you go to work."

"Yeah, okay." But I knew he wouldn't. He rarely woke up when I left for work and if he'd had a heavy night the night before, I knew he wouldn't surface before midday. That gave me another twenty-four hours to think about my 'options', as Dr McIlwain had put it.

*

But there were no options. If I was completely honest with myself, then there never had been. I would have the baby. It only remained for me to tell Seth.

"I have news," I said, as we lay in bed the following Saturday. "I went to see a doctor last week—"

"Oh wow, babe. Are you pregnant? That's fantastic! When?"

He's been expecting this. He decided he wanted a baby and it never occurred to him that it wouldn't happen. "I'm not sure yet, it's early days. Are you really pleased?"

"Of course I am, and it's what you wanted too, isn't it? Wow, how amazing are we? We made a baby."

"Yes, we did." I tried to make my voice as excited as his. "We really did."

An hour later we were both still lying on the bed, enjoying the winter sunshine streaming through the windows.

"Of course, we'll have to get married."

"What?" I sat up quickly and turned towards him. "Why?"

"Why? Because no child of mine will be born a bastard, that's why."

"Nobody thinks like that anymore. Why rock the boat? We're happy, aren't we? What's the point of getting married?" I stood up and walked across to the window. Marriage had never crossed my mind and I wasn't sure I wanted it. No, now I thought about it, I was very sure I didn't want it.

"Don't you love me?" Seth sat on the edge of the bed, very still.

"You know I do. But, marriage? That's really grown up."

"And being parents isn't?" He regarded me quizzically.

"Of course it is." I smiled and went back to sit beside him on the bed. "It's just that it's all so… Life changing. Can't we just think about one thing at a time?"

"Sure thing, babe. Whatever you want."

Of course he wanted to go shopping straightaway. Even though it would be months before we needed anything for the baby. But it was fun and he bought me a beautiful locket and chain from a shop in The Lanes.

"Look, you can put a picture of me on one side and one of Junior on the other."

"Why would I want a picture of you?" I teased. I see your ugly mug every day. Although I suppose when I'm the size of a house, with swollen ankles and piles, it would be good to have a reminder of whose fault it is."

"Charming, anyone would think you'd been forced into having this baby."

"I'm sorry, darling. I am pleased, it was just a bit of a shock that it happened so quickly."

And I was pleased. I really was and the more I thought about it, the more confident I became that this baby would bring us closer together. We would be a little family.

"I love you, Seth." I caught hold of his hand.

"Of course you do. I am the amazing and fabulous father of your child, aren't I?"

"So modest and unassuming, too." I laughed.

"It goes without saying. Let's go home and celebrate properly."

*

"Stu, what's this? You have me booked out for the day on April 17th." I was going through the diary, checking it for clashes with antenatal appointments.

"Yes, darling. There's a possibility of a filming thing that day. Not sure if I want you or both of us to go; just wanted to make sure you didn't book anything else."

"Oh, okay."

"Problem?" Stu peered at me over the top of his glasses.

"No, not really, it's just that it's Seth's birthday. I think he wants to make a big thing of it."

"Sorry, Roz, it can't be helped. You'll be back for the evening, I'm sure."

"Fine, no worries, I'm sure he won't mind."

*

When I got home that evening, Seth was stretched out on the sofa with a glass of wine in front of him.

"Busy?" I enquired, raising my eyebrows.

"Don't start. I have been, I've been out schmoozing and networking and I'm knackered. You're late."

"There was a suicide at East Croydon and the trains were all over the place."

"I hate it when they do that, it's so fucking selfish."

"Seth, someone died. How unhappy must you be to do that? And I always feel for the poor driver."

"Yeah, well, he'll be having time off with full pay while he recovers." He made that ridiculous gesture to indicate quotation marks when he said 'recovers'. "I wouldn't feel too sorry for him."

"God, you're so cynical. Anyway, when I finally did get a train it was standing room only all the way home. I'm so tired and I'd kill for a cup of tea."

"You should have played the pregnant card. Got one of those lazy fuckers to give you their seat. Stick one in for me while you've got the kettle on, and what about dinner?"

"Didn't you get anything?"

"I was waiting for you. Shall I get the Indian menu?"

"That'll take ages, and I don't think I'm that hungry now to be honest. I'll probably just get some beans on toast."

"That sounds good, I'll have cheese grated over mine."

"So that's a tea with two sugars and beans on toast with cheese. Anything else?" I deliberately tried to inject some sarcasm into my voice, but it sailed right over his head.

"Nah, that'll be fine." I gave up and headed into the kitchen.

As we sat and ate our beans on toast at the table, I remembered the filming thing. "Oh, Seth, by the way: Stu has booked me for a filming thing on the 17th, so we'll have to do your birthday in the evening."

"What? No fucking way."

"It can't be helped. We'll go out in the evening, it'll be lovely."

"No, it's my birthday. How dare you make other plans?"

"Because I work for a living, that's how. What's the big deal? We'll go out in the evening."

"What you mean is, you work and I don't. I am trying. And it's a big deal because… It's. My. Fucking. Birthday." The blood was starting to drain from his face and his eyes were starting to darken, but I carried on regardless.

"You're behaving like a child, and a spoiled one at that. It's just a day, it's not as if it's an important one or a milestone. You're going to be thirty-three, for God's sake."

Seth stood up, sending his chair flying backwards into the wall. He thumped the table with both fists and leaned over so he was staring into my face. "It's important to me." His voice was low and very controlled. "But obviously you don't care, so forget it." He turned, kicking the chair out of his way, and walked out of the apartment, slamming the door behind him.

I was too shaken by this exchange, and too tired, to think straight. I picked up the chair, took the plates out to the kitchen and washed them up, together with the cups and glasses he had left around the apartment during the day. Then I went to bed. I thought I wouldn't sleep, but I didn't even get around to turning the light out as I had crashed as soon as my head hit the pillow.

The alarm went the next morning and I rolled over to say sorry, but he wasn't there. I lay awake, deciding whether to ring Stu and plead morning sickness and wait for him to return. *Should I? I have so much to do at work, and what if he's gone AWOL for days? Do I really want to sit around here and wait for him? No, I have no time for childish tantrums. Just let him get on with it.*

*

"Roz, darling, I'm taking you to lunch." Stu perched himself on the edge of my desk.

"I'm busy, Stu."

"No, you're not. Not with anything worth stressing over, anyway. Come on, it's Friday and we haven't had a good old Friday long lunch in years and years."

"I'm not in the mood."

"Maybe not, but I am, and I'm not taking no for an answer."

In the pub, I stared at the menu without enthusiasm. "When this is all over, I'm going to stuff myself on pate and soft cheese and then swim in alcohol." I sighed. "I'll have the Waldorf salad and an orange juice."

"Don't pout. I'll go and see if Waldorfs are in season."

I smiled weakly as he went off to place the order.

"Now," he said as he returned. "I've had Seth on the phone this morning."

"Oh?"

"He's a bit scared to come back."

"Scared?"

"He's worried what your reaction's going to be, how cross you are."

"Crosser now that we seem to have strayed into the playground. Where the hell does he get off, ringing you?"

"He was worried about you, bearing in mind your condition."

My condition didn't seem to bother him when he was kicking the furniture and getting in my face. "He was the one who walked out. He was the one who behaved like a bloody five-year-old."

37

"Hmm, well, it's a stressful time for both of you. Anyway, he's told me about the mix-up over the 17th so we've sorted that. I hadn't realised it was an issue, I'm so sorry."

"That's just it, it wasn't an issue. It's just him being childish." I could hear my voice rising; I was starting to sound like a petulant child myself.

"Okay, well, it's sorted now." Stu took my hand across the table. "I know he can be difficult sometimes but I told him that you shouldn't be stressed at the moment."

"So is he going to be there when I get home?"

"I do believe he is. Are you going to be kind?"

"I suppose so." I sighed. The urge to stick out my bottom lip and sulk was very strong. Why had no-one told me that all these hormones would reacquaint me with my inner teenager?

"Good. So, after you've eaten your lunch, go home and make things up with your man."

*

"Come on sleepyhead, rise and shine. It's your birthday and it's a beautiful day. Look, I've brought you breakfast in bed, and here's your present." The Big Day had dawned and, ever dutiful, I was entering into the spirit.

"Thanks babe, what's the present?"

"Like you don't already know. Never let it be said I can't take a hint, especially one that's been repeated several times a day for weeks."

"Wow, a mobile phone. Thanks babe."

"I have no idea why anyone would want to carry a telephone around with them. Why on earth would you want to be contactable 24/7?"

"I wouldn't expect you to understand, you're such a Luddite."

"A Luddite who isn't constantly plagued by people wanting to get in touch with her." I smiled, taking the edge off the sarcasm. "So, now we both have a day off in your honour, what would you like to do?"

"I have it all planned." He put all the phone stuff to one side and checked his watch. "Glad rags on, we're going out."

"Where?"

"It's a surprise. Why don't you wear that new suit, with the blouse that shows off your gorgeous pregnant tits?"

"But—"

"No buts, it's my day. You can't refuse me anything today."

*

When I had got home after the row a few weeks before, I had been greeted with flowers, champagne, chocolates and a very contrite Seth (who had obviously forgotten that I couldn't drink, or that I hated chocolate). He had also bought me the new suit that he was now trying to persuade me to wear. Over dinner at our favourite Greek restaurant he had justified his behaviour.

"When I was a kid, my mum and dad were always too busy fighting with each other to acknowledge my birthday and, even if they had, there was no money – what with Dad's gambling and Mum's drinking – for presents or parties. All the other kids would have parties and stuff. I just never told anyone when it was my day, but I swore that when I was a grown up I would always make a big deal of my birthday."

This was the most he had ever told me about his childhood and I leaned across the table and stroked his hand. "I'm so sorry, I had no idea."

"No reason why you should, I should have explained earlier. I just hate talking about it."

That night when we went to bed, we made love and he cried as he came. I held him in my arms until he fell asleep. It felt like we had passed some sort of important milestone in our relationship. I lay awake, watching him sleep, and felt a rush of love and compassion for the little boy who had grown up believing no-one loved him.

*

"Roz, hurry up, we're going to be late."

"Late for what?"

"The birthday surprise I've organised. Come on."

"Er, why have you organised your own birthday surprise?"

"I just have. Ready? Good, let's go."

We left the apartment and walked up Fourth Avenue. As we crossed over Church Road, I caught hold of Seth's arm. "Isn't that Stu over there? Yes, it is. What's he doing here?" I waved and we walked over.

"So, my sweet, are you ready?" Stu enveloped me in a huge bear hug.

"Ready for what?" I asked.

"Haven't told her yet, mate." Seth grinned.

"Told me what? What's going on?"

Just then, Gavin appeared with Donna. She was wearing a bridesmaid's dress and carrying a posy of flowers. Slowly, my brain began to process the information it was receiving and I realised we were outside the Town Hall.

"Hello darling." I bent down to give Donna a hug. "Don't you look pretty? What are you doing here?"

"I'm your bridesmaid," she lisped. "For your wedding."

I straightened up and looked at Seth.

"Surprise." He smiled and shrugged sheepishly.

"Er, how have you organised this?" I was still trying to form my thoughts into a coherent pattern.

"Well, I did have to, um, forge your signature a little bit. But I didn't think you'd mind. Ends justifying the means and all that."

Forged my… "But I thought we'd agreed we weren't going to do this."

"Yeah, but that was just jitters on your part, wasn't it? I've organised it all, so you don't need to worry."

"But—" *No! This is happening too fast. Come on Roz, get a grip, say something.* I opened my mouth to do just that and then caught Seth's eye.

"Roz, you're not going to spoil it for everyone, are you? Donna's been looking forward to this." He gripped my hand tightly and I saw his eyes start to darken. My stomach sank.

"No." I sighed, and then put on my brightest smile. "I won't spoil it. Thank you, darling, it's a very romantic surprise. It's just a shock, that's all."

"I thought you'd be pleased." His voice was low and exaggeratedly calm. "Look, I'll call it off. Wait there. Gavin, can you look after Donna? I have to go and talk to the Registrar. Stu, come with me."

"No wait, it's fine, let's go." I forced a huge smile and took Donna's hand. "It's exciting, I just wasn't expecting it. Blame the hormones."

40

So, we did it. We got married and came back out into the sunshine as Mr and Mrs Seth Peterson. As Stuart and Gavin hugged me and took photos, and Donna ran around throwing confetti, I told myself that I was overreacting. Over lunch at Wheeler's, I held my husband's hand and set my stepdaughter on my lap and I began to believe that we really were a family after all.

*

It had been nearly four months since the wedding and life is carried on as usual. I came in from work one August evening, after a particularly hot and sticky day in London, to find Seth in his usual position on the sofa surrounded by the detritus of his day – mugs, newspapers, plates. The sink was full of washing-up and there were no signs of any sort of preparation for dinner.

I took a deep breath and let it out in a sigh. "Seth, I'm finding everything so hard with all this travelling, and I'm so tired."

"Poor you, shall I run you a bath?"

"That would be nice, but I'm talking about every day up and down to London. It's exhausting, especially in this heat. I'm thinking of giving up work sooner rather than later."

"Is that a good idea, babe?"

"I'm just so tired and that can't be good for the baby. And it would be fun to have a few weeks to get everything ready, spend some time together."

"The thing is, babe, we need your money coming in for a while."

"What? But we had thousands left over from the sale. Surely we could use some of that?"

"Well, yeah, but I've had expenses and the wedding wasn't cheap."

"It couldn't have been much cheaper. And what expenses?"

"Oh, you know, studio time for Mobius Strip and Angharad. Promo shoots, all that sort of stuff. Business expenses."

"But Angharad isn't even your act! And I thought the Mobius guys were having 'artistic differences'? How could you have spent all that money? How much is there left?"

"A couple of hundred, maybe five." His voice was casual, but then he saw the look on my face. "But I've got a new potential I'm going to see tonight, so we could be back in the money soon. Actually, Christ, is that the time? I'll be late. See you later, babe." And he was gone.

I cleared the mess, washed up and then hauled myself into the bath, which I'd ended up running for myself, and lay down to soak. I was trying to dispel the feeling of despondency that seemed to accompany me most of the time these days. I had occasionally bought a pregnancy magazine to browse through on the commute home, but they were written in a sort of breathless, optimistic tone I was finding it very hard to feel myself. I usually abandoned them, feeling there was nothing relevant for me in them.

I'd met a couple of girls at antenatal classes, but I had stopped going to them since the 'birth partners' had been expected to attend. Seth always managed to have a meeting which clashed.

Dragging myself out of the bath, I went through to the kitchen. Opening the fridge, I spotted the bottle of wine that Seth had been drinking the night before. I took a deep breath and poured myself a glass. Sancerre, my favourite. I sat on the sofa, pulled my legs up and took a sip of the wine. As I felt it slip down, it was as if it was spreading calm all the way through my body. I leaned back and closed my eyes, feeling all the tension leave me.

Sometime later the phone rang. "Is that my big, fat, pregnant sister?" Ce-ce's voice sounded so clear.

"Sure is. But not so much of the fat, you. How are you? How's California?"

"Oh, you know. I've just about forgiven you for getting married without me. California is hot, sunny, shallow and enormous fun. But how are you?"

"I told you, it's not like I had much choice. It didn't feel right without you, but it was a surprise. How am I? I'm tired, hot, terminally grumpy and hormonal, but other than that absolutely fine. Less than two months to go now. I could do without England being quite so hot and sunny, particularly when I'm on the train home from town."

It was so lovely to chat to her and when I finally replaced the phone the effects of the bath, the wine and the chat had made me completely relaxed. I washed up the glass and replaced it in the cupboard and went to bed. For once, I fell asleep easily.

*

The next few weeks went by so quickly. All of a sudden I had a week to go before the baby was due and Stu had organised a farewell drinks party at the office. Some of my old bands were there, some musicians I had known for almost as long as I had known Stu. Gavin was even there, although usually he avoided our office at all costs ("too random, darling"). Seth had promised to be there, but at the last minute called to say he had an unavoidable meeting.

"But you were going to help me carry everything."

"Get taxis, babe, I'll pay. I'll see you later."

Stu's eyes were grave as he watched me replace the handset. "You okay, sweetie?"

"Yes, I'm fine." I smiled. "See? Happy face." He looked doubtful. "Honestly, Stu, I'm fine. It's probably better that he's not here, he'd only be trying to pinch the talent, and I can get all emotional about leaving you without him giving me a hard time."

"As long as you're sure."

"I'm sure."

I'd developed a new habit on the commute home for the last few weeks. I'd pop into the off-licence and pick up a bottle of wine and a bottle of Lilt. Once at the station I'd go into the Ladies, empty the Lilt down the pan and replace it with the wine. I could then sit on the train and drink without drawing hostile looks. I had found it hard to accept that since becoming pregnant it seemed that anyone and everyone was entitled to an opinion on my welfare, and felt quite at liberty to voice it. That and the fact that my swollen belly seemed to have become public property, with perfect strangers seeing no reason why they couldn't pat it at will.

Sometimes it seemed that the only person who didn't have a compelling urge to touch my burgeoning body was Seth. At first, he said that he was afraid he would hurt the baby. When I proved to him that this wasn't so, eventually he confessed.

"I just don't find it a turn–on, babe. I know some men do, but to me you're just fat."

I had no response to that and so for months we had carefully avoided the subject, and I had avoided going to bed at the same time as him or undressing in front of him.

I knew that alcohol wasn't good for the baby, although it was worse in the first trimester and I hadn't drunk then, but I also knew that stress wasn't good for the baby. I reasoned that if, by having a little drink on the way home, I took the edge off the stress of dealing with Seth when I got there then that had to be good for both me and the baby, surely?

I didn't drink the whole bottle. Trevor was a homeless man who used to hang around outside Hove station of an evening. I would give him my Lilt bottle and a couple of pounds and we had become quite good friends. I would miss him now that I wouldn't be catching the train anymore.

"Last time tonight, Trev," I said with a sigh as I handed him the bottle. "That was my last commute."

"God bless you, darlin'," he said and caught hold of my hand. "And the best of luck with the little one."

"Thanks, Trev. You take care of yourself now, okay?" As I walked away, I felt an urge to cry.

*

"Hello, minty." Seth was in the kitchen when I got home and gave me a quick peck on the cheek. "Still craving the extra-strongs, then?"

There was no point in giving him more reason to criticise me, so I hadn't told him about the wine. "Don't tell me you're actually cooking?" I looked around the kitchen.

"Don't be ridiculous. But I am ordering, how does Chinese sound?"

"I thought we were on a budget?"

"We're celebrating, Mobius Strip signed a deal today. They're going to be big, babe, and we're going with them."

"I'm really pleased for you, that's great news."

"I even bought champagne. I'm sure one glass can't hurt. After all, he is fully cooked in there."

"A tiny one, then. When the Chinese arrives."

"Good girl."

*

Eight days later, I opened my eyes to see Seth standing beside the bed wearing a surgeons outfit.

"Nice hat." I tried to smile and then to sit up. "Whoa, ouch."

"Careful, babe, you've had a Caesarean. You'll be woozy from the anaesthetic and the stitches may hurt."

"Is the baby all right?"

"He's fine, we've got a little boy. You'll be able to go and meet him soon but they just needed to make sure he's okay. You've both had a bit of a time, by all accounts."

"I don't remember. I just remember walking to the shop and feeling weird. Where were you? I kept trying to call your mobile."

"You know there's no signal out at the studio. I didn't get the messages until I got back into town."

"But why were you at the studio? I thought you were going to stay close to home, once he was due, in case I needed you."

"I'm here now, aren't I? And you're both okay."

"I was so frightened."

"For God's sake, Roz. You've had the baby, you're both fine. Don't go spoiling it by whining."

"Sorry, Seth. I love you."

"Yeah, I love you too."

*

We called the baby Toby. Mainly because we liked the name, but also because he had this look sometimes when he was really thinking about something – his face would screw itself up and he reminded me of a Toby jug. But without doubt, my little boy was the most beautiful baby ever born to any woman in the whole world.

'Beautiful' couldn't possibly describe me. My C-section scar was huge, like a sickly grin carved into my belly. The staples reminded me of the teeth of some horrible monster. I couldn't bear to look at myself, let alone let Seth see it. Not that he was showing any signs of wanting to, which suited me.

"Seeing your son born must have been awesome." Fergus, one of the lads from Mobius Strip, was round at the apartment a couple of weeks later, picking up some stuff. He was having a cup of tea while I gave Toby his bottle.

"Dunno, I didn't see it." Seth was looking through some papers and glanced over at Toby and me briefly.

"Didn't you?" I couldn't hide the surprise in my voice. "I could have sworn you said…"

"I came in after it was all over. I was outside the door. It looked like they had enough to deal with without me getting in the way."

"Oh." I tried not to sound hurt.

"It's not a big deal, babe. I was there to hold him as soon as they'd cleaned him up, while they were sorting you out."

"Yeah, I suppose." Poor Toby! His entrance into the world had been violent and stressful, and only strangers had been there to greet him. I was knocked out and his father couldn't, or rather didn't want to, overcome his squeamishness enough to play his

45

part. I cuddled him extra close as I gave him his bottle. "It must just have been a bit of a frightening start to the world."

"Like he knew anything about it. And you're one to talk about bad starts – what about breastfeeding? She's never even tried it, Fergus, despite what all the books say about it being the best thing."

"I did try. It hurt the wound and I couldn't produce enough. You know that." I could feel my tears welling up and Seth could obviously hear it.

"For God's sake, don't start. That's all she seems to do these days, Fergus, cry. And if it's not her, it's him."

"My mammy had eight of us." Fergus came over, stroked the top of Toby's head and winked at me. "She seemed to be crying for most of my childhood."

"Eight? I'm not surprised." I laughed. "She must have been exhausted."

"I think she was but, sure, she had my sisters to help. And she never breastfed either. It didn't do me any harm." He was right there – a strapping lad who loved his rugby on Sunday mornings almost as much as he loved playing guitar. "Anyway, I have to go now. I'll see you guys later. Seth, are you coming to the club tonight?"

"Yeah, I'll be down later."

As Fergus left the apartment I said quietly, "You're going to be out for most of the day, do you have to go out again tonight?"

"It's my business, babe, it's what I do. You're asleep most of the time, anyway, why should you care?"

"I'd just like us to spend some time together, that's all, as a family."

Seth snorted derisively, grabbed his phone and his keys and took his leather coat off the hook. "I don't know what time I'll be back."

"What about dinner? Will you come back for that?"

"I don't know."

"I'll make some anyway. Please try. And can you leave me some money, please? I need to get milk and nappies and stuff."

"For Christ's sake, how many nappies can one baby use? I seem to be forever giving you money." He took out his wallet, glared at it and then extracted a note and placed it on the table.

"I could always look around for a job."

"I've told you; I don't want you working. You have a job – looking after Toby."

"But I've always earned my own money. Do you think I like having to ask you?"

"It may be old-fashioned, but that's the way I want it. See you later."

After he'd gone, I smiled at Toby. "He can't stop us having fun, can he? Beach? Let's go and get the shopping first, though." I put him into the baby sling and we strolled up the hill to Church Road and the Little Shop.

"Hi, Syed," I greeted the young guy behind the counter. "How are you today?"

"I'm very well, Roz, and you? And young Toby?"

"We're off to the beach, so we need sustenance." I made my way around the shop, took the nappies I needed and picked up two cans of cider and a bottle of Lucozade. I hadn't been strictly truthful with Seth, we had plenty of baby milk but the only way I could get any money of my own was to lie. I was rather alarmed at how good I was at it. "And my usual please."

Syed reached behind and took down a packet of ten cigarettes and a pack of extra-strong mints.

"Thanks, Syed, see you soon."

"Goodbye, lovely lady, enjoy the beach."

We went back down the hill and across the road to Brighton Lawns. We made our way through the late holidaymakers to the pebbles beyond. I sat down and released Toby from his sling, laying it out flat so he could lie on it and kick his legs. Considering it was the end of October, the sun was still warm and he revelled in it, smiling and gurgling.

I tipped the Lucozade out onto the pebbles and then filled the bottle with one of the cans of cider from the shopping bag. Then I lay back, using the nappy bag as a pillow, propping myself up so that I still had eye contact with my baby.

"Cheers, precious boy." I opened the cigarettes, took one out and lit it. "Probably best not to mention this to Daddy. He's gone a bit fanatical since he gave up himself."

I wasn't proud of myself that my secret drinking had continued in the weeks since Toby had been born, or that I had started smoking again. But after the trauma of the Caesarean, and Seth's barely disguised hostility, the drink had become an essential way of getting through the day, whether Seth was home or not. And it was only one or two cans a day, no big deal. In fact, I could keep it down to one if Seth was out. It was just when I heard the door close downstairs and then his steady trade on the stairs that I would crave the second drink. It would calm my nerves and I could be cheerful to him and, usually, manage not to cry at the silliest things.

*

"Roz, not only is he beautiful but he is thriving. And he's such a happy little thing, aren't you, bubba?" Helen, the Health Visitor, leaned forward and blew a raspberry on Toby's tummy. He rewarded her with a throaty chuckle.

"Thanks. Here's your tea, I'll put it up on this bookshelf."

"And how are you? Eight weeks in?" She laid Toby gently down on his play mat and put his baby gym over him.

"Oh, you know, tired."

"That goes with the territory, I'm afraid." She sat down on the sofa next to me. "Is that all?"

"Yes, I'm fine." I smiled. *But even more tired because I got up at stupid o'clock this morning to make sure that the apartment was clean and tidy for your visit.*

"It's okay to ask for help, you know. It can be difficult when you don't have any family close at hand."

"I'm okay." *Please stop being nice. I'm not sure I can handle nice.*

"But Seth's good, isn't he? Helps you out?"

"Yes." *I can't take much more of this. He's no help at all and most of the time I'm out, keeping us away from him, so we don't make so much noise and disturb him.*

"It's good that you've got him, it's such a help to have a supportive husband."

"Mmm."

"I probably shouldn't tell you this, but he did call me. He's very worried about you, he thinks you're drinking."

"What?"

"He was asking if there was anything more he could do to help you."

And that's when the floodgates opened. Everything came out. How I had started to have terrible dreams about Toby: of people interfering with him, of him being kidnapped or hurt in some way. Of walking away from him or leaving him on the beach without caring at all. How sometimes I had almost managed to convince myself that I am incapable of looking after him properly and that I shouldn't let myself get close to him in case something happened to him. The thoughts and feelings that made me feel so bad that I had sometime started to think he would be better off without me. And how this terrified me, because my mother had died when I was young and I knew the effect it had on children.

"You poor thing." Helen patted my back as I sobbed into her shoulder.

"And no, Seth doesn't help me. I don't know what he's been telling you, but most of the time it feels like Toby and I are a hindrance to him. Oh God, please don't tell him I said that."

"Of course I won't. But we do have to tell him that you're feeling low. He's going to have to do more to help out. And we're going to get you an appointment with the doctor this afternoon. But I'll tell you one thing, Roz: no way would that little boy be better off without you. Look at him, he hasn't taken his eyes off you since you started crying. He obviously loves you."

"About the drinking, Helen…"

"Let's get you some help and it can all be worked out then. The main thing is that you've reached out."

*

"And did you get the help?" Detective Sergeant Wood's voice was strangely gentle.

"After a fashion," I replied. "Seth wasn't much help, but there were a couple of mother and baby groups – not that that's really my scene – but the best help came from Trev…"

"Who's Trev?"

"The homeless guy from Hove Station. I met him a couple of times down on the beach, with his partner Dolly, and they became my best friends. They loved Toby and were brilliant with him."

"Did Seth know about them?" She raised a quizzical eyebrow.

"I did tell him at first, but he went ballistic. He was convinced they'd give Toby some terrible disease, or fleas, or they'd force alcohol down him, or inject him with drugs. It was ridiculous. So they became another secret I had to keep."

"Difficult," she murmured.

"Very," I agreed. "But I swear I owe my sanity to those two, if not my life. And I'm not exaggerating."

"Okay, go on."

*

We were doing okay in Brighton. Toby was toddling and was still the cutest baby ever, Fergus's band – Mobius Strip – had had a top ten hit and were in the studio recording an album. Seth divided his time between them and another new act that he had signed up: a girl singer who I didn't reckon much, but he thought she was amazing. Either way, he didn't spend much time in the apartment with us which made our life quite calm.

I had cut down on my drinking and had made a couple of friends through a toddler group I had joined. Toby and I also used to spend a lot of time on the beach with Trev and Dolly and their mates. Seth would have had a fit, knowing Toby was hanging out with all the 'down and outs', but I always felt totally safe in their company and they loved my little boy almost as much as I did.

I kept in touch with Stu, although I felt a little awkward as Seth had signed Mobius Strip with another record label. I had suggested, mildly, to Seth that maybe the label he had chosen was not as responsible as Stu, but when he shot me down in flames I left him to it. Fergus and the boys were enjoying their success and who was I to query the money being spent on limousines, entourages and all the other accoutrements of fame? Seth loved it – he loved being invited to all the parties and events, and didn't even seem to mind that I didn't want to go with him. Most of the time, he took Bianca – his singer – to give her exposure.

Toby and I were just setting out one day to go and meet Trev and Dolly when there was an insistent ringing on the entryphone buzzer. "Who on earth can that be?" I said brightly to Toby. "Hello," I sang into the phone.

"Roz, it's Bianca. Is Seth there?"

"No, I thought he was with you today?"

"He was supposed to be, but I haven't seen him…" She started to cry. "I'm really sorry to come round but I didn't know what else to do."

"You'd better come up." I buzzed her in.

I had only met Bianca once or twice, but the one thing that stood out about her was how gorgeous she was. She was tiny, but curvy, with enormous blue eyes and a cloud of blonde curls, almost like a halo. When I opened the door this afternoon, though, there was no sign of her ethereal beauty. The waif in my doorway had mascara running down her cheeks, her hair looked matted and filthy and her clothes were hanging off her. "I'm so sorry," she sobbed. "I know I shouldn't have come here but I couldn't think where else to go."

"You'd better come in." Puzzled, I took her arm and led her over to the sofa by the window. She sat down and I knelt on the floor in front of her. Toby clambered up beside her and patted her knee, gazing up at her with his thumb in his mouth. She gathered him up and cuddled him, sobbing into his hair.

"What on earth has happened? I'll call Seth." I picked up the phone and dialled his number, but all I got was his voicemail message. "Seth, it's me. I'm not sure what's happened, but I've got Bianca here and she's very upset. Please can you call me as soon as you get this?"

"I've been trying all day," Bianca said over the top of Toby's head. "But he's not picking up, I think he's ignoring me."

Toby was starting to look quite distressed to see Bianca crying like this.

"Come on, sweetie," I said to him. "Let's go and make Bianca a cup of tea." I took him by the hand and we went to the kitchen area. I sat him in his highchair while I busied myself making the tea. "How about we put your Barney video on while Mummy and Bianca have a chat? We'll get the duvet from your bed and you can bundle yourself up and watch, while the grown-ups talk." He nodded and went and collected his current favourite teddy. When I had got him sorted out, I took the tea over to Bianca.

"I don't think it will take very long for him to go to sleep," I said. "Now what's all this about?"

"He's so cute," said Bianca. "Seeing how cute he is just makes things worse."

"Why would that make things worse?"

"Oh, you know, the whole 'might have been' thing." This brought on a fresh bout of crying.

"You're not making any sense." A small pit was starting to open up in my stomach.

"I know you and Seth are only living together because of Toby, and that you'll be divorced very soon, but I thought it would have been nice for Toby to have a little brother or sister. I know my career is important, but we could have managed both, I'm sure."

That small pit had become quite a large chasm.

"Oh?"

"But Seth said we had plenty of time for that. He was supposed to come with me this morning, to support me. I kept thinking he was just running late and then I thought he would be waiting for me when I came out, but I haven't heard anything from him and he won't answer his phone."

"Come with you, where?"

"To the clinic, of course. He told me he'd told you."

"It must have slipped his mind," I said dryly. "Along with the fact that we are getting a divorce. Are you trying to tell me you're pregnant?"

"Not anymore. Oh my God, you mean you're not getting a divorce?"

"What do you mean, not anymore?"

"Roz, I'm so sorry. I honestly thought, I mean, he told me… Oh, how can I have been so stupid?" She put her head on her knees, linked her hands behind her neck and cried, deep heart wrenching sobs.

I waited until she had calmed down a little. I walked over to the window and stared out over Brighton Lawns. I could see Trev and Dolly sitting on the grass. He looked up, saw me and waved. I went to wave back but my arm felt heavy. There was a rushing sound in my ears and the world felt in slow motion. I turned back to the child on my sofa, for she was a child – she was no more than nineteen – and I went and sat down beside her.

"I think you'd better tell me everything," I said. "Start at the beginning."

*

"What did Seth say?" DS Wood asked, as I paused for breath.

"I need another word with my client." Ian Dillon placed his hand flat on the desk in front of me.

DS Wood opened her mouth to speak, but closed it as she looked at DI Nixon and her shoulders slumped slightly.

Is it my imagination, or is she enjoying this?

"I'll fetch some tea," she muttered as she and DI Nixon left the room.

"Roz, at the moment you're describing a very clear motive." Ian spoke quietly, but firmly.

"It must have been a long time in the planning, then. This all happened over fifteen years ago. I have nothing to hide, as I didn't do anything. Please let me just tell my story, it's a relief to get it off my chest."

"As your solicitor, I would be negligent if I allowed you to incriminate yourself."

"Trust me, if you let me finish, I won't. But we may as well take advantage of the tea break." I smiled as DS Wood re-entered the room with a tray. "And look! They found some biscuits. All I need now is a cigarette and my life will be complete." So, after a tea break, some biscuits and a stroll outside to have a smoke with Ian, we continued.

*

1994, Kings Gardens

Seth didn't return for a week. He didn't answer my calls and I had no idea where he had gone. I had just started to think (hope?) that he might not come back when…

"Babe, it's me."

"Oh." I pressed the entryphone buzzer and went out onto the landing. "Where's your key?" I said as he came sheepishly up the stairs.

"Here." He held it up. "But I wasn't sure if I'd be welcome."

"And why would that be?" I asked dryly, as I went and sat on the floor with Toby, who had barely noticed his father. Now I came to think about it, I wasn't sure he'd even registered his father's absence.

"Where's Bianca?"

"She's gone to the country, to her mother."

"Good. She needs help, that one. It's all lies, you know that." He sat down on his armchair, dumping the piles of ironing I just finished this morning onto the floor.

"Really? You've had a week and that's what you've come up with? 'She's lying'?" Pointedly, I started re-folding the ironing and placing it on the sofa while murmuring quietly to Toby.

"Of course she's lying. It wasn't me; I was trying to help her." He picked up a T-shirt and attempted to fold it.

"Of course you were." I took the T-shirt from him, folded it and placed it on the pile.

"Babe, I was. It was some kid from the backing band. She came to me saying that her parents would kill her and would I help? How did I know she was going to fixate on me?"

"Oh please."

"Don't you think that if I was lying I would have come up with something better in a week? I'm telling the truth. I thought it better to keep out of the way, so that you guys could sort something out."

"You could have let me know that was your plan. You could have phoned me. You keep insisting that you must have the latest tech, but when I need to reach you it's switched off."

"Roz, why do you think she came to you? I figured it out this week. She obviously saw our lifestyle – our home, our child – and wanted that for herself. And she didn't care how she went about getting it." He reached down, picked up Toby and set him on his lap. "It was best I kept out of the way, although I hated that you had to go through it on your own. But you're so good at that stuff, I knew you'd sort it out."

All the tension of the past week started to catch up with me. I had held myself together, dealt with Bianca – arranging for her mother to come and collect her – and had kept Toby and me going without falling apart. At least, I didn't fall apart during the day when we could go and spend time with Trev and Dolly. They loved Toby and would keep him entertained while I dashed to the shops or did child-unfriendly chores. I offered for them to stay, although I knew Seth would freak out if he knew, but they had gently refused. They'd enjoyed the shower and laundry facilities, though.

But at night, after they'd gone and Toby was asleep in bed, it was different. That was when the fear took over. The fear that I would be on my own forever, that I was all my little boy had and that I wasn't going to be enough. My mind had gone into creative overdrive and conjured up nightmare scenarios, the best of which had us living on the streets with Trev and Dolly. The worst – even now I can't contemplate the worst. The only way I had got any sleep for the past week was to drink myself into oblivion every night.

"I'm not..." I tried to speak, but the words got caught in my throat. *Dammit.* I took a deep breath and tried again. "Seth, I'm not..."

He got off the chair, still holding Toby, and sat down on the floor beside me. He put his arm around me and pulled me towards them. "I know, babe," he murmured into my hair. "She should never have put you through that. You've been strong, but I'm back now. It's going to be all right; I'm going to take care of you. There's no way I'm going to let some little nobody spoil what we have. You go ahead and cry, I'm here now and I'm strong enough for both of us."

*

And so I betrayed the sisterhood and we settled back into our version of normality. Bianca wasn't the last, I'm sure, but it never darkened our door again like that. At least until... but I'm getting ahead of myself.

Toby was four and at full-time nursery when the next blow came.

"Mrs Peterson, may I have a word?" The manager of the nursery was waiting as I arrived to collect Toby.

"Please call me Roz, is everything all right?" *Oh God, what's happened to Toby?*

"There's nothing wrong with your son, Mrs Peterson, don't be alarmed. Could we have a word in my office?" She held open her door for me.

"What seems to be the problem?" I asked as she followed me in and closed the door.

She crossed the office and walked round behind her desk. "Please sit down, Mrs Peterson. I'm afraid we need to talk about your bill, which is now three months in arrears."

"My husband takes care of all of that, you'll need to talk to him."

"Your husband is being quite… elusive, Mrs Peterson. We've sent a number of letters and tried many times to call him. I do see, from Toby's file, that there was an express instruction to only talk to him about financial matters, but we have reached a point now where we have to ask you to pay or withdraw Toby from the nursery."

"What? You can't, Toby loves it here. Let me talk to my husband, I'll get this sorted out. It must be a mistake." *Surely it's a mistake. We're doing well, Seth would have said if we were in trouble.*

"I can give you until the end of the week, Mrs Peterson. Then I'm afraid we'll have to let Toby go."

*

"It's true, babe." Seth didn't seem surprised when I raised the issue with him later after Toby had gone to bed. "Work's dried up, I can't seem to find a decent act and I blew a load of money with all that shit over Möbius Strip."

"But they got a Brit Award, Seth, I don't understand." Fergus's band had been riding high with their first album and the music press had loved them. There'd been some contractual issue which required Seth being out nearly all the time and a lot of shouting over the phone, but I tended to zone out when he was being 'Shouty Daddy' and concentrated on keeping Toby and me out of his way.

"Yeah, but the label fucked me over with the second album. So the band sacked me. The lawyers' fees alone are eye-watering." Seth's ultra-calm voice was even more worrying than his shouting.

"How bad is it? What can we do?" I emphasised the 'we', to show that I was on his side. I just needed to know how bad things really were.

"It means a lot that you want to help, babe. It's not huge. If we mortgaged my half of the apartment that would more than cover it." I was sitting on the sofa and he came across and crouched in front of me, taking hold of both my hands and looking up at me.

"My apartment?"

I felt his hands tighten around mine momentarily and heard him take a deep breath. "Our apartment," he said quietly. "We're married now, remember? It's half mine."

"Of course," I said quickly, not wanting to give him any reason to be angry. "How would we go about that? I've never had a mortgage before."

"Don't worry, I've already been looking into it. We could go into the bank tomorrow and sign the papers."

"Okay, I'll give Andrew Dillon a ring in the morning." I dreaded having to tell my lovely solicitor that I had been reckless with my mother's inheritance. I knew it wasn't my fault, but it still felt like it was.

"Oh, we don't need to bother the old boy with this, I know a good local guy who can deal with it."

Relieved that I could avoid an awkward conversation with the man I had adored since childhood, who would no doubt have been sympathetic but disappointed in me, I nodded.

"Good girl." Seth kissed my forehead. "Now, how about we get a nice bottle of wine and order a takeaway and have a good old-fashioned night in?"

I'd say it was like old times but truthfully, now I think about it, I'm not sure we ever were the sort of couple to sit cuddled on the sofa watching a video. Whatever, it was a nice gentle evening and that night Seth made love to me for the first time in as long as I could remember. It seemed that everything was going to be all right.

*

Seth was a different person to 'Shouty Daddy' the next day. Dressed in his good Italian suit, he seemed taller and walked straighter somehow. He was business-like, self-assured and confident. To see him, you would have thought that he was a successful businessman completing another in a series of deals. Which was, of course, the image he wanted to portray.

We'd dropped Toby at the nursery and, while I was nervous facing the manager, Seth had strolled in and acted as if yesterday's conversation had never taken place. As far as he was concerned, it hadn't.

"Ah, I'm glad we caught you," he said smoothly when the manager came out of her office as we were leaving. "My wife has told me of your conversation yesterday. An oversight and I apologise for that. We are just going now to get it sorted and you will have your money within your deadline. Under the circumstances, I won't be pursuing you for breaking the condition that my wife is not to be disturbed with financial matters. But I would ask you to remember that she's fragile and easily upset."

I'm right here. I flashed a weak smile at the manager, who stood open mouthed as he swept past with me scurrying behind, slipping easily into the role he had clearly designated for me – dutiful, fragile wife.

Next stop was the solicitor Seth had found. His offices were nothing like Andrew Dillon's, which had been old-fashioned and as sturdy and comforting as the man himself. These were brash, bright, open plan and with a computer on each desk. Seth greeted the girl at the front desk by name.

"Hello, Fay, we're here to see Chris."

"Hi Seth," she purred. "I'll let him know you're here." She picked up her phone and murmured into it, casting an inquisitive sideways look at me. Across the room, a tall blonde man emerged from one of the glass walled offices that lined the edges. He smiled and waved us over.

"Seth, mate, good to see you." He shook Seth's hand. "And this must be Roz." He flashed me a brief but brilliant, expensive smile and then turned to guide Seth back into his office, one arm around his shoulders. I followed in their wake and stood awkwardly in the doorway until Chris directed me to one of the chairs set around a glass topped table in the centre of the room.

"Let me just call up your file," Chris said. "Then it's just a question of getting it all signed up and you can be on your way." He turned to Seth. "Thanks for getting me those tickets, mate. The gig was brilliant and she was well impressed... Well impressed." He emphasised these last two words and winked at Seth.

Seth laughed and said "No problem, mate. Anything I can do to help." I was becoming slightly nauseous with all the testosterone flying around the room, but suddenly the printer on a low table by Chris's desk started to spew out sheets of paper. Chris gathered them up, put them in order and brought them to the big table.

"It's all fairly standard stuff," he said. "I just need your signatures here, here and here." He marked the places with a pencil cross. "And I'll get one of the girls in to witness and you can be on your way."

Seth bent over the papers and signed, then came to stand behind me with his hands on my shoulders. He dropped a kiss on the top of my head. "Okay babe," he murmured.

I looked down at the papers in front of me. I could see the words 'Deed of Transfer', but everything else seemed to be quite small. "Shouldn't I read this through first?" I asked. "Or call Andrew Dillon to check it out?"

I felt Seth's hands tighten on my shoulders. "Don't worry, babe. I've read through it and it's fine. And Chris is here so that you don't need Andrew, right?"

"Of course," Chris said smoothly. "But if you want to ring him you can use my phone, Roz. I don't want you signing anything you're not happy with."

"I, er…" I started, but then felt Seth's hands tighten even more on my shoulders. I twisted and looked up at him. His eyes were turning black, although he was smiling down lovingly at me. "No, it's fine," I said brightly. "I trust you." His hands relaxed and he gave me a kiss on the cheek.

"That's my girl," he said. "Of course you trust me, it'd be a pretty poor show if you didn't." He gave a short laugh.

I picked up the pen and signed, then Chris called in one of the girls from the office outside to witness our signatures. Distractedly, I wondered how he could tell them apart, his girls. They all seemed to be young, blonde and pretty – maybe he had a room at the back where he turned out clones every time he needed a new office girl.

Chris handed Seth two of the copies we had signed, placing the other one in a buff file on his desk. "Great, so I'll see you later, mate." He shook Seth's hand and slapped him on the arm, then he turned to me.

"Pleasure, Roz," he said, taking my hand briefly. "I'll walk you both out."

Call-me-Rob, the personal banker, also seemed to be expecting us. "It's good to meet you at last, Roz." We sat down in front of his desk and within minutes he had produced some paperwork – more forms. Seth handed him the papers we had brought from Chris.

"Is your name really Rob and you work in a bank? In Wales, you'd be called Rob-the-Bank." He and Seth stared at me as I giggled nervously. "Sorry," I said. "I talk too much when I'm nervous."

"There's no need to be nervous, Roz," said Rob. "It's all sorted. Today we're just signing on the dotted line and crossing the T's."

"Oh?" I said. "I thought we were just applying for a mortgage today." I looked questioningly at Seth.

"No, I told you, babe, I've sorted all that. This is the bit where we get the money." He took my hand and gave it a tight squeeze. "I didn't want her fretting over the application process," he said to Rob. "She gets stressed easily."

"It's all cool, Roz," Rob said reassuringly. "As it's a fifty percent job, and the other half is free from charges, then it's all quite straightforward. You should have the money by close of play today."

I didn't feel reassured. "That's a lot of money," I said in a small voice.

Seth flashed me a quick look. "We've talked about this," he said quietly. "Remember?" His hand tightened around mine and I could feel the bones being pushed together.

No we haven't, not really. "Of course," I said quickly. "It's just me being silly." I smiled at them both. "Ignore me." Which I'm pretty sure they would have done anyway.

*

We came out of the bank into bright sunshine. Seth checked his watch. "It's a couple of hours till lunchtime. I've told Chris to meet us at The Grand in a couple of hours for a champagne lunch – on us – to say thank you."

"But we don't actually have the money yet," I said nervously. "Shouldn't we at least wait? And isn't this money to cover your debts? We'll have a mortgage to pay now, too. Shouldn't we be economising?"

"God!" Seth spat out. "I can always rely on you to put a downer on everything, can't I? For once, just once, can't you go with the moment and stop bleating on about everything? I mean, for fuck's sake, Roz…" He dropped my hand, that he had been holding since we signed Rob's papers, and strode away.

I scuttled after him, caught up and took his hand again. He threw mine away and swore under his breath. I took it again and stood in front of him. "I'm sorry, Seth. It's just that I've never had a mortgage before. Come to think of it, I've never had debts before either and the thought of both terrifies me. Don't be angry with me, we'll go and have lunch. It'll be fun. I've never eaten at The Grand, is it very posh? Should I go home and change?"

"No, babe, I've got a better idea. We've got a couple of hours, let's go shopping. Let's go to The Grand really fucking looking the part."

Shopping is not my idea of fun, but I got into the spirit of it for Seth's sake. Two hours later we walked into The Grand – Seth in an eye-wateringly expensive Italian designed suit and shoes and me in a dress that wouldn't have looked out of place at a Royal wedding, with shoes and bag to match. Seth had even persuaded me to have my make-up done at one of those beauty counters in the department store we went to, but I drew the line at buying it all knowing I would never wear it again. Besides, we were doing all of this on my credit card – Seth's being maxed out of course – and I was mindful that we still had to pay for lunch. I had a good credit limit and paid it off every month, but I would have been mortified if we'd gone so far that we couldn't cover lunch.

Seth insisted on champagne - and ignored Chris's attempts to pay for himself and Fay, who he had brought along – and he made jokes about being a 'kept man' when I produced my credit card at the end of the meal. He told Chris – amid loud guffaws – about my Rob-the-Bank comment, even though he didn't seem to find it funny at the time. He would have settled in for the evening too, I think, but I had to get back to

61

collect Toby from nursery. He walked out of the hotel with me to the taxi he had ordered for us.

"Okay babe, I'll see you later," he said as it pulled up.

"Aren't you coming with me?" I'd assumed we would be spending the evening together at home, like last night, if we couldn't stay on where we were.

"Places to go, people to see. There's a couple of gigs tonight that I want to go and have a look at. Don't wait up." He gave me a perfunctory peck on the cheek and strode off, leaving me to get the taxi fare myself.

*

The next morning I went up to our local bank and made sure that the funds were indeed in our account. Seth had also arranged for me to get a draft made out to the nursery, which I dropped off when I took Toby in, and a transfer to my credit card company to cover our spending from yesterday.

"It would be so much easier if you gave cheque-books on this account," I sighed to the girl behind the counter.

She gave me a strange look. "We do," she said, her brow furrowing slightly. "Your husband has one."

"Of course, I'm sorry. I'm getting muddled up with something else." I don't think she was fooled for a moment, but I was too embarrassed to admit that Seth had always told me that there was no cheque book, and therefore it was easier for him to get the cash out for a week and let me have it as and when I needed it.

After I had dropped off Toby, I went to the local branch of the bank that held my own account from my working days, which I had never closed, although Seth believed I had. Whenever I could, I deposited any spare money from the 'housekeeping' that Seth gave me. It was Toby's and my security fund in case anything ever happened to Seth or we found ourselves on our own for any reason.

I checked the balance. There wasn't much in there, but it made me feel slightly better when Seth did one of his disappearing acts. It also occurred to me now to open a savings account in Toby's name; that Seth wouldn't be able to touch. I had always thought that at least we would have the apartment but now, with a mortgage hanging round it, I couldn't even rely on that.

*

I turned to look at Ian with an ashamed smile. "I never did get around to explaining it to your father. Mainly because the explanation was obvious – I'm an idiot."

"He knew something had happened," Ian replied. "And he's tried to keep a weather eye on you since."

I could feel tears coming to my eyes and tried to blink them away.

DI Nixon gave me a shrewd look and then checked the notes in front of her. "We have your address in Suniton. When did you move from the apartment in Hove?"

"Another reason for me to be ashamed. You know the saying, 'Fool me once…'?"

"He did it again?" DS Wood cut in.

"Yes, but of course it was easier this time because now he actually owned half the apartment."

*

My beloved boy was coming up five and would be starting school in September. I had assumed that he would be going to the local primary school and had registered him accordingly. Seth, however, had other plans.

"He should go to private school," he announced one rare evening when he was at home.

"What? No!" I reacted instinctively. "We can't afford it, and anyway I don't believe in private education."

"It's not about what you believe but what's best for my son," he said smoothly, his eyes doing their familiar darkening thing. "And don't worry about the money, I've got it under control."

"What's that supposed to mean? I thought we were broke?"

"Not broke, no. But if we move to somewhere cheaper than Brighton, we could clear the mortgage and still have some cash left to cover the first year if we need it, but we won't."

"Won't we?" I was confused.

"You know I told you about this old biddy I've met? Marjorie? Well, she and I have decided to set up a charity project together. She's going to fund it initially and I'm the paid Project Manager."

"Er, when was all this decided? And did you not think of talking to me about it first? I haven't even met this Marjorie woman."

"Why on earth should I discuss it with you? It's my work, my career. It doesn't affect you, except that it will be a regular income instead of relying on the music biz."

"Sorry, but I think it has quite a lot to do with me..." I started, but then I caught the expression on his face darkening. "Oh, never mind. Can I at least meet this woman? If she's going to be working with you."

"Yeah, she's been on at me to meet you and Toby anyway. I'll arrange it."

*

There are many words I could use to describe Marjorie – my personal favourite is Ellie and Toby's 'Concrete-haired Witch' – but 'old biddy' would never even have been on the list. The woman Seth introduced to me the following Sunday, over lunch at a rather nice carvery deep in the countryside, was polished and very much in control. She was a good deal older than me and told me that she had been widowed a couple of years before.

"I've been looking about for a project to give some meaning to my life," she explained, while regarding me with a cool gaze. "When I met Seth and heard about his ideas, it seemed like the perfect match. With you two planning to move over near me for Toby's school—"

"Sorry?" I interrupted, but Seth placed a hand on mine and I could feel it pressing down hard.

"We haven't finalised the details yet, have we, darling?" The pressure increased.

"Er, no," I stammered, blushing furiously.

"Well, I think it's a lovely idea," Marjorie continued without batting a perfectly made-up eyelid. "And it would be such fun for us to be living closer together. I would love to see more of Toby."

"Oh, I see." I felt like I had stepped into a play for which I had learned the wrong script and everyone else knew it but me. I picked up my wine glass and took a gulp. *Hang on, Roz. This is going to be important, I think. You need to keep a cool head.* I put the glass back down and Seth refilled it immediately. Marjorie's eyebrows flickered momentarily as Seth glanced at her with a barely perceptible shrug. The exchange was over in a millisecond and I wasn't sure whether I had imagined it.

"You'd like that, wouldn't you, Toby?" Marjorie went on, turning to him. I was so proud of him; he had behaved beautifully all through lunch, although he must have been so bored. She ruffled his hair (something he usually hated) and he smiled at her uncertainly. Then she turned back to Seth. "He's so lovely, and he's the image of you."

Seth visibly preened himself, although Toby was nothing like him as far as I could see. "Thanks."

"Perhaps we should let him outside for a while," I suggested. "This is a long time for four-year-old legs to be keeping still. I'll take him out for a run around that garden." I needed to get outside for a smoke and to try to process the subtext of what had been going on for the last ten minutes.

By the time we came back in Marjorie was at the counter settling the bill, and Seth was waiting to one side holding her coat. I strapped Toby into his buggy and went to join him. "Want to tell me what all that was about?" I asked in a whisper. "What is going on here?"

"Ssh," he whispered back. "I'll tell you later."

"Okay, this is the plan," he said later at home. "We sell the apartment, clear the mortgage and buy something smaller, over Suniton way. Property is much cheaper over there—"

"I'm sorry, what? Whose plan? And don't I get a say?"

"Let me finish. Marjorie has offered to front up Toby's fees for the first year while we get things sorted and, anyway, the salary we have agreed on is much better money than I've ever been on before."

"Why on earth would she be prepared to pay the fees for a child she barely knows?"

"She's just a good person, all right? Anyway, why should you care? At least we don't have to pay."

"I just don't get it. It all seems a bit… odd… no, creepy… to me."

"Look, she has no grandchildren of her own – no kids, even. Her husband was a lot older and they never had children. I think she's lonely and where's the harm? It's not like Toby has any grandparents so it's a win-win."

"I guess…" I said, my voice trailing off. Now I was not only doubting Marjorie's motives, but Seth's as well.

"Good girl. Just don't make waves, okay?"

*

A couple of days later Seth called me to say that he would collect Toby from nursery and that he would 'probably take him for a pizza afterwards'.

"After what?" I asked the empty phone line. I spent the afternoon down on the beach with Trev and Dolly and told them about Marjorie and all the other stuff. They were as sceptical as I was.

"Is she doing the horizontal tango with your man?" Dolly asked.

"Eww, yuck, no! She's a good twenty years older than him, I think." I couldn't imagine Seth doing that with someone old enough to be his mother. More to the point, I didn't want to imagine it. Although he and I never got it on these days, I'd hoped he was at least being faithful now.

"There must be something in it for her," Trev reasoned. "But I'm buggered if I can think what. There's no such thing as true altruism."

"You, Trev, are an old cynic. I prefer to accept that she is just a very kind person. Until I get proof of anything else, that is."

"And are you really going to move, pet?" he asked. "Sure, we'll all miss you and the small fella."

"I'll miss you too," I said, stroking his arm. "When Seth says Toby doesn't have any grandparents, he's wrong. You've been like a grandpa to my boy and he loves you like one. But you could always come and visit – Suniton's only a few miles away."

"You're right there, pet. Perhaps we will, but we won't be expecting a bed in your guest room so don't worry about that."

"You know I wouldn't mind, but Seth would definitely have something to say." I smiled. "He doesn't know we hang out with you guys."

Dolly let out a raucous laugh. "Probably for the best. We don't exactly fit the demographic he's trying to cultivate." She scratched her head, belched loudly and knocked back the last of the can of cider I had brought her.

"Honestly, woman, you are so uncouth," Trevor admonished, but with real affection in his eyes. "I can't take you anywhere."

She cackled and slapped him hard on the arm. "Sure, don't we go to the finest places anyway? Look, our bedroom has the best sea view in the whole of Brighton, the rent's dirt cheap and we are practically next door to all those highfalutin celebrities."

*

I was still smiling at the thought of those two when I let myself into the apartment.

"Mummy!" Toby cannoned into me, hugging my knees and nearly sending me sprawling on the floor. "We have had such a good time! We went to Pizza Express and I had a whole pizza to myself and chocolate ice cream after."

"You'll burst," I laughed. "Was it a nice surprise to have Daddy pick you up?"

"And Granny Marjorie," he said.

"Granny Marjorie?" I looked at Seth who shook his head and mouthed 'later'.

"Yes, we went to my new school, which is really cool with a swimming pool and everything."

"Your new school?" I was gaining appreciation for the troops in Helmand, with all these bombshells flying at me.

"Hey Toby," Seth said, guiding him away from me towards the sofa. "How about we let Mummy sit down and catch her breath? Want to help me make her a cup of tea? Or perhaps she'd prefer a glass of wine?" Was I imagining that slight edge in his voice?

"Okay," Toby sang. "But then can I tell her about the new school?"

"Yes, then you can." Seth ruffled Toby's hair and didn't seem to notice him flinch. "We can tell her together and you can show her that book they gave you. Can you remember what it was called?"

"A puss-pecker?" Toby said doubtfully.

"Well, that would be a stupid name for it, wouldn't it? It's a prospectus, remember?"

"Seth, we don't say 'stupid', do we, Toby?"

"No, but, Mummy, the book's got loads of pictures in it of the school. You'll really like it."

"I'm sure I will, darling. But I could really do with that cup of tea now, please."

But Seth brought in a bottle of wine, poured me a large glass and settled Toby on the other sofa with a Thomas the Tank Engine video. Then he came and sat beside me with the (he thought) disarming, quasi-guilty smile he always put on when he had done something he knew would upset me.

"New school?" I hissed. "Granny Marjorie?" I was shaking with suppressed anger.

"Yes, what's wrong with Granny Marjorie?"

"You really don't know? Or are you being deliberately obtuse?"

"Look," he said in a calm voice. "Marjorie wanted to help us out by getting Toby into the school. She's already said she'll pay the first year, I told you that."

"Yes, but I haven't actually agreed!" My voice was getting higher and louder.

He frowned at me and nodded his head in Toby's direction. "Keep your voice down, Roz. Don't upset the kid—"

"The 'kid' is your son, who you seem to be quite happy to pimp out to some old woman you barely know as a pseudo-grandson. How do you know she'll stick around? Or that she isn't some kind of nut-job? How can you put Toby at risk like that?" I took a huge gulp of the wine and immediately felt calmer.

"Roz, she handed over a cheque for the whole of the first year's fees this afternoon. He'll start there in September."

"But I haven't even seen this school. I know nothing about it, I don't even know where it is."

"It's in Suniton, and you can see the prospectus that we brought home. Toby loved it."

"Of course he did – it's got a swimming pool and you showed him all the good bits. How am I supposed to get him to Suniton every day? I don't drive. Oh God, he is a day pupil isn't he? It's not a boarding school? He's too young for boarding. I definitely won't let you do that."

"No. He could board, after a year or two, but he's just a day pupil at the moment. As for getting him there, I've seen the ideal house and it's ten minutes' walk away. I put in an offer this afternoon and it's been accepted, subject to us selling this place."

"You did what? But I haven't seen it. What if I don't like it? How could you do all of this without consulting me?" I was on the verge of tears now; I was so frustrated and angry.

"I've booked another viewing for the weekend; you can see it then. Can you make sure you're in tomorrow and you get some of this mess tidied up? The agent is coming round to value the place and get the details done so we can put it on the market. I'm off out tonight, I've got a business dinner with Marjorie." He pecked me on the cheek absentmindedly and got up. "See you later, dude," he said to Toby and ruffled his hair, seemingly not noticing that Toby's hand came up immediately to bat his away and straighten his fringe. "Don't forget to show your mum that book," he said as he headed out of the door.

When he'd gone I drained the glass, took a deep breath and went over to sit next to Toby, putting my arm around him and squeezing him tight. "What a busy day you seem to have had," I said brightly. "Want to tell me all about it?"

"Yes, Mummy, after Thomas." He snuggled into me and looked up, a confused frown on his face. "Are you cross with Daddy?"

"A little bit, darling, but only because I would have liked to come and see the school with you."

"Never mind, Mummy," he said, his eyes straying back to the TV and Thomas. "Granny Marjorie said it will still be there when you get around to seeing it."

"Did she? How kind of her to think of me."

*

Later that evening, after I had given Toby his bath and put him to bed, I finished the bottle of wine and phoned Ce-Ce in California. She sounded so happy and carefree when she answered and I felt terrible that all I could do was cry and whinge about my worries.

"I'm coming over," she said as soon as I had finished telling her. "I'm due some vacation time and I'll be there within the week. I'll let you know when I'll be arriving. Until then, don't sign anything or agree to anything, okay?"

The house in Suniton was sweet, I have to admit. Not far from the beach and a short walk along the seafront from the school that Seth (and Marjorie) had chosen. Which, I also had to admit, had a quaint, old-fashioned air about it. It didn't have a swimming pool but it was located opposite the town pool. The only drawback was that Marjorie lived in an art deco mansion block between the house and the school.

"Good for babysitting," she pointed out when we were walking from the viewing to the school. Like Seth ever took me out these days, I'd wanted to reply, but didn't.

And once again, Seth seemed to have the luck of the devil when it came to selling the apartment. The second people to view it offered the asking price. Seth wanted to take it off the market and put it back on at a higher price, convinced that the agent must be doing the dirty on us, but Marjorie talked him out of it. He'd fallen out with Chris, the super-smooth lawyer – I didn't ask why – but Marjorie had a man she used, so of course that's who we went with.

Ce-ce came over for a week and dealt with the solicitor on my behalf. Somehow, she got the sale to proceed with each of us owning separate halves of the new house, rather than owning it together. It meant that Seth couldn't do to me again what he'd done with the apartment. Toby and I were secure. Of course, she sold it to Seth that it was to his advantage and so he went along with it. She didn't run a successful TV network for nothing.

It seemed like no time at all before we were in Windsor Road and I did my best to make it feel like a proper home. In doing so, I discovered some surprising things about myself: I enjoyed decorating and I seemed to have a flair for it; and I fell in love with gardening. I even started growing my own vegetables which – because more often than not he had put as much effort into them as I – Toby was happy to eat.

And he blossomed at school. Where once he had been quiet and shy, he became more confident in himself and less jumpy. Of course, another reason for that might have been that Seth was out of the house a lot, and when he was with Toby he was usually also with Marjorie so 'Shouty Daddy' wasn't around much. Even when Seth was in he had taken to spending all his time in his study – including sleeping in there – which meant less tension all round.

Marjorie and I had also reached an unspoken truce. There was no love lost on either side, so we just avoided each other. And I had no qualms about playing the 'I am his mother' card when her interfering became too much. A couple of play dates clashing with times when she had planned to see him usually brought her back into line.

*

I missed Trev and Dolly, of course, but one bright February morning, when I was walking back along the prom after dropping Toby off at school, I heard a familiar cackling laugh and there they were sitting on a bench in the park next to the swimming pool.

"Oh wow, you two!" I ran over to them. "Boy, have I missed you!"

"Didn't we tell you we'd come to visit?" said Trev. "Didn't think it would be this easy to find you, though."

"I always had faith," said Dolly. "We're linked telepathetically, don't you know?"

"It's telepathically, you daft mare," grumbled Trev. "Although you're right, you are pretty pathetic." But the smile he gave her took the sting out of his words.

"Aw shut up, you old goat," she grinned toothlessly. "You know you love me really."

"I'd invite you both back to the house," I said. "But I never know when Seth is going to pop home unexpectedly."

"Step into our parlour instead," grinned Trevor and led the way to a block of chalets right on the prom, which I had always assumed were abandoned, with a paved patio in front of them. There were a couple of sleeping bags rolled up and tucked into one corner, along with Trevor's canvas bag which he had carried since I'd known him. Dolly took the sleeping bags and laid them out on the pebbles in front of the chalets. Trev reached into his bag, bringing out three bottles of Strongbow cider. "We couldn't have come without bearing gifts," he winked. "Is this still Madame's preferred choice?"

"Most certainly, but please bear in mind that Madame has to collect her son from the extremely posh school this afternoon. I have to take things very easy these days."

It was just like the old days back in Brighton. We sat on the beach in the early spring sunshine, drinking cider and setting the world to rights. At lunchtime I went and bought sandwiches and teas for them from a little café nearby, and a strong black coffee for me.

"God, I've missed you guys," I said and started to tear up. "I hardly know anyone over here and the other mums at the school barely talk to me. Which is no great loss, to be honest, but still…"

"We thought we'd stick around for a while," said Trev. "Brighton's getting a bit dodgy these days."

"And isn't Suniton supposed to be the place for old people?" Dolly cackled. "Should suit us down to the ground."

When I picked up Toby from school I crossed the road with him and then bent down and whispered, "I've got a surprise for you, but it's a secret."

71

"What?" he whispered back.

"You have to promise not to tell Daddy or Marjorie," I said. "It's just for the two of us."

Toby crossed his heart, then spat on his hand and held it to me. "Shake, Mummy. Then it's a sacred vow."

I shook his hand, smiling. "Where did you learn that?"

"School. Seb made me do it when he shared his sweets with me that he'd got from the Pick and Mix when his mum wasn't looking. Oh, oops." He blushed as he realised what he had done.

"Right, well, we'll have a talk later about stealing and don't worry, I won't tell Seb's mummy. But you must never keep secrets from me, okay?"

"Okay, Mummy, what's the secret?"

By this time we had walked through the little park to the prom and I could see Trev and Dolly sitting on the beach waiting for us. I pointed to them. "Over there."

He squinted, then his eyes lit up and he gasped. "Is it…?" he asked excitedly. Trev and Dolly had spotted us and were standing up.

"Go and see," I said. He ran over and threw his arms around Dolly's waist. She reached down and hugged him back.

"Well, if it isn't my special boy," she declared. "And grown all big and smart! Let me look at you." She crouched in front of him and spun him round, admiring his school uniform. "You'll be too hoity-toity for the likes of us soon."

"Never," Toby said fiercely and gave her another hug before turning to Trev, who held out a hand for him to shake. Toby shook his hand formally before throwing his arms around Trev as well.

I had caught up to them now. "Trev, is that a tear in your eye?" I teased.

"No," he said gruffly. "I must have got a bit of sand in it."

"Oh yes, that'll be it." I nodded my head solemnly. "This pebble beach is notorious for its sandstorms."

We stayed on the beach with them for another hour and then I walked Toby home to have his tea and do his homework.

*

Seth came home a couple of hours later.

"Nice day?" His voice was low and slightly menacing.

"Yes thanks," I trilled as if I hadn't noticed the darkening eyes and the icy calm in his voice.

"What did you get up to?" He was talking to me but staring at Toby, whose head was down over his homework although I knew he could hear us.

"Nothing much, the usual," I replied in the same bright tone.

"Really?" he growled. "You didn't meet any friends?"

"No," I said, shaking my head. I put my hand on Toby's shoulder and could feel him trembling. "Tobes, sweetie, why don't you go and do your reading in your bedroom? I'll call you when tea's ready." Toby smiled at me gratefully, grabbed his bookbag and scuttled out of the room.

I turned to face Seth. "What's up with you?"

"You were seen," he said, still with the same calm voice. "One of Marjorie's neighbours was on her balcony and spotted Toby in his school uniform on the beach. She phoned Marjorie when she realised the type of people he was talking to. Street drinkers and hobos. She didn't realise that his own mother was one of them."

"Oh."

"Is that all you've got to say for yourself?"

"Trev and Dolly would never drink when Toby is around," I said quickly. They—"

"You mean it's that bloody Paddy you used to see in Brighton?" He exploded. "What the fuck is he doing in Suniton?"

"He and Dolly came to see us. They missed Toby."

"They missed blagging money off you, you mean. I won't have it, Roz. I'm trying to set up this project and I can't have you hanging around with degenerates. Not to mention teaching our son that it's acceptable to scrounge off the state and spend the money on getting drunk and pissing in gutters."

"Please keep your voice down, you'll upset Toby," I said as calmly as I could. "Trev and Dolly don't claim benefits and they don't piss in gutters either—"

"I don't fucking care. Shut your smart mouth, you stupid bitch." He strode towards me and then smiled when he saw me flinch. "You're not even worth the energy," he sneered. "Just make sure it doesn't happen again."

God, Roz, don't let him hit you. Toby will hear and he'll be terrified. "I'm sorry, I didn't think—"

"No, you never think, that's your problem. Now, Marjorie and I have an important meeting tonight. Don't wait up." He left the house without even saying goodbye to Toby.

My hands shaking, I went to the fridge and took out a bottle of wine. I grabbed a glass from the cupboard and filled it before putting the wine back. I sat at the table and downed it. Then I heard a noise outside the kitchen door.

"It's okay, Tobes," I said. "Daddy's gone out for the evening, you can come in." The door opened and Toby sidled in, his face a picture of anxiety. "Hey, what's with the worried face? We know Daddy's not keen on Trev and Dolly. He was just a bit cross with me, not you. As it's Friday night, let's stay up and watch Toy Story on the video."

He nodded his head slowly and we spent the evening curled up on the sofa watching Woody, Buzz and the rest do their thing. Gradually, I felt the tension go out of my little boy's body as he sat cuddled into me, sucking his thumb. After he went to bed, I finished the bottle of wine, which didn't fully ease my own tense nerves but did at least mean I was crashed out, fast asleep, before Seth came home.

*

The following day Toby had Saturday School in the morning. Seth was still asleep when I got up, but he came into the kitchen while Toby was having his breakfast.

"I'll pick you up from school," he growled. "Okay?"

"Yes Daddy." Toby's reply was barely audible.

"We'll be going out with Granny Marjorie this afternoon, so you have to be on your best behaviour. Understood?"

Toby flashed a quick nervous smile at me and then nodded.

"That's nice," I said brightly. "Where are we going?"

Seth turned to me with a sneer on his face. "You're not going anywhere. It's just me and Toby who are invited and I think, following on from yesterday, he could do with a couple of positive role models. Instead of the down and out degenerates you hang out with."

I opened my mouth to argue but then it occurred to me: this was a punishment and the more I kicked against it, or defended Trev and Dolly, the longer it would go on. "Okay," I said meekly. "What time will you be back?"

"Why do you need to know?" His eyes were dark again and he seemed to be quietly simmering, just looking for an excuse to have another go at me.

"So I know what time to put dinner on for," I said with a frown, as if I couldn't perceive that any other reason I might want to know.

"Don't bother, we'll eat out."

"Okay, but don't forget that Toby has been looking forward to the next episode of Doctor Who, haven't you darling? They're repeating the old ones and I can't record it, because the recording bit isn't working properly and I think it's going to be exciting. It's the Daleks."

"For God's sake," Seth spat out angrily. "It's only a TV show."

"Toby, sweetie, if you've finished your breakfast, go and clean your teeth and brush your hair," I said. I could see his lip beginning to tremble. "We need to leave for school soon." He nodded and slunk out of the room as if trying to make himself invisible.

"Seth, can't you remember what it was like to try and fit in at school?" I kept my voice deliberately calm. "All of his friends are as mad on Doctor Who as he is. If he has to admit that he missed it then it's going to single him out for the whole week. Plus, anyway, he really loves it. Please could you try to be back in time?"

"Yeah, whatever." He rolled his eyes. "But I can't promise anything."

"Promise me you'll try." I tried not to sound as if I was pleading.

It was a very quiet little boy who left the house with me to go to school that morning. He slipped his hand into mine as we left the house and there was no skipping or running.

"Don't you worry about Daddy being cross last night," I said as we walked along the road. "He wasn't cross with you, just with me. And I've had an idea – why don't you tell Marjorie all about Doctor Who while you're out, and that you'd really like to be home in time to watch it? I'm sure she wouldn't want you to miss it."

He smiled at that thought. "I can tell her about my Doctor Who pyjamas. We have to wear our special pyjamas when we're watching Doctor Who, don't we Mummy?"

I squeezed his hand. "Of course we do. And I like having you there in case I get scared, because you're so brave."

"I am, aren't I? Even when it's the cyber men."

We stopped round the corner from the school – so that I could kiss him without his friends seeing – and he shouldered his backpack and ran on ahead of me without looking back. I hugged my arms around myself and watched until he disappeared inside the building. Then I headed for the beach.

*

I found Trev and Dolly in their shelter. As soon as I sat down beside them, Trev narrowed his eyes. "What's up, pet? You look upset."

"I'm fine." I sighed heavily. "Just one of those days. How long are you planning on staying around, both of you?"

"Why?" Trev sounded suspicious.

"No reason, just curious. I didn't know if you had plans to spend your summer in the south of France?"

"What happened? We were thinking of stopping here for a while, weren't we Doll? Spending some time with you and the little fella."

Despite myself, I felt my heart sink. I loved these guys so much but, if they were going to stick around, it was going to make life awkward for me and Toby. How could I tell them?

Dolly must have picked up on my hesitation because she reached across and took my hand. "We don't want to embarrass you, or cause you any problems with your new friends, Roz, lovey. We just thought it would be nice to see Toby as we hadn't seen him for so long. We've seen him now, we can clear off tomorrow."

"No! Please don't go. And you could never embarrass me; you know how much I love you guys. It's just…" I trailed off.

"Just?" Trev frowned at me. "Come on girl, spit it out. Is it that fancy-schmancy husband of yours? Is he giving you a hard time? You know you're too good for him."

Dolly gave my hand a squeeze. "Now don't you worry, my darling. The last thing we want to do is make trouble for you, so we'll be on our way tomorrow."

"But I don't want you to go!" I wailed. "And Toby will be heartbroken if you do, he's missed you so much. So have I." And with that I burst into tears.

Of course, the whole story came out: about Seth and Marjorie, how Marjorie's friend had seen us and how I was being punished by Seth taking Toby out for the day without me. "And I don't have any new friends," I sniffed at Dolly. "In fact, I think you two are my only friends. Proper friends, that is. Not just other mums at school."

Trev started rolling up their sleeping bags and gathering their few possessions together. "Come on, Doll, get yourself together."

"Please don't go," I cried, as Dolly and I exchanged anxious looks.

"Go? The only place we're going is to find a new spot that isn't right under that stuck-up cow's window. And don't you be hugging me, Rosalind my dear, because she might be watching." He put his hand up to stop me as I walked towards him with my arms out and gave me a huge wink. "Now, you go home and play the dutiful wife and we'll meet you at the pier at lunchtime. If we haven't found anywhere we'll all go looking together. Go on, off you go, and try to look like you given us our marching orders."

I tried to wipe the delighted grin off my face and turned to walk away with my head down.

∗

Luckily, I didn't have to try and wipe the smile off my face when I got home, as Seth's car was gone. There was, though, a familiar figure sitting on our doorstep, a guitar strapped to his back, rolling a cigarette.

"Fergus!" It had been some time since I've seen him. "Come to visit the little people, now you're famous, huh?" I hugged him.

"Not exactly." He grinned ruefully. "We lost our deal last year. Didn't Seth tell you?"

"Since when did Seth tell me anything?" I kept my voice light. "What happened?"

"Sure, who really knows? Accountants, lawyers and managers, they all speak a language I can't understand. How are you, anyway? You're looking bonny. Thin, but bonny." He smiled. "Spare a cup of tea for an old friend?"

We went inside and caught up. "Anyway, you haven't told me to what I owe the pleasure of this visit." I teased him when we finally stopped swapping news.

He looked surprised. "I had a meeting here with Seth this morning. I'd only stopped to roll a cigarette when you turned up. Don't you two ever talk to each other?"

"Not if we can help it." I rolled my eyes. "What was the meeting about? Surely you won't let him manage you again? I'm amazed you're even still talking to him."

"He called me. He wanted to know if I'd be interested in helping him out with the project. I was dubious about working with him again, but couldn't resist a trip to the seaside to hear him out."

"And?"

"Well, it looks okay, and if it means seeing more of you and the little fella then how can I say no? I'll have to meet this Marjorie though. She seems to be the one who's really in charge."

"Yeah, good luck with that. I'll be interested to know what you think. I just hope that 'Granny Marjorie' fully appreciates the importance of Doctor Who in the world of a small boy." I recounted the events of the morning to him.

By the time I left to catch up again with Trev and Dolly, Fergus had sorted out recording Doctor Who and had promised to keep me updated on what was happening with Seth. He also walked into town with me, along the prom, to say hi to Trev and Dolly and 'maybe do a little light busking in the sunshine.'

Trev and Dolly had found themselves another little niche at the other end of the prom – an old Victorian shelter a good mile away – and so in the end Fergus joined us and we spent the afternoon sitting on the beach drinking cider, listening to Fergus strumming on his ever present guitar and putting the world to rights. I had never seen either of them get fiercely drunk – like me, they just maintained a permanent buzz to take the edge off the world. Their lifestyle wasn't one that many people would choose but they seemed content and, as they did no harm to anyone, who had the right to judge them?

*

I was feeling very mellow as I walked home in the sunshine, but as I turned into our road my heart sank when I saw Seth's car parked outside the house. I let myself in through the kitchen door and could hear Toby crying in his bedroom. I found Seth in the sitting room, pacing.

"He wouldn't shut up about bloody Doctor Who," he ranted. "The whole bloody afternoon. Marjorie tried to pretend that she was interested, but I could see that she was as hacked off with it as I was. So I brought him home and – surprise, surprise – you weren't here. Where have you been?"

"Out. Where is Toby? Has he eaten? Have you?"

"No, I haven't. We've got a table booked for later – business meeting. I sent him to his room and told him to stay there, with no dinner. I'm so bloody fed up with him."

"I'll go and see if he's okay. And you can't send him up there with nothing to eat, Seth."

"It never did me any harm."

I spoke more gently. "Please try to remember he's only six. Grown-up afternoons and that sort of stuff are boring to him. I'm probably to blame because I suggested he talk to Marjorie about Doctor Who, so that he would have something to talk about and she would understand why it's important to him." My heart contracted as I thought of my little boy trying to make conversation with the hard-faced woman, imagining her unsmiling face.

"I might have known that it would come back to you and the way you baby him. He spoiled and he needs to learn how to behave. The old ways had it right – children should be seen and not heard."

"Was he rude?"

"Not exactly, no. He just wouldn't shut up. She tried to get him to talk about school – she is paying for it after all – but the ungrateful little brat had nothing to say about it, beyond telling her about his friends and saying that he liked circle time, whatever the hell that is."

"Seth, that is him talking about school!" I burst out. "What was she expecting, an OFSTED report? Or don't they have those in the private sector? And for your information, circle time is when they can sit together and chat about things that are important to them. It's a reward for being good all week."

"That's what I mean. They're in school, they shouldn't have to be enticed to behave. They should just bloody do it, or get punished."

"Well, if they don't behave they get circle time taken away. In Toby's class, as there are eight boys, that's when they talk about things like Doctor Who."

"That's what playtime is for, surely?" he growled.

"I don't know about you and Marjorie, but I'd prefer that he spend playtime running around getting lots of exercise and fresh air." I didn't mention that, as far as I knew, Toby and his friends spent their playtimes re-enacting previous Doctor Who adventures.

"He was still very annoying, so I brought him home before Marjorie got completely fed up with him. And now I'm going back out to dinner." With that, he turned on his heel and left, slamming the front door behind him.

I sighed, went to the fridge and poured myself a large glass of wine which I drank quickly. Then I went upstairs to Toby's room, tapped on the door and went in. He was lying on his bed with his thumb in his mouth, clutching his toy TARDIS. His face was streaked with tears and as he looked at me he was a picture of misery. I sat on the bed beside him and stroked his hair. "Oh, Tobes, I'm sorry. That was my fault. I thought that Marjorie would like to hear about the things that you like, but maybe she just wasn't ready for Doctor Who."

"Have we missed it now, Mummy?" His voice was so sad and quiet it made my heart hurt.

"Not exactly, sweetie," I said with a smile. "I've got a surprise for you. Go and wash your face, put your special pyjamas on and then come downstairs."

His face brightened and he padded off to the bathroom. I nipped into my bedroom and put on the leggings and oversized Doctor Who T-shirt that did for my 'special pyjamas' and headed downstairs. My mobile started ringing and I saw it was Fergus – we'd swapped numbers this morning.

"Hello, lovely lady," his Irish lilt was a welcome, soothing influence. "How did the little man enjoy his programme?"

"He hasn't yet." My voice was wobbly and I poured the story out to him.

"That man!" I heard him swear under his breath. "So you haven't started watching yet?"

"No, I'm going to start cooking tea in a minute and then we'll settle down after to watch it."

"Can you give me half an hour? And don't worry about cooking. Seth will be out for the evening, will he?"

I agreed to give him half an hour and ended the call just as Toby came downstairs. I got a glass of milk and we sat on the sofa. "What's the surprise, Mummy?" he asked.

"You'll have to wait and see, my darling. Just for a little while."

Twenty-five minutes later the doorbell rang. Toby ran to answer it and I followed him into the hall. A delivery boy from the local pizza restaurant stood at the door, clutching two large boxes and a carrier bag.

"We haven't ordered anything." I said, confused.

"Well, it's all paid for and this is definitely the address," he replied.

Toby was peering around him to another figure coming up the driveway. "Fergus!" he shouted.

Fergus appeared in the doorway behind the pizza guy. "Man, that was quick." He grinned at him, taking the boxes and the bag. "You beat me here. Do you have the other order, too?"

"Yeah, I do," said the youth. "But are you sure about these directions?"

"Definitely, and there's an extra fiver in it for you if you deliver these as well." He handed a six pack of beers to the pizza guy and, as he did so, I saw recognition dawn on the lad's face.

"Wait, you're…" He grinned and stuck out his hand. "Man, I love your stuff."

"Cheers, dude." Fergus grinned back, handing over the five-pound note. "Don't let them go cold, now."

"Sure thing." The lad's face was red and he was smiling the widest smile. "I'm off there now." He backed off down the drive.

Fergus turned to me and Toby. "It always amazes me when I still get recognised, but it comes in useful sometimes." He crouched down and gave Toby a high-five. "Yo, dude, how's it going?"

"Yay, Fergus." Toby's face lit up.

"Other order?" I queried.

"Are you going to let me in," he stood up again. "Or shall we just stand here all night?"

We went inside and, once in the living room, he put the pizza boxes down on the table. "This needs to go in the freezer," he said, handing me the carrier bag. "Now then, dude," he went on, turning to Toby. "I understand that there's a bit of an event planned here for tonight. So, as I've gate-crashed, I brought the supplies and made sure I dressed for the occasion." With that he whipped off his coat and revealed a cricket jumper, brightly coloured scarf and a bow tie. "I wasn't sure which doctor you were up to, so I mixed a few up. What do you think?"

"Cool," said Toby. "But we've missed Doctor Who and our recorder thingy isn't working."

Fergus looked confused and shot a look at me.

"That's the surprise, sweetie. Fergus fixed it."

"So it's Doctor Who, pizza and ice cream for afters," said Fergus. "Some wine for Mummy and me, and coke for you, Tobes. What do you say?"

"YES YES YES!"

*

It was a lovely evening. We watched Doctor Who, gorging ourselves on pizza. And then we watched it again – 'because we can', as Fergus and Toby decided. About 9:30, I started to get nervous about Seth returning, but would have felt churlish to ask Fergus to leave. I was starting to fidget and was trying to think of a way to say something to him when suddenly he jumped up.

"Right," he said to Toby. "It's high time we Time Lords were in bed. We need our sleep if we're going to be ready to save the universe. Off you hop, I'll just collect up all these boxes and the ice cream tub to take with me…"

"Why are you doing that?" Toby asked.

"I have a secret plan to run my car on leftover pizza boxes." Fergus winked. "It'll save me a fortune on petrol."

"You're just silly." Toby gave him a hug, then came over to me.

"You won't be saying that when I'm the world's biggest pizza box fuel millionaire," Fergus replied.

"Okay, sweetie," I said, giving Toby a kiss. "Go clean your teeth and I'll be up to check on you in a minute." He disappeared and then we heard him thumping up the stairs. I turned to Fergus. "Thank you, it's been a fun evening."

"You're welcome, lovely lady. And I will take these away with me." He held up the boxes in his hand. "No point in giving himself something else to fret about, is there?"

At the door, he turned to smile at me and I suddenly remembered. "Hey, you never did tell me what the other delivery was?"

"Ah, that. Sure, I couldn't have sat here all warm and toasty like, knowing that our friends weren't doing the same. Although I didn't think that Trev and Dolly would appreciate ice cream, in their circumstances. I thought lager would be more to their taste."

Instinctively, I gave him a hug. "You are such a lovely person, I'll bet your mother's proud of you."

He tightened his arms around me for a second and then stepped away, regarding me with his head tilted over slightly to one side. "I hope so." He seemed to be about to say something else, but then stood straighter and gave himself a little shake. "Well, good night to you, fair Rosalind, and adieu until we meet again."

"Adieu, kind sir," I replied, with a little curtsey. "And as Toby would say, yeah whatev's…"

We both laughed and then he was gone. I went back inside and cleared up before heading up to bed. I looked in on Toby and he was spark out, the TARDIS clutched in his hand. I gently removed it, kissed his forehead and tucked him in. Then, for the first time in a long while, I went to bed and fell asleep without having had to anaesthetise myself with alcohol, and with a smile on my face.

*

The following weekend, I'd arranged for one of Toby's friends from school to come for a play date. Toby had been looking forward to the visit and had planned all sorts of activities for them. Alice, Benji's mum, brought him round and we all had lunch together and then the boys went up to Toby's room to play.

"I hope you don't mind me staying too," Alice said as we settled down with coffee. "It's just that sometimes Benji finds new situations stressful, and I like to be on hand just in case." She smiled nervously and took a sip of her coffee.

"Of course not, the boys aren't the only ones who like making new friends. Has Benji always been nervous?"

"It's not so much nerves, it's more that he is uncomfortable when he breaks from his normal routine. And that can lead to problems. I'm sure you've heard we've had some trouble at school sometimes."

"I'd heard something." I smiled sympathetically. "But I have an aversion myself to idle gossip. And every kid has a moment now and then."

"It's a little bit more than that, we think." She stared out of the window as she was speaking. "The school are talking about autism spectrum disorder." I could hear the catch in her voice and I reached across the table and squeezed her hand.

"Hey, whatever, he's still your little boy, right?"

She nodded and I busied myself refilling the cafetière to give her a moment to collect herself.

Just then Seth arrived home. I heard him go straight to his study without calling out a greeting. Then he appeared in the kitchen. "What the hell is Toby doing up there?" he grumbled. "It sounds like a pack of elephants is doing a tango. Oh, hello." His demeanour changed as he noticed Alice.

"I'm pretty sure that elephants move in herds," I said brightly. "And it's probably more Riverdance than Strictly. Toby is playing with Benji and this is Benji's mother, Alice."

The boys burst into the room. Toby was brandishing my guitar and Benji had a set of tom-tom drums. "Listen to this Mum," Toby shouted. "We've made up a song!" They threw themselves onto the sofa and grew serious as Toby counted them in.

Of course it was just a cacophony, but they were loving every second of it. Alice and I both laughed, but more than watching the boys I was enjoying watching Seth's face as he struggled with his conflicting urges to shut the boys up and charm Alice.

The decision was made for him when Alice turned to me, delightedly clapping her hands. "Look at Benji! He is totally engaged and happy. I don't think I've ever seen him like this. Where can I get a set of those drums?"

"You can take those with you for now," I said. "We don't use them. And there is a music shop in town where you could probably pick some up."

"But they're…" Seth began, but Alice didn't let him finish.

"Oh, thank you, thank you! You have no idea how lovely it is to see him like this. Wait until his dad sees him."

"Our pleasure," Seth said stiffly. "Now, I really have to get going. Sorry Alice, but I have a business meeting. It was good to meet you." He turned to me, "I'll be back later, darling. Not sure yet what time. See you boys," he called as he left the room.

"Yeah, Dad, bye." Toby barely glanced up from the guitar. Benji had his eyes closed, obviously lost in the music he was creating.

I knew Seth didn't have a meeting, he just wanted to get away from the noise. And by the time Alice and Benji left, a couple of hours later, my head was ringing but it was worth it to see the smile on both their faces. I don't think we'd have been able to prise the tom-toms away from Benji even if we'd wanted to, although I did whisper to Alice that I thought she could get mufflers for them from the shop in town if she felt the need.

"Mummy, when are we seeing Fergus again?" Toby asked as we waved goodbye. "I told Benji that he might let us join his band."

"I'm not sure, sweetie, and I don't know if he has a band anymore."

"Oh, that's okay," Toby said airily. "We'll let him join ours."

"That's very sweet of you, darling. I'm sure he'd love that."

*

I was expecting Seth to kick off about the tom-toms when he came back – he could be quite childish about 'his' things when he wanted to be – but he was all smiles as he asked me for Alice's number.

"Why?" I tried not to sound as suspicious as I felt. If Seth could be said to have a type, she was it – petite and blonde, with an air of vulnerability.

"Because Benji is exactly the sort of child we want to target with our project, and I think it would be useful to have a chat with her."

"I see. She's quite nervous, Seth, and the subject of Benji's possible autism is quite a sore point for her."

"Bloody hell, Roz!" he exploded. "I only wanted to get together with her for a chat with me and Marjorie, not white-slave them both to Africa."

"Okay, well, why don't I arrange another play date here next weekend and then you and Marjorie can come and talk to her here? She might feel more relaxed than if you appear to be interviewing her. She could bring her husband along too."

"I suppose," he said slowly. "As long as you keep the boys quiet while we're talking. That racket this afternoon was deafening."

"What exactly is this project? There seems to be an awful lot of talking and planning going on, but I still don't know what it's all about."

"Well, Marjorie wanted it to be a charity that would benefit children, but we were a bit stuck for a USP. Meeting Benji has given me a great idea, I've spoken to Marjorie about it and she agrees."

"What's a USP?" I asked, but he just rolled his eyes and went into his study.

A charity to benefit children sounded like a good thing, but neither Seth nor Marjorie struck me as the altruistic type and I couldn't help but suspect their motives. But then, I couldn't see Fergus getting involved in anything dodgy. I decided to curb my natural scepticism where Seth was concerned and give them the benefit of the doubt.

*

We invited Benji and his parents over the following weekend and they met with Seth and Marjorie. I wasn't in on the discussion as it was my job to keep the boys out of the way. But it seemed to go well and Seth was certainly busy over the next couple of months.

I saw Alice a few times at the school gates and she seemed very excited about the plans. One afternoon she and Benji came back after school and she talked about Seth's proposal. He had barely mentioned it to me. "It's such an amazing thing," she gushed. "You must be so excited."

"Actually, I'm not that involved." I felt somewhat embarrassed by my lack of interest in what Seth and Marjorie were up to and resolved to get more involved and be more supportive. After all, Toby was involved too and perhaps it would help us to become closer as a family. It might even help me get more used to Marjorie. I was increasingly feeling that I should keep an eye on what they were up to - I just couldn't shake that nagging suspicion in my gut – so when Seth came home that evening I asked if there was anything I could do to help.

"Yeah, I suppose there is. We're building up to a Launch in late June or early July, ready to start in the new school year, and there is quite a lot to do. I'll ask Marjorie if she's got any ideas."

Marjorie had plenty of ideas, most of which involved me doing grunt work – all the grotty stuff she didn't want to do – but I didn't mind. It did seem to bring Seth and me to a better place and our house was calmer and even a little bit happier.

Seth had said he wanted to make a video of Benji and Toby playing music together to illustrate the thinking behind the Project. Alice approached me one afternoon as we were collecting the boys from school.

"Are you ready for your close-up, Mrs DeMille?" She laughed and then looked confused at my puzzled expression. "I mean the video shoot this afternoon," she went on, frowning. "Aren't you going to be there? I was going to offer you a lift."

"Of course," I lied. "And a lift would be great, thank you. Do we have time for a coffee beforehand?"

"I should think so, although I may need your help finding this place that they're using as an office. Seth's given me the directions but it seems to be in the middle of nowhere."

I wasn't aware they had an office. So much for the spirit of openness and togetherness. And why is he luring Alice out there alone? Or am I being too suspicious?

"I'll just give Fergus a ring," I said. "I'm sure he must know the way and it would be silly to do the music stuff without the musician. He must be going."

"No, lovely lady," Fergus said when I got him on the phone and explained. "I haven't been asked, but now you come to mention it there is some stuff I need to do at the office. I'll meet you at the coffee shop and then you can all follow me out there."

"I hope your man isn't up to his old shenanigans." I heard him mutter as we met at the coffee shop. "I hope he wasn't planning for Alice to go the same way as Bianca. That girl is still a mess."

I glanced at him in surprise, but he shook his head as Alice approached us. "Now, let me buy you ladies a couple of coffees and some disgustingly fattening cakes. The boys have already given me their orders. Then we can go to the offices."

*

Alice was right – the offices were in the middle of nowhere. They appeared to be an old farmhouse, complete with kitchen and what appeared to be a sitting room with a couple of sofas.

If Seth was surprised to see all of us turn up then he hid it well. Having Fergus there to interact with the boys proved to be a great success and I could see that Seth was pleased with the footage he was getting.

I was standing next to him at one point while Alice and Fergus played music with the boys. "Marjorie's not here, then?" I asked casually.

"No, she has a meeting. It was already arranged and then Alice said that this was the best time for her, so the logical thing was for Marjorie to keep the meeting and for me to meet Alice for the filming. We thought about rearranging but then we talked about it and decided this made more sense."

"I see." Unwittingly he had confirmed my suspicions; Seth had a habit of over-explaining when he was lying. "She'll be sorry she missed this, I expect."

"Probably." He shrugged. "Are you okay to go back with Alice? I'd like to stay and get on with some editing."

"Sure, it's time we got going anyway. The boys have school tomorrow and there's still homework to be done. Will you be back for dinner?"

"No, I'll probably be here until the small hours. I may even kip here on the sofa. Don't wait up."

"I never do." I laughed, but there was an edge to my laughter. I didn't drive – I'd never learned and, anyway, my drinking habits prohibited it – so he knew I had no way of checking whether he was telling the truth or not. It crossed my mind that he and Marjorie may have chosen the location of the office deliberately for that reason, but then I shut the thought down as being suspicious to the point of paranoia.

Alice and Benji dropped Toby and me home and I settled him at the kitchen table with his homework while I started cooking dinner. I wasn't surprised when the doorbell went and it was Fergus. He stood on the doorstep looking slightly nervous.

"If you want to stay for dinner, you'll have to do homework duty," I said breezily, before he could say anything. "And the grown-ups don't get to talk until after bath and bedtime."

It was a fun evening. Once Toby was in bed, and I was sure he was asleep, I got a beer out of the fridge for Fergus and poured another glass of wine. Then I sat down at the table. "So, you're still in touch with Bianca? How is she?"

"She's okay. She'll be fine eventually, but she's given up any idea of a music career. She's planning to go to College next year to do beauty therapy. Roz, about what I said…"

"Don't mention it."

"No, I shouldn't have said anything. It's not my place. I mean, if you ever want to talk I'm happy to listen, but other people's marriages…"

"I'm fine," I said firmly. "It's not a subject that is open for discussion, but I'm glad Bianca is going to be okay. Now, tell me everything you know about this project of theirs."

"You know, it's really not a bad idea. I'm excited about it…"

He talked for a couple of hours and, by the time he'd finished, I was quite excited about the Project too. I just couldn't figure out what was in it for Seth or Marjorie.

"I was also puzzled at first," Fergus said. "But I think, for Marjorie, it's the kudos of being involved in a charity for children, particularly kids with special needs. For Seth, it's money of course. He's got a cushy number going here with her money backing it up. Whatever, as long as the kids benefit, let's not rock the boat."

"Trev and Dolly think…" I couldn't bring myself to finish the thought. "Well, you know…"

"Yeah, it's not that." He put his hand on mine across the table, reassuringly. "It's not sexual, their connection. God, even Seth wouldn't stoop that low. I mean, she's got twenty years on him, and he's hardly toy boy material, is he? I haven't figured it out yet, but I honestly don't think you need to worry about her. And now I'd better get home to bed. I've got quite a day tomorrow."

I lay awake, that night, turning it over in my mind. I resolved to try and get to know Marjorie better and see if my suspicions were ill-founded. Maybe I had misjudged her? Maybe she would turn out to be a good influence on Seth.

*

The Launch date was about six weeks away when Seth came home one day with a folder containing designs for an invitation and flyers and such.

"What do you think of these?" He laid them out across the kitchen table. "We've got a new girl on board, an artist, and she's done these for us. I'm quite excited about her, she's really good, and she's deaf which will score points with the PC brigade."

"They're great designs," I replied. "But surely it shouldn't matter whether she's deaf or not? And how is she going to communicate with the children?"

"Sign language. The kids at the state schools all learn Makaton, which is a basic form of sign language. But, anyway, she's an amazing lip reader. Honestly, you wouldn't know she was deaf most of the time. As long as you're facing her when you speak, she's great."

"Does she have a name, this amazing woman?"

"Ellie. Eleanor Chandler. She is going to be a great addition to the team. And did you know that Fergus can do sign language? We had to put a ban on them signing to each other in the office."

"Why?"

"Because none of us knew what they were saying. Marjorie didn't like it, I think she thought they were talking about her."

"Probably," I muttered under my breath. "So when do I get to meet her?"

"She's coming to the Launch. Her boyfriend is something to do with the Council and they're giving us a lot of funding. We help them achieve a lot of their policy targets, and because we are an independent charity it's extra kudos to them for engaging with the 'third sector'. There's money to be had if you know how to spin it."

And if anyone would know how to spin it, it would be you. "How fortunate. For both sides," I said dryly. I couldn't help but think about the soup kitchen that Trevor and Dolly had told me had lost its funding. They were in the process of persuading the manager of a local café to help them out by donating the leftover food at the end of the day. Trevor was hoping that if they got a couple of the local food shops involved, as well, they might be able to get a small food bank going. But, of course, homeless people weren't as 'sexy' as disabled children. And, if Fergus's theory about Marjorie's motives was right, wouldn't score nearly so high on the kudos.

*

I'd told Seth about my plan to get to know Marjorie better and he told me he was doing his best to get us together more. She was always perfectly pleasant to me and it was clear that she was genuinely fond of Toby, but I still couldn't warm to her.

Half term was due a few weeks before the launch, and Seth announced that she had borrowed a friend's house in France for a long weekend at the end of half term. "She thought that we could all do with some downtime before, hopefully, we get really busy," he explained. "We can fly over on the Thursday evening, then back on the Monday evening. There's a pool and stuff and it'll be nice for us all to have some time together as a family to make up for how hard I've been working, don't you think?"

But we're not a family. I bit down on the thought and nodded. He was sitting at the kitchen table while I got dinner ready. "We'll have to talk to the school about Toby having the Monday off."

"Don't worry, babe, Marjorie's already fixed it," he said casually. "She spoke to the Head last week."

"Last week? But I hadn't agreed it then. I'm only learning about it now."

"Yeah, she didn't want you to be bothered and I forgot to mention it."

"It's kind of important, don't you think? I mean—"

"For God's sake, Roz!" He exploded. "She's paying for us to go away for a fucking weekend. Can't you just be grateful, for once?" He thumped the table hard and I jumped.

"Sorry, I am grateful. It's a lovely thing for her to do. I'm just surprised that the school would grant him leave on her say-so."

"Well, they know who's paying the fees."

She who pays the piper… "Yeah, I guess they do."

*

Les Peyroux was beautiful and only forty minutes from Bergerac airport. The house was on the edge of a neighbouring vineyard, with a stone terrace and a beautiful, kidney-shaped pool which had been built with tiny, mosaic-like black tiles so it looked more like a natural pond than a swimming pool.

Toby and I played in the pool while Marjorie read magazines and Seth spent most of his time on his laptop or on his phone, usually inside the house. His redhead's complexion kept him out of the sunshine but I think it also made him feel important to still be doing business even while we were on holiday.

"I hadn't realised this project was so in-depth," I said to Marjorie on Saturday afternoon, when Seth once again disappeared inside the house after lunch.

"He's very engaged with it. I knew I'd made the right choice for my Project manager almost as soon as I met him, and he knows how important it is to me." She pushed the sunglasses to the top of her head and stared directly at me. "I wanted a charity that would help children and when he came up with this idea it was perfect."

"Did you never have children of your own?"

"Sadly, my husband was much older than me and unable to father children…" She stopped abruptly, replaced the sunglasses and concentrated on watching Toby in the pool.

"I'm sorry," I said. "I didn't mean to pry."

"It's not something I like to dwell on." She sighed. "But, as we are now practically family, I suppose you deserve an explanation at least."

Practically family? "Marjorie, you don't have to tell me anything that makes you uncomfortable. It isn't any of my business."

"No, I want to tell you, because I want you to know why Seth and Toby – and you – have become so important to me. Is there any of that wine left from lunch?"

I poured us both a glass as she moved her chair closer towards me.

"My husband and I couldn't have children, as I said, but I had had a child – a son – before I met him. He would be about the same age as Seth is now, but I was seventeen and to be an unmarried mother in those days was just about the worst thing I could have done to my family. When I told my parents they were horrified and they made me go and stay with an aunt until after he was born and then they had him adopted." She took a large mouthful of wine.

"What about the father?"

"We were a wealthy family and he was an under-gardener on our estate. But he was ambitious, he had plans. By the time I realised I was pregnant, he had moved to France – here." She gave a little shrug and an ironic laugh. "He went to work with the War Graves Commission somewhere, but they have so many places all over Europe. I tried to find out where he had gone, but I couldn't, so he never knew. I returned to my family after the baby was born and eventually went to train as a nurse at the Royal London. That was what girls like me were expected to do." She squared her shoulders and took another gulp of wine.

"Marjorie, that's awful. Did you ever find out what happened to the baby?"

"No, it was a private adoption. My parents took care of everything. When I moved to London I tried to find Drew – the father – and also to find out what had happened to my son, but I came up against dead-end after dead-end. Then I met my husband, a surgeon at the London. Don't get me wrong, Roz, I was extremely fond of my husband but a small part of me couldn't help being quite smug about marrying a man my parents couldn't disapprove of, who couldn't give them grandchildren."

"But that meant you didn't have any more children of your own?"

"If I couldn't have Drew, I didn't want any."

"Is that what you called him?"

"Yes, after his father, but he could have been given any name after he was taken away from me."

I reached across and squeezed her hand, feeling quite sympathetic towards this woman I usually disliked so much.

"Anyway, he would be about the same age as Seth is now. When I met Seth and he told me about having no mother, I just felt it was fate somehow. I had often wondered whether I had grandchildren and I thought I could help with Toby in so many ways. I have all of this money and no-one to spend it on."

Marjorie being vulnerable, sounding pathetic, was a new concept for me. I still couldn't totally warm to her, but I did understand a little more.

Toby – with impeccable timing – chose this moment to climb out of the pool and stand in front of us, shivering. Marjorie grabbed a towel and started vigorously drying him off to warm him. Ordinarily, this would have grated on me but I told myself that she was just a lonely old woman who loved my boy.

The rest of the weekend went by smoothly and we flew back to Southampton on the Monday. I resolved to talk to Seth about my chat with Marjorie, and to maybe establish some boundaries that we were all comfortable with.

*

The opportunity came sooner than I'd thought a couple of days later. Seth was home to have dinner with Toby and me for once and, after Toby had gone to bed, he poured me a glass of wine and sat on the sofa opposite me.

"I hear Marjorie told you her story?" he asked casually. "What did you think?"

"Apart from the fact that I wasn't aware that your parents were dead? I thought you said you'd run away from home because of their drinking and violence."

"It might as well be the same thing." He shrugged carelessly. "It's only details."

"No, it's not. Marjorie thinks you're an orphan, which isn't true."

"I'm as good as," he snapped. "What the hell difference does it make to you, anyway?"

"None, I suppose. I just don't see why you had to lie about it."

"I didn't lie. She assumed my parents were dead and I didn't correct her. She's a lonely old lady looking for a son-figure and I felt sorry for her."

"She's a rich lonely old lady."

"Look, where's the harm? She wants a family, we've got one. She's happily paying for Toby to go to that school, she paid for us to go on holiday and she's given me an extremely well-paid job. As far as I can see, it's win-win."

"It just feels dishonest."

"Since when did you get a conscience? Just don't rock the boat, okay babe? Toby loves that school, it would be awful if he had to leave." His tone was calm, but I could hear the underlying threat.

"Okay, but you had better hope it doesn't come back to bite you on the bum."

"How could it? If I play this right, we could be set for life. She won't last forever and she needs to have somewhere to leave all that money."

I downed my glass of wine and stood up. "I'm going to bed." I didn't like Marjorie much, but I couldn't help feeling sorry for her. I looked at Seth, trying to hide my distaste. "I'm assuming you'll be sleeping in your study again tonight?" I picked up the wineglass and the bottle and took them both upstairs with me. But even after I had finished the bottle I couldn't sleep. I knew I wouldn't betray Seth, but not out of any sense of loyalty. I was just too scared of what his reaction might be.

*

I tried my hardest with Marjorie over the next couple of weeks, mainly out of guilt, but there was still something about her that left me cold. We were busy with the Launch, though, so I didn't have to spend too much time alone with her.

Launch night came and Seth was flat out. I picked up Toby from school, took him home for his tea and we were then going to walk to the Assembly Rooms after he had done his homework. He went up to his room as soon as we got home and came down looking mystified.

"Mummy, what's this?" he asked, holding a set of clothes that looked like they had been made for a miniature old man.

"I don't know, darling, where did you find them?"

"On my bed, but they're not mine. They're really weird."

"Never mind," I said brightly. "Let's get on with homework and tea." I realised that Seth had left the clothes for Toby to wear that evening. No doubt Marjorie had bought them, but they were ridiculous clothes for a small boy to wear. He would look like a tiny old fogey. But Seth would have a fit if I vetoed them. Then, suddenly, I had an idea.

"Actually, Tobes, perhaps you should try them on. I think Daddy has left them for you to wear tonight."

He made a face but disappeared upstairs obediently while I loaded the bedding I had stripped that morning into the washing machine. I had just set it on a long cottons wash when he reappeared, walking stiffly and looking miserable.

"Do I have to wear these tonight? The shirt is really itchy and the trousers are too big."

"They're not that big. Sit down, sweetie, and get your juice. Then we'll do your homework, okay?" I went into the kitchen and mixed up a big jug of Ribena, while Toby sat down at the table. As I returned to the table, my foot caught on the rug

93

underneath it and I lunged forward, tipping the whole jug all over Toby. "Oh, Tobes," I said in a rush. "I'm so sorry – all over your lovely, new clothes. You won't be able to wear them tonight, now."

He looked down at the clothes that were now wet and pink, then looked at me. His face broke into a grin.

"It's not funny, Toby," I said, trying to look serious. "And if we don't get those clothes into the washing machine right now, they will probably stain and you won't be able to wear them ever again. Oh no! I've just put the bedding on, it will be a couple of hours at least and by then we'll be out." I widened my eyes in a mock expression of horror. "What can we do?"

"I don't know, Mummy," he replied, looking equally horrified and trying not to laugh. "Shall I go and get changed?"

"You'd better have a bath as well, otherwise all that Ribena will be really sticky. I just hope it doesn't make us late." I had a nasty feeling that Seth and Marjorie had a plan to parade my boy in front of all the bigwigs they had invited to the Launch. Knowing that meeting all these new people in one go would make Toby anxious, I decided that we would get there just as the presentation started.

When Toby came down again, this time dressed as a proper boy in his smart jeans and a sweatshirt, I announced, "You know, it's a special occasion tonight and I think you deserve to go out to tea beforehand. Let's go to the café and then we can go onto the Launch after that."

As we left the house, the home phone started to ring but I ignored it. It was only when we got to the café that I 'realised' that I had left my mobile back at the house. "The thing is, Toby, if we go back for it we're going to be really late." He smiled nervously and I hugged him to me. "None of this is your fault, my darling. I'll explain it all to Daddy and if he's going to be cross with anyone, it will be with me. Okay?"

"Okay, Mummy, we can tell him it was a series of unfortunate events." He smiled as he quoted the title of his current favourite books.

"Yes we can," I said. "And if he gets too cross, I'll remind him how many times I've asked him to stick that rug down in the kitchen." Then I kissed the top of his head.

*

Seth came out to meet us as we hurried up the steps of the Assembly Rooms with five minutes to spare. His eyes were dark as he hissed at me. "Where the hell have you been? I've been trying to call you."

"I'm sorry," I said, keeping my voice light. "We had a bit of a disastrous afternoon, and then I left my mobile at home. But we're here now. We haven't missed anything, have we?"

94

"We're just about to start the presentation," he said through clenched teeth. "Marjorie wanted to take Toby on stage with us…" He glanced at Toby. "What the hell is he wearing? Where are the clothes I left out for him?" He didn't even greet his son.

"We've had a series of unfortunate events," announced Toby in his most portentous voice. "Sorry, Daddy."

Seth looked like he was about to explode and I put a placatory hand on his arm. "It's all my fault…" I started to say, just as Marjorie hurried up.

"Seth, we have to start now," she said firmly. She looked at Toby and me. "Well, at least you're here, I suppose. We'll have no time to rehearse Toby now," she said to Seth. She looked at Toby again. "And he's hardly dressed for it, anyway. Hello, Toby darling." At least she had acknowledged his presence.

"We'll be fine, sitting at the back and watching," I said. "Go on, or you'll miss your big moment." I smiled in what I hoped looked like a supportive way.

Seth looked like he had a lot more to say, but Marjorie strode off and, with a last withering look at me, he scuttled off behind her.

I looked down at Toby beside me. "Phew," I whispered. "I think we got away with that. Let's go and watch the show." We slipped inside and found a couple of spare chairs at a table near the back. A movement from the next table caught my eye and I turned to see Stu waving at me. I hadn't known that Seth had invited him. I felt a little twinge of guilt that maybe he had done so for me and my sabotage tactics had spoiled the surprise. Then, with a little shiver, I pulled myself together and told myself that probably Seth had invited Stu to keep me occupied while he and Marjorie paraded Toby like some sort of prize cow.

The presentation was actually very good and I learned quite a lot more about the Project from it. Towards the end, Seth announced that two of the leading members of Mobius Strip – "who some of you may remember from the Top Forty a few years ago" – would be working with the charity and were going to give a short performance now. I saw Fergus and Olly take to the stage and figured I would slip out for a cigarette and a quick drink. I squeezed Toby's shoulder and pantomimed going outside. He nodded and turned back, enthralled, to watch the band.

Outside, I found a bench and sat on it with my knees to my chest. I took a sip from my lilt bottle, enjoying the warmth as the cider spread through my body. A woman came out from the Assembly Rooms, sat on a nearby bench and rolled a cigarette. She was striking, with long, curly, strawberry blonde hair, but what really struck me was how colourfully she was dressed – with a hand knitted jacket and some ethnic looking scarves and high-heeled boots. *That's how I used to dress… Before I met Seth. When did I stop caring what I looked like?*

95

"Are you enjoying the show?" I asked, feeling drawn to her and wanting her to notice me. She ignored me – probably not realising I was talking to her – so I moved a little closer and repeated the question.

She caught the movement and turned, putting her head on one side and smiling at me. "I'm sorry, did you say something? I'm deaf, but I lipread. I didn't catch what you were saying."

Immediately, I realised this was the woman I had been hearing so much about over the past few weeks. "Oh, are you Ellie? I'm pleased to meet you." I moved to sit on her bench and made sure I was facing her. "I'm Roz, Roz Peterson. I'm Seth's wife." I held my hand out to shake hers and couldn't miss the momentary flash of confusion across her face. I smiled. "You've never heard of me, have you?" I was unsurprised, Seth had long ago abandoned the habit of introducing me to his latest intended conquests. "Don't worry about it, I'm Seth's dirty little secret. I'm a drunk, don't you know?" I tried to keep my voice light, but I was still quite hurt. "I'm sure Marjorie will fill you in. She does enjoy giving people the gory details, but in a caring and concerned way, of course." I finished sarcastically, then realised any tone of voice was lost on her.

She grimaced and wrinkled her nose. "She'd have to bring herself to speak to me in order to do that," she said in a surprisingly low, even tone. "And then, of course, I'd have to be interested in anything the old witch wanted to say, providing I could drag my gaze away from that ridiculous concrete helmet hairdo."

I burst out laughing. "Concrete helmet hairdo! I love that." Chuckling, I took a cigarette from my pack. "Do you have a light?"

Just then Stu came out and joined us. I introduced him to Ellie and we laughed about the concrete hairdo.

When Toby came out I was enjoying myself so much I had forgotten about the cigarette. I didn't like to smoke in front of him. Apart from it being a bad influence, I didn't want to put him in a position of having so many ongoing secrets from his father.

"Mummy, are you smoking?" He snuggled in beside me on the bench.

"Yes I am, darling." I took a deep breath of fresh air and dropped the cigarette on the ground behind the bench. "Toby, this lady is Eleanor. Do you remember, Daddy told you about her? That she can't hear very well and so she watches your mouth to see what you're saying."

"Yes." Toby took his thumb from his mouth and smiled at Ellie. "It's nice to meet you."

"And you, Toby. Are you enjoying yourself?" I was pleased to see that Ellie leaned towards Toby so that her face was level with his and she smiled broadly.

"Yeah, I love the band and I love Fergus." Toby looked up at me. "It's all right, Mummy, I won't tell Daddy that you were smoking." My heart broke a little as I thought about all the secrets and worries that my baby was balancing in his head.

*

I'm not sure if Detective Nixon heard the catch in my voice, but she raised her hand. "I think this would be a good point to suspend the interview. We've been going quite a while and I'm sure you're tired. We have Ms Chandler coming in next and I would like some time to prepare before that. If it's all right with you, Roz, we'll pick this up again at a later date?" She looked around the table, nodded at DS Wood, picked up her file and left the room.

I was left staring at Ian. "Is that it? Or do I have to stay here? I don't understand."

"It's certainly very unusual," he replied. "DS Wood?"

"You can go home, Roz. We'll be in touch when we need you again."

Within ten minutes we were outside the Police Station. "I definitely need a drink," I said to Ian.

"Good plan, let's go and debrief in the pub."

* * *

Beatrice

I grabbed a cup of coffee and was in my office with my shoes kicked off, rubbing my feet, when Alex came in.

"Er… Guv?" She stood in the doorway. "What's going on?"

"A complete waste of my time," I replied. "Clearly, this Marjorie woman has some sort of influence somewhere and has kicked up a stink. We have a post-mortem conclusion of suicide and the Coroner has signed it off; this Seth was obviously a shit of the highest order and the world is a better place without him; and I have six weeks to go until retirement. So why not give it to good old Billie Nixon to give her something to do, to stop her getting under everybody's feet while she's waiting to shuffle off to Shady Pines. Or wherever it is that retired detectives go." I took a mouthful of coffee and then continued. "That's okay and I'm happy to play the game, but I'll be buggered if I'm going to waste any more time or resources than I have to on this."

"But what if she's right? What if he really was murdered? Surely, we have a duty—"

"I'm not saying I'm not going to investigate it," I sighed. "I'll go through the procedure, but I'm not going to waste the Department's scant resources on some sort of PR or political exercise. We'll talk to the Chandler woman tomorrow, then that other one with the double-barrelled surname, and take it from there. We'll call in this Marjorie woman too. No reason why she should get away without being interviewed if she's prepared to put everyone else through it, and if we get any sniff that there might have been a murder then we'll deal with it appropriately. Do you have a problem with that?"

"Sounds fair enough to me. He certainly sounds like a grade A shit, from what the wife says. But we only have her word for that. Let's see what the Chandler woman says tomorrow."

"Right now, I'm heading for a glass of wine and a bubble bath. What are you up to tonight?"

"Oh, the usual I expect. We'll get the kids bathed and put into bed before wine o'clock, then dinner in front of the TV. You know, it's just so rock 'n' roll chez Wood."

"Don't knock it, at least you have a family to go home to. I even found myself thinking that I ought to get a cat when I retire, and that really is the slippery slope." I gave a little laugh. "I'll be a mad cat lady before the year is out, you wait and see."

* * *

ELEANOR

Fitch and I presented ourselves at the Police Station as requested. The officer on the desk tried to tell me that Fitch couldn't come into the station, but I played the deaf card and explained that she was my hearing dog.

"Really? A Jack Russell?" He was obviously completely up-to-date on the Police sarcasm training.

"Yes, a Jack Russell. Why should labradors and retrievers get all the glory?" I glared at him and took the seat he had indicated.

After twenty minutes, I went back to the desk. "Look, if your Inspector Nixon is too busy to keep the appointment she made with me, perhaps she should come to me when she can spare the time. She has my number."

"Please wait there, Ms Chandler. I'll call and see what's holding them up."

I mentally gave them another five minutes and at the end of that was just about to leave when the young Detective Sergeant appeared. "I'm so sorry for keeping you waiting, Ms Chandler. Please follow me. Oh, I'm not sure if the dog can come in—"

"She's an assistance dog. She comes everywhere with me."

She shrugged and led the way to an interview room. It was painted the same shade of early 70s civic-building-grey as the rest of the station and contained a Formica-topped table with four utilitarian chairs, presumably from the same era as the decor. There were no windows and a black panic band around the walls at waist height completed the look.

Inspector Nixon was already in there, sitting at the table and studying the contents of a buff folder in front of her. She stood up to greet me and we went through some preliminary formalities before beginning the interview. "Before we start, Ms Chandler, I need to ask if you require a sign-language interpreter?"

"Thank you, no."

She gave a little shrug and smiled. "Probably a good thing. We only have two BSL interpreters listed on our books, and one of them is you. Is there enough light in here for you?"

"Yes, thank you."

"And you are aware that you are under caution?"

"Yes."

"Now, Eleanor… May I call you Eleanor?"

"What may I call you?"

She looked surprised, momentarily. "Inspector Nixon."

"Then you may call me Ms Chandler. Best to keep things on an equal footing, don't you think?"

She smiled, as if at a private joke. "Okay, Ms Chandler, let's start with your comments at the graveside."

Now it was my turn to smile. "I thought we probably would. Obviously, with hindsight, and knowing what I now do, I would have been a little more circumspect."

"And what is it you know now?"

"That Seth didn't die of a heart attack, as I had assumed."

"Why had you assumed that?"

"Well, because I 'assumed' it was natural causes and, as he wasn't fifty yet, I 'assumed' a heart attack."

DS Wood finally joined the conversation. "Are you aware of the circumstances surrounding Mr Peterson's death?"

"Yes, I am now."

"And what do you think about that?"

"In what way? Why should I think anything?"

Inspector Nixon leaned back in her chair. "From what you know about Mr Peterson, does it surprise you?"

I took a deep breath. "Nothing about that man could surprise me anymore. But I suppose you could say that I'm surprised that his instinct for self-preservation must have let him down."

"You didn't like Mr Peterson, did you?" DS Wood said.

"You worked that out? I can see why you're a Detective."

"And yet you worked for him for some years. If you disliked him so much, why did you stay with the Evans Foundation?"

"For a start, I didn't work for him. I worked with him, there's a difference. As for why… For that, I'd have to take you right back to the beginning. Any chance of a cup of tea and some water for Fitch? It's a long story."

∗

Why am I here? I hate these bun fights. Where the hell is Mark? I turned to see Mark, smiling broadly, coming towards me.

"Are you okay, my darling? Come and meet some people."

"Do I have to?" I groaned. "I'm happy just standing here drinking."

"I know you are, but you're far too lovely not to show you off."

"Oh, fun-ny."

"Come on, you should meet these two." He led me over to an older woman and a man about our age. "This is Marjorie Evans and Seth Peterson. They're setting up a new charity and we are giving them a grant. I've told them about your artwork and they'd like to meet you."

I leant forwards and shook both their hands. "What's the charity?"

"Music therapy for disabled children. We'll be…" Seth Peterson turned away as he was talking to acknowledge someone in the crowd.

"Sorry, I missed that."

He turned back and gazed at me curiously.

"I'm deaf. I lipread, but it does mean you have to be looking at me when you speak."

"Oh, I'm sorry, I had no idea."

"No reason why you should."

Mark smiled at Seth sympathetically. "She doesn't like getting special treatment. I'd be in huge trouble if I 'warned' you."

I mock-glared at him, then turned back to Seth. "So tell me again about your charity."

"Well, it's very exciting. My background is in the music industry and we want to bring music into schools as therapy for disabled children, both learning disabled and physically, to help integrate them with their non-disabled peers."

He certainly has the jargon off pat. "Sounds good."

Seth paused and looked slightly awkward.

"I'm not a great believer in political correctness for its own sake, Mr Peterson. I'd feel silly saying that something you said 'looked' good."

"Please call me Seth."

"Seth, then. Please continue, why would you be interested in my art?"

"We are still putting our promotional material together." Marjorie Evans broke in. "We may be interested on that account." She was an extremely elegant woman, obviously well (and expensively) maintained. It would be hard to put an exact age on her, but I would say she had about twenty years on me, putting her in her mid-fifties. An image of the Wicked Queen in Snow White came to mind.

"Well, let me give you one of my cards." I fished around in my bag and pulled out a card. As I passed it to Marjorie, I realised she had been saying something.

"Sorry, missed that." I grinned.

Irritation flashed momentarily across her face but was almost instantly gone. "I said, we'll be in touch."

Wicked Queen or Grumpy the Dwarf? Seth Peterson wasn't the tallest of men, but he had managed to find a partner who only came up to his shoulders. *I wonder if they are only business partners? Surely not, she's old enough to be his mother.*

"Can I have one of those, too?" Seth held out his hand. As I handed it to him, did I imagine that his fingers brushed mine? I glanced at Mark, who didn't seem to have noticed anything amiss.

"That's beautiful." Seth was looking at my card. "Is this one of your designs?"

"No, I thought I'd use a picture downloaded from the Internet."

"Really?" His head came up and he stared at me, confused.

I smiled. "Sorry, strange sense of humour. Yes, it is one of mine."

"I see." He didn't smile back.

Oops, blown that, Ellie. You and your so-called sense of humour.
Mark stepped in. "Ellie, my sweet, let's go and talk to James. He's been very keen to meet you. Nice to see you both again."

"Yes, nice to meet you." I smiled. Marjorie had already turned away, but Seth flashed me a smile as Mark led me off to meet his friend.

*

A couple of days later I was working at home when the phone rang. "Hello, Eleanor Chandler."

Eleanor, hi. It's Seth Peterson – we met at the Council get together on Tuesday.

"Yes, I remember. Hello."

I'm not quite sure how this works. The phone, I mean.

"Me neither. I think it's something to do with electrical impulses being sent along millions of fibre-optic cables"

Sorry? Ah, the famous sense of humour.

"No, I should apologise. I can see everything you say on a screen, but it's too boring to explain. What can I do for you?"

I wanted to continue our chat from the other night. I think there may be some interesting ways we could work together. Would you like to get together for lunch sometime?

I'm not a business lunch sort of person. I don't understand it. If you want to do business with me, tell me what you want – preferably in a phone call – and I'll tell you how much it will cost. If that's agreeable, fine. If not, we haven't both wasted an hour or so of our lives making polite conversation and worrying about our table manners. But I pulled out my go-to excuse.

"I'm snowed under this week."

Next week, then? It's on me. Or rather, it's on the William Evans Foundation. How about Tuesday? There's a nice pub out near Bishmenham. I'll book a table.

"Can we not just talk about it on the phone?"

But Seth Peterson was determined.

I've got quite a lot I want to talk about, it would probably take too long. And anyway, I prefer to conduct these sorts of meetings face-to-face. And you have to eat. You do eat, I suppose?

"Yes, I eat."

So it was arranged.

"You do eat, I suppose?" I repeated later when Mark popped round after he finished work.

"Hmm." Mark was checking his phone.

"I don't get what he wants to talk about. What can I possibly do for a music therapy charity?"

"Mmm, dunno."

"Of course, then I told him to stop beating around the bush, that I couldn't wait and why didn't he come round right then so we could spend the afternoon having hot, sweaty sex."

"And did he?"

"Yes, in fact, he's still upstairs waiting for me to get rid of you so we can go again. He's just setting up the handcuffs now."

"O–kay… Er, what?" Mark finally dragged his gaze away from his phone as I threw a tea towel at him.

"I get the impression you're not giving me your full and undivided attention."

"Sorry, my darling. There's just a lot going on at work right now. So, will you have lunch with him?"

"I guess so, I just hope Grumpy won't be with him. She doesn't like me."

Seth didn't have Marjorie with him when we met the following Tuesday. We placed our orders at the bar and then went and sat at a corner table.

"So, what did you want to talk about?" I was determined not to drag this out.

"Well, I would like to talk to you about designing some of the posters and teaching materials that we take into the schools. We want very basic images, bright colours… You know the sort of thing."

I grabbed my bag and took out my notebook. "And what will they need to say?"

"I've got the details in my briefcase in the car. Let's enjoy lunch and then we can talk specifics afterwards. I'd like to fill you in a bit more about the charity."

With a deep inward sigh, I resigned myself to not getting away for at least an hour and a half. But he talked easily and with compassion about the work they were hoping to do and I found myself being drawn in by his enthusiasm.

"How did you get involved in the first place?" I asked when there was a pause in the conversation.

"My son, Toby, has a friend who is on the autistic spectrum. He was round at our house one day when I was playing around on my guitar. Benji – the friend – and Toby were singing along and drumming with their hands on the table, so I gave them an old set of tom-toms I had lying around. They had so much fun. Later, Benji's mum said she had rarely seen him so engaged so we started having him around more often."

"How old is your boy?"

"He's six. Anyway, I'd met Marjorie a couple of years ago and she was looking for something to do since her husband died and so it kind of grew from there. I recruited some musicians from people I knew in the local scene and we started by going into Toby's school a couple of times."

"And now you're going global?" I smiled.

"Well, we thought we'd start with West Sussex at least." He returned the smile.

Oh my word, I do believe that's the first time he's actually got one of my jokes. Actually, he has quite a nice smile.

"Baby steps? I'll drink to that." I raised my glass of orange juice. We chinked glasses and, as we did so, he turned the full force of his smile on me. *I think you're quite a dangerous man, Seth Peterson. I can't imagine many people turn you down.*

"So, Eleanor, tell me about yourself. You and Mark, are you married?"

*

"Can you believe it?" I ranted at Mark later. "By the time he'd insisted on pudding as well, taken any number of bloody text messages, we got out to the car and he didn't have enough time to show me the stuff."

"Oh dear." What was it about me losing my temper that always made Mark smirk? "So what did you do?" he asked.

"He's going to call me to make another appointment." I rolled my eyes. "I'm not wasting my bloody time over lunch again so I've told him I'd like to see their offices."

"Good idea. Perhaps he fancies you? And that's why he's stringing out the meetings?"

"Yeah right, well, he can go whistle. And I told him that you were the love of my life, so he knows he has no chance."

"What did you tell him that for?" Mark raised his eyebrows.

"Because what goes on in my bedroom is no concern of his. And as for the love of my life, Sam Lewis in 4A holds that title and will do for ever more."

"And on that devastating blow, my darling, I'm afraid I must leave. I have some work to finish at the office." Mark stood up and put on his jacket. "Seriously, though, when we were chatting at the Council thing the other night, he was talking about maybe branching out into art therapy. That's why I introduced you, I thought it might be right up your street?"

"Yes, it probably would be, if he ever gets around to asking me."

"Hang in there, my darling. See you tomorrow." Mark left me to take out my exasperation on the washing-up.

*

The following Monday found me driving through the depths of the countryside, trying to find the William Evans Foundation offices. I had just pulled over to phone for directions when I spotted a tiny sign on a farm gate: 'WE Offices'.

"Thanks for bloody nothing," I growled as I pulled into the farmyard. "Don't make life easy for anyone, will you?" I got out of the car and stomped over to what had

109

obviously once been the farmhouse. I found the door. "Unbelievable. The sign here is bigger than the one on the bloody gate." As I reached to ring the bell the door opened.

"Ellie, lovely to see you again." Seth stood in the doorway. "Come on in. Are you okay? We were expecting you a bit earlier."

"Directional issues," I snapped. "Or the lack thereof." I glanced around at the entrance hall. "I'm sorry, I'm rubbish at Monday mornings. You should ignore me until I've had my third cup of coffee and my second cigarette, at least. So, show me round."

"Let's rectify the coffee situation first." Seth opened a door marked 'Rehearsals'. "Come and meet the team."

We entered a large room, which I think was the former farmhouse kitchen. Seated on one of two overstuffed sofas, each with their feet on a low coffee table strewn with magazines and empty mugs, were two young men. They were both wearing jeans and T-shirts and each had long hair, although one had beautiful dark curls whilst the other's was more straggly. *Sort of Brian May against Francis Rossi… Way to show your age, Ellie.*

"Eleanor, this is Fergus and Oliver. They are our musicians in residence. Guys, this is Ellie." They both waved.

"Which one is which?"

I'm Fergus and this is Olly. Brian May signed.

Wow, you sign! I gave him the thumbs up.

I'm a bit rusty. My baby sister is deaf. She had meningitis when she was younger.

Like me. How old was she?

Ten. We count ourselves lucky, she nearly died. His face was sombre for a moment and then it brightened. *Welcome to our humble offices, Ellie.*

You can call me… I showed him the sign for my name.

"Hey, you two, no secret signing." Seth frowned. "Ellie, do you remember Marjorie?" He gestured over towards the kitchen area, where Marjorie had her back to the room and was engaged in filling up a coffee machine.

"Of course. How are you, Marjorie?" She didn't turn round.

Puzzled, I turned to Seth in time to see him say "… you have to face her when you speak."

Marjorie turned and although she smiled as she waved the coffee jug at me I didn't feel particularly welcomed by it.

"Black, no sugar, please." I tried my most winning smile – the one I reserve for doctors' receptionists and bank managers – but she turned back to the coffee machine. *Okay, lady, so that's how it is, is it?* I sat on the other sofa, facing the boys.

What's her problem? I asked Fergus.

No idea, except she can be grumpy on Monday mornings.

"I think we're going to have to have a rule that you two only communicate by talking." Seth frowned at us both. "At least in company."

"I'm not accustomed to having people set rules for me," I said, keeping my voice low and calm, as if trying to control my temper. "And I'm unlikely to stick to them. But if it makes you feel more comfortable, we were talking about the coffee."

"Sorry, I didn't mean to offend you." Seth looked awkward. "Olly, please don't do that in front of me."

Olly paused in the middle of rolling a cigarette. "Chill out, Seth, I'm only rolling it in here. I'll smoke it outside."

"Can I come too?" I fished my own tobacco tin out of my bag. "And then we can get on with the tour?" I questioned Seth, who looked somewhat put out. Nevertheless he smiled and nodded.

I followed the boys outside and we stood in the shelter of an open-sided farm building while we smoked.

"So you're joining our happy band?" Olly asked.

"Am I? I thought I was just looking around and maybe doing some artwork."

"Oh." Olly looked puzzled. "Seth told us that you are coming to join us." He glanced at Fergus for confirmation.

"It's just Seth," said Fergus. "He has this belief that if he says something it automatically makes it fact."

"I'm not saying I won't," I said lightly. "I'm just here to see what it's all about. So what do you two do?"

"That's easy to explain." When Olly smiled he looked years younger. "We play the music and encourage the children to join in."

"Yeah, we love it." Fergus threw his cigarette down. "Come on, we'd better get back inside."

I spent the rest of the morning looking around the offices and recording studios. Seth had some videos of the work they had already done in schools. I studied these and started to sketch some ideas for promotional material in my notebook. At lunchtime I gathered my things together in preparation to leave.

"Let me buy you lunch." Seth picked up his car keys from his desk.

Marjorie threw herself back in her chair and rolled her eyes. "But I've brought in lunch for you." She didn't bother to hide her exasperated sigh.

"It'll keep, won't it? I thought I could take Ellie to the pub and talk over her involvement. You could come too," he added as an obvious afterthought.

Remembering Mark's comments about Seth fancying me, and my own discomfort at him trying to impose rules on me earlier, I felt it better to be strictly professional with Seth Peterson. "Please, don't worry." I smiled at them both. "I have to get back anyway, I need to get started on these." I indicated my bag, which contained my notebook.

Marjorie flashed a brief, reluctant smile. "Good, that's decided then. Goodbye Eleanor, thanks for coming." She turned back to her computer screen.

"At least I'll walk you out to your car." Seth went to take my arm as Fergus came back into the office, which gave me the opportunity to make the sign for 'okay?', thus avoiding Seth being able to grab me.

"Oops, sorry, naughty me for signing. Fergus," I enunciated slowly. "Would you like a quick smoke before I go?"

"You read my mind, lovely lady." He turned towards Seth. "We are all finished in there, Seth, so we'll head off too. See you tomorrow." He peered round Seth. "Bye, Marjorie." She waved, but carried on typing.

So it's not just me, then. "Lead on then, Fergus, and we'll go for a spot of slow suicide. 'Bye Seth, I'll be in touch when I've got some preliminary drawings done." We left him standing in the doorway of the office.

*

Ellie, Seth Peterson.

"Seth, hi. How were the designs?"

They were excellent, thanks. We're going to use them and I wondered if we could get together to discuss them?

"Great! I'll come to the office. Let me just grab my diary."

I'm going to be near your place tomorrow. How about lunch?

But I haven't told you where I live. "Tomorrow? I guess so. Will you have Marjorie with you?"

No, she's snowed under with the arrangements for the launch. It will just be me, I hope that isn't a disappointment?

"No, that's fine, but all these lunches must be expensive. I'm sure it's easier for me to come to the office."

It's all on expenses, don't worry. I could come to you, though?

Yes, but someone has to pay those expenses and you're a charity. "Not possible, I'm afraid. I work from home and make it a policy not to let clients intrude on my space. No offence."

None taken, although I had hoped that we were going to be more friends than business acquaintances. But I understand about wanting to keep your own space sacrosanct.

Friends? Let's wait and see, Mr I'm-so-smooth Peterson. I'm fussy about who my friends are.

*

"You'd have been proud of me," I told Mark the next evening. "Your management technique is obviously rubbing off on me. I made him do all the business stuff before we ordered and then we only had time for a sandwich each." I giggled. "He wasn't altogether happy."

"Yeah, well the Council have given them a fairly substantial grant," Mark grumbled. "I'm not altogether happy myself if it's all going on bloody lunches. And this launch isn't going to be cheap. He certainly knows how to spend money."

"Well, here's a saving. It's our invitation to the launch – I'm designing them, so this is an original. You never know, it could turn out to be valuable when they become an international charity." I winked, but Mark just scowled.

"I'm not holding my breath."

*

The Launch day arrived and it was a beautiful June evening as Mark and I made our way to the Assembly Rooms.

"At least the Council gave him a deal on this place," Mark was grumbling again. "Otherwise, who knows where he might've booked? Wembley Arena, probably."

"Come on, let's go and find a seat and then you can buy me a very big glass of wine."

The evening went very well. The place was plastered with WE CAN banners, posters and other materials, all with the logo I had designed for them. I liked the play on the initials of the Foundation that Seth had come up with for the name of the Project and I was proud of my design.

Fergus and Olly had written a song for some of the children to perform, which seemed to go very well. There were some presentations, one from Seth himself, and then the finale was a set from a band called Mobius Strip who had had a couple of hits a few years back. I was stunned to see Fergus and Olly take the stage with them. I hadn't recognised them when I met them and now felt rather embarrassed, especially when Fergus spotted me in the crowd and waved.

I grinned, and waved back. *Going for a smoke, see you later.*

Outside, I found a bench and sat down to roll a cigarette. I smiled at a pretty, but painfully thin, woman who was sitting on the next bench. Her legs were drawn up against her chest and she was chewing at her thumbnail, so I wasn't sure if she said something to me.

"I'm sorry, I'm deaf," I said. "I can lip-read, though, but I need to be able to see your face."

"Oh, are you Ellie?" She moved over to my bench and turned to face me. "I'm Roz Peterson, Seth's wife. I've heard a lot about you."

"Oh!" I was startled, but managed to recover. "How nice to meet you." In all our conversations, Seth had not once mentioned a wife. I had assumed that he was divorced.

"You've never heard of me, have you?" She took a sip from the Lilt bottle she was holding. "Don't be embarrassed. I'm Seth's dirty little secret, I'm a drunk, you know."

I was just trying to work out how to respond to this when she laughed. "Don't worry, I'm fine. I'm sure you'll hear all about me eventually. Marjorie usually enjoys filling people in." She rummaged in the pocket of her jacket and produced a pack of cigarettes. "Do you have a light?"

I lit her cigarette for her. "She'd have to bring herself to speak to me to do that," I said, icily. "And then, of course, I'd have to be interested in anything the old witch wanted to say, providing I could drag my gaze away from that ridiculous, concrete-helmet hairdo."

Roz laughed again. "Good one! Concrete helmet, I love it!"

Just then a portly, kind-faced man approached us. He leaned over and said something to her as he gave her a kiss.

"Stu, this is Eleanor. Ellie, Stu. Stu used to be my boss back in the days when I was a sane human being. Stu, sit, but make sure Ellie can see your face. She lip-reads."

"Nice to meet you, Eleanor. I'm sorry I interrupted. Who has a concrete helmet, Roz darling?" He perched himself on the arm of the bench.

"You mean you can't guess? Marjorie, of course, henceforth known as the Concrete-haired Witch."

"Mummy?" A small boy had approached from the same direction as Stu. "Are you smoking?"

"Yes I am, Toby darling." Roz drew him to her and as he allowed himself to be enveloped, his thumb went straight into his mouth. "Toby, this lady is Eleanor, do you remember, Daddy told you about her? That she can't hear what you say, so she watches your mouth to see what you're saying."

"Yes." Toby took his thumb from his mouth and nodded his head. "It's nice to meet you, Eleanor."

"And you, Toby. Are you enjoying yourself?"

"It's okay, I guess. I love Fergus and Olly and I love the band." Toby twisted round and looked up at his mother. I didn't see what he said but guessed it was something to do with the cigarette as Roz dropped it quickly.

"Good boy." Stu said. "Your daddy doesn't have to know everything, does he?"

"You're not a fan of the band, then?" I asked Roz.

"I've known them since they started out. I love Fergus and Olly to bits, but their music brings back some mixed memories for me. They had their first hit just after Toby was born, when Seth was their manager.

This was certainly turning into a night for surprises. "I had no idea he was their manager."

"Oh yes," said Stu. "He managed to ensure that they were a one-album wonder."

I frowned, trying to understand this comment, as Roz placed her hand on Stu's leg. "Another time, Stu."

Just then, I saw Mark heading out of the building and looking around for me so I stood up. "I have to go. It's been lovely to meet you all. Roz, I hope to see you again soon?"

"Sure thing. Well, as long as it's okay with my dear husband. Take care, Ellie."

"And you." I gave Toby a little wave, but he was almost asleep and he just smiled round his thumb.

"Come on, let's go," Mark said as I reached him. "I've made our goodbyes. Seth said to say he'll call you on Tuesday."

"Oh, lucky lucky me. Shall we pick up a pizza on the way home?"

*

A week later, I pulled into the car park of Saint Crispin's School and noticed that Seth's car was already there, as was the old transit van that Fergus and Olly used to transport all their gear around.

"Hells Bells," I cursed. "Late, late, late." I had agreed to spend the morning watching them all. Fergus and Seth were still trying to persuade me to join the Charity but I wasn't sure where I would fit in. This morning I was going to see how they all worked, what they did, and see if there was any way to bring my art into the mix.

I presented myself at Reception. "Hi, I'm here to see—"

"You're a bit late, dear." The grey-haired woman behind the desk checked the clock as she came round to take me by the arm. "But—" she strode off down the corridor, apparently still talking.

"Excuse me." I just about managed to stop myself being propelled along the corridor. "I'm deaf. You need to look at me when you speak to me."

She turned around to face me. "Oh. Yes. Your. Boss. Did. Tell. Me. Sorry."

My boss? "It's okay, and you don't need to slow down what you're saying. I just need to be able to see your face."

"Yes, well. You're with our Downs kids. The headmistress is holding them for you." She set off down the corridor again.

"Sorry? Down with whom?" But she had arrived at the door to a classroom. She knocked once and walked straight in. I followed behind, still perplexed. Fifteen or so small faces turned towards us expectantly. At the front of the class was an attractive blonde woman, who greeted us with a smile. I turned to face my companion in time to catch the end of what she was saying.

"— deaf, but she lip-reads, so she says. I'm not sure she knows what she's doing, but I'm sure you'll sort it out, Mrs Jakes." With that, she turned on her heel and left the room.

"You must be Eleanor," Mrs Jakes came forward to shake my hand. "And this is Willow class." She swept her hand towards the small people sitting on the floor. "Willows, say hello to Eleanor."

I directed my attention towards the class, who all greeted me with the sign for 'hello', as well as saying it.

Oh, dear God, not 'down with'… Downs Syndrome. That old cow — she actually referred to them as the Downs kids.

Hello everyone. I smiled at them and waved.

"Well," said Mrs Jakes. "I'll leave you to it, then. The children can show you where everything is, Eleanor, can't you children?"

"Sorry, wait! Where what is? I'm here to observe."

"Oh! Oh dear. Seth told me you were coming to do some artwork with the children. I'm afraid I have a meeting. Is there anything you can do with them? They've been so looking forward to this."

What the…? "I'm not sure…" I looked at the children all lined up on the floor, gazing up at me expectantly. "Yes, of course there's something we can do. Isn't there, guys?"

Mrs Jakes left the classroom to a huge chorus of "Yes!"

*

When she came back, an hour and a half later, we were hard at work putting the finishing touches to the posters we had designed to advertise a musical concert that the children had told me would be the final part of the day with WE CAN.

"It's break time now, children. You'll see Eleanor later."

I stood at the door and thanked each child as they left. Some were happy to speak to me, but some of them hurried past with a quick sign for 'thank you'.

"Eleanor, come and join us in the staff room for a coffee." Mrs Jakes smiled. "You can build yourself up for the next lot."

117

"The next lot? Mrs Jakes, how many classes do you have me scheduled for today?"

"Please call me Katie, and there's… Let me see…" She consulted a printed timetable she had in her hand. "Four classes, that one being the first."

"May I see that?" I held out my hand for the timetable. It was a printed sheet with the WE CAN logo at the top. It was quite clearly set out and there was my name in several places, with the title of the lesson I was apparently giving: Art Therapy. I fumed. How dare he? The arrogance of it. He had already printed this up and yet he told me I was just coming in to observe. I followed Katie Jakes to the staff room and when we entered Seth and the rest of the team were already tucking into coffee and a plate of biscuits.

"Ellie, hi, how did it go?" Seth greeted me.

"Surprisingly well," I replied through gritted teeth. "Can I have a word outside?"

"Oh dear, looks like I'm in trouble," Seth joked, looking around at the others. Fergus seemed to be taking a great deal of interest in the floor at his feet, Marjorie was smirking and Olly just looked confused. I turned on my heel and strode out of the door, Seth following behind.

"What exactly is this?" I thrust the timetable at him once we were in the corridor.

"Ah, yes—"

"How dare you do that to me? Who do you think you are? What if I hadn't shown up? Or I couldn't work with the children? You had no right to put me – or them – in that position."

Seth held up his hand. "Whoa, wait. The thing is that you did show up. There was never any doubt that you wouldn't be brilliant with the children. I know I shouldn't have been so presumptuous, but we were desperate."

"But you should have asked me! I told you I wasn't sure about working in the schools."

"Yes, but you didn't really mean it, did you?" Seth flashed me a grin, like a naughty schoolboy caught with his hand in the cookie jar. "You just needed a bit of persuasion. Come on, Ellie, was it so bad?"

"No, but that's not the point," I grumbled.

"It's exactly the point. I did it for your own good, you see? Come on, let's grab some coffee before break finishes." He went back into the staff room.

I followed him in, still quietly seething. I wasn't used to being manipulated. Fergus caught my eye as I sat down.

You okay?

Yes, just feeling a bit used and abused.

Marjorie had been sitting and talking with one of the teachers. "Now, you two, remember the rules. No signing in company."

Was she smirking? I bit back a smart reply and sipped the coffee that Seth had brought over to me.

"So what do you have planned for the next class?" he asked.

"How many more classes do I have?" I enquired icily.

He either missed the tone, or chose to ignore it. "Just another double session before lunch and then one afterwards. Then the concert at the end of the day."

"Do you have any suggestions? Seeing as I have had no preparation for this."

"Actually, yes I do." He produced a folder with the WE CAN logo on the front. "I put these ideas together yesterday."

Not that I would have told him, but his ideas were good and the rest of the day went well. The concert at the end of the day was great fun and showed that Fergus and Olly both had a good rapport with the children.

"Am I forgiven?" Seth walked me to my car at the end of the day, and flashed me a mock-sheepish grin.

"Don't do that to me again," I said through gritted teeth. "I don't like being ambushed."

"I'm right, though, aren't I? You enjoyed yourself. So will you become part of our team?"

"I'll think about it." I got into my car and started the engine. "I'll call you."

*

I have to admit the next few weeks were fun. I worked with WE CAN on and off in schools until the end of July, when the summer holidays started.

"Right, that's it," I said to Fergus and Olly as I packed up my things for the last time at the end of the summer term. "I'll see you both in September."

Seth was carrying a box of tambourines out to the van, but he stopped. "I thought you'd be helping us out over the summer, Ellie?"

"Doing what? No, don't answer that." I picked up my bag and shawl. "I don't want to know."

"Got something better to do?" Fergus grinned at me.

"Absolutely!" I smiled back and turned to Seth, who had put down his box and come to stand in front of me. "And don't you dare try to trick me into something else. I'm going for some much-deserved peace and quiet, to recharge my batteries."

"For the whole summer?" He was looking decidedly grumpy.

"Yes. Did you know that your eyes go darker when you're cross? The whole summer. And I will most definitely be out of contact, so don't even try."

"But—"

"No, don't you dare! I am off to Oxford, to my boat, to do some real painting and you are not going to change my mind."

"Boat?" Seth queried. "I didn't know you had a boat."

"Why should you? But yes, I have a narrowboat which is moored on the Oxford Canal. My old art tutor keeps an eye on it for me – it's at the bottom of his garden. My summer is spent pottering around the canals, painting and generally chilling out."

"And will Mark be going with you?"

"No, why would he?" Too late, I remembered that I had told Seth Mark was the 'love of my life'. "He would just be in my way."

"But if I need you, and will you have your mobile on?"

"What could you possibly need me for? An emergency sketch of something?" I laughed. "I'll be switching on the mobile occasionally but, Seth, I warn you now: if you try to disturb me, I will not be a happy person."

"What about us?" Fergus gestured to himself and Olly. "Can we come and visit?"

"Maybe, if you ask nicely and you're good at locks and stuff, I'll see."

Seth narrowed his eyes. "What have they got that I haven't got?"

"It's more what they haven't got. Neither of them has a wife or child who need you at home. And stop sulking; you look like a little boy. May I remind you that I am a volunteer in the schools? I can do what I like with my time otherwise. I'll see you all in September." I blew air kisses at them all and headed out to my car, passing Marjorie on the way. "See you in September," I sang. I didn't wait to see if she replied.

*

"So, you're back then?" Marjorie said, as I walked into the offices at the beginning of September. "We wondered if you might have fallen overboard."

"Why would I...? Oh, I see. I should point out, Marjorie, that being deaf I can't actually tell when you're being sarcastic. I could have mistaken that for genuine concern and then where would we both be? Anyway, how was your summer?"

"Busy. I was working."

"Oh, poor you. Well, I had a great time and got loads of painting done. I feel fully recharged now." I turned away from her and smiled at Fergus and Olly. "Hello, you two. Good summer?"

"Yes thanks." Fergus was restringing a guitar while Olly was tuning another, but he stopped and smiled at me. "Sorry we didn't make it to Oxford in the end, it would have been fun. But every time we thought we'd cleared some time, something else came up that Seth needed us for."

"And where is our beloved leader?" I enquired.

"Out schmoozing some new head teacher, I believe." Fergus looked to Marjorie for confirmation. She nodded, without turning away from her computer screen.

She's not very happy about it, Fergus signed.

Why not?

We'll tell you outside. I'd never seen Olly sign before. I wasn't aware that he could.

They stood up. "We're going out for a smoke," Fergus informed the back of Marjorie's head. "See you in a bit."

Outside, I grabbed Olly and spun him around to face me. *Look at you with your signing!* I smiled and he blushed from the neck up, then stared fixedly at his feet.

It was one of Seth's projects for the summer, Fergus explained. *He got a tutor for a couple of hours a day. It was supposed to be a surprise for you.*

It certainly is! I couldn't hide my delight. *And you've learned well, Olly.*

Yes, he and Toby were the star pupils.

Toby?

Yes, Seth brought him in for the lessons and he loved it. Seth, not so much.

Oh?

Yes, he couldn't get the hang of it at all. Fergus was obviously relishing the tale of Seth's discomfiture. *We had lots of slammed doors and cursing.*

Olly grinned. *Yeah, it was funny. He and Marjorie were both rubbish, and you know neither of them likes to fail.*

Marjorie was learning? It was just one surprise after another.

She had no choice, Seth told her she had to. Something to do with our 'inclusion policy'.

Our what?

His way of justifying the cost of the tutor. We now have policies covering all sorts of stuff, which allows him to spend money on courses and suchlike. It should all become clear in the meeting tomorrow.

I switched to speaking and signing, thinking this might be getting a bit too technical for Olly. "I wasn't aware we had a meeting."

"Yes, the inaugural meeting of our Executive Board."

"Executive what? Nothing to do with me."

"But I'm sure—" Fergus looked confused and then turned away from me as Seth appeared behind him.

"—chance to explain it to her yet." I caught the tail end of what Seth was saying. "I was going to do it today."

"Best you do it quick, then," I said, dryly. "Before I begin to think I am being bamboozled again."

"Heaven forbid." Seth laughed. "I wouldn't dare."

And so, by the end of the day, I found myself on the Executive Board despite my protestations that I wasn't board material. Mark roared with laughter when I told him over dinner that night.

"I don't know why you find it so funny," I grumbled.

"I just want to know what Seth's got that no-one else has." He was still chuckling. "You're on a committee!"

"Executive Board." I was still grumbling. "You know I don't do committees."

"It's a committee by any other name, my sweet. Priceless. I must ask him how he did it. I thought you loathed things like that."

"I do. And I don't know how he did it either. I believe it was a carefully planned strategy involving flattery, surprise and Seth's usual 'I have said it and therefore it will be so.' That, and the fact that it became apparent that Marjorie didn't want me anywhere near it."

"So, the reality is, they've got you because of your perverse nature and because you don't like Marjorie."

"Yup, that's about the truth of it."

*

Nobody was more surprised than me that I took to regular working hours, and my place on the grandly-named Executive Board, with ease. I enjoyed working with Fergus and Olly and being a subversive element in the numerous meetings that Seth liked to call. He had now taken the title of Chief Executive Officer and the boys and I considered it part of our duty to prick his pomposity every now and then. And he did love a meeting. Fergus and I had a pet theory that he called them mainly to show Marjorie he was doing something.

It was during one of these meetings, in early spring of the following year, that his ever present mobile rang. He picked it up, looked at the caller display and cancelled the call. Almost immediately it rang and once again he cancelled it. When it rang for the third time, Marjorie let out a dramatic sigh. "I think you'd better take it, Seth. They're clearly not going to stop."

He grimaced. "It's Roz, she can wait." And he cancelled the call again.

"Come on, mate," said Fergus. "It's probably important, you should answer it."

It rang again and we all nodded our agreement with Fergus. Seth answered it with a terse "What?" and strode out of the room. He came back in after a couple of minutes. "Something to do with Toby and the school," he said. "A lot of fuss about nothing, I expect."

"It didn't sound like nothing," Fergus said. "She obviously needs to talk to you. I think you should get back there, we can finish this another time."

"Yes," agreed Marjorie. "I'll drive you back now."

"It can wait until we've finished," Seth snapped. "It sounds like she's started drinking already, so if I give it another hour she should be just about ready to pass out. Then I can get the full story from Toby."

"But he —"

"Leave it, please, Fergus. I'm sure that Seth knows what he's doing." Marjorie interrupted.

"Surely, if she's drunk, you need to get back there as soon as possible," I said. "Aren't you worried about Toby?"

"Believe me, the last thing Toby needs is to see his mother drunkenly haranguing his father," Marjorie said. "Let's get through this as quickly as possible and then I will drive you home, Seth."

So we finished the meeting. After they had gone, the three of us went outside for a cigarette. "I don't understand," I said. "If she's so awful – although from what I've seen of her I don't think she is – why is he apparently happy to leave Toby alone in the house with her?"

"Because she isn't that awful." Fergus finished his cigarette and ground it out with the heel of his boot. "It suits Seth to badmouth her and get sympathy from Marjorie."

"But surely it can't be good for Toby?" My thoughts went back to the little boy curled up on his mother's lap outside the launch party, thumb in mouth. Did he look like a troubled child? Would I even know what one of those looked like?

"Ellie, I've known Roz since before that little boy was born. I don't know what else is going on in that house, but no way would she hurt him. And he adores her." Fergus looked concerned and started to roll another cigarette. "There's not a violent bone in that woman's body and, while she does drink, I've never seen her drunk in front of Toby."

∗

I volunteered with WE CAN for a couple of years, then became a full-time paid employee. I still had my summers off, though, which didn't please Marjorie but I had insisted on it being put into my contract. I loved working with the children, but I needed my time on the canal to decompress.

We were due to start a new school year – my fourth with the Project – and I was finishing up a painting I had started during my break. At least, that's what I told myself I was doing. In truth, I had been sitting and staring out of the window of my little studio shed to the trees at the end of the garden.

"Ellie?" Seth appeared in the doorway and waved his hand to attract my attention. "I've been trying to call you. Is everything okay?"

"Not really. And I know you've been trying to call. I've been ignoring you, can't you take a hint?"

"Ignoring me? Why? Have I done something to upset you?"

"Oh, please don't take it personally, I've been ignoring everyone. It's just been a crappy couple of weeks."

"Best you put the kettle on, then, and tell me all about it. Work starts again on Monday and we can't have our star artist being upset." He turned and headed back towards the cottage, brooking no argument.

"I'm your only bloody artist," I grumbled, following him. "And you can put the kettle on. In fact…" As I came into the kitchen, I opened the fridge and took out a bottle of Sancerre. "… I have a better idea than tea."

"So," he said as we settled in my little sitting room. "What's up?"

"I thought I'd got a gallery exhibition, but it fell through. Then my cat died. She was eighteen, so it wasn't completely unexpected, but still it was sad. Then, to cap it all, it would have been my wedding anniversary today."

"I didn't know you were married?"

"Why should you? It wasn't for long and it was a very long time ago. Not a topic for general conversation. I don't come out of the story very well."

Seth smiled sympathetically. "Are you okay, though?"

"I will be. It's at times like these that I thank God for wine and chocolate."

"I'm happy to join you for that. Although, have you eaten?"

"No, nor do I intend to. If you're thinking of your bloody stomach, as usual, then you're on your own."

"Charming. I'll get a takeaway delivered and then, if you do want something, you can have some. I think you should if you're on the wine. Where do you keep the menus?" He stood up.

"In the kitchen, in the drawer."

"Which drawer?" He stood in the doorway. "There are several."

"The small one. It's 'The Drawer'." I mimicked quotation marks with my fingers.

"Huh?"

"You know, everyone's got one. It's the drawer where everything without a home ends up: menus, fuse wire, odd screws, instruction manuals etc."

When the takeaway arrived he fussed around with plates and spoons and forks. I sat and drank my wine and watched him. "Won't Roz be wondering where you are?"

"No, she'll be in a drunken stupor somewhere. We are officially separated, you know, although we live in the same house. Neither of us can afford to buy the other one out at the moment."

"How does that work?" I was starting to feel a little fuzzy with the wine and was relishing thinking about someone else's life, other than my own.

"I have what used to be the study as a kind of bedsitting room; we share the kitchen and bathroom. I've had to put a lock on my door, because of her drunken rampages."

"I still don't get why you feel comfortable leaving Toby with her."

"Because when all is said and done, she's a good mother. In fact, that's the only reason she married me – to have a kid. She was pregnant when we married, you know."

"No, I didn't, but then why would I?"

"When we first met, she had a good job and we had a nice place in London, but she wanted a kid and she got pregnant without me knowing. Then she wanted to move to the coast, so we sold up in London and moved to Brighton. I had to relocate my business and she didn't want to work. It was about this time that she started drinking."

This was the most he'd ever opened up to me and I was starting to feel quite sorry that I hadn't taken the time to listen to him before.

"Then, with the drinking and the unstable behaviour and everything else, my business began to suffer and we ended up having to sell up in Brighton and move here. But let's not talk about that, I'm supposed to be cheering you up. This is a lovely cottage, by the way."

"Thanks, I love it here. The light's great and there are lots of walks around when I really need to think."

"Bit of a nightmare when it rains, I should think?"

"Are you always so pedantic? But, yeah, that's why it doesn't pay to have a flashy car here… Like yours." I grinned.

Seth's eyes had flashed when I teased him, but now he leaned forward to drain the rest of the bottle into my glass. "So, Ms Chandler, are you going to take me to bed, or not?"

I burst out laughing, moving backwards away from him. "That is such a cheesy line. Has that ever actually worked?"

Again, his eyes flashed dark and he looked angry. I continued in a more conciliatory tone. "I'm sorry, but you have to admit it's pretty bad." I tried a smile, but he was still looking pretty thunderous.

"Look, Seth, there are any number of reasons why you and I are not going to jump into bed. The first, and most important as far as you are concerned, being that you have a wife and child at home."

"I told you, we're separated."

"I know, but they're still a fact of your life. Also, you're not my type."

"Really?" Seth's boyish good looks didn't work when the boy appeared to be sulking.

"Trust me, you're not my type. Let's just call it a night for now, shall we? We've got to work together on Monday and I wouldn't want an awkward situation." I leaned towards him and squeezed his hand. Our faces were inches away from each other and he went to kiss me, but I kissed him on the cheek and stood up. "Are you going to wash or dry?"

*

The next morning my phone was flashing with a text when I woke up.

Good morning! Lunch today? XX

Really? I had knocked him back last night, although we had finished the evening friendlier than we had ever been. Now here he was asking me to lunch. I messaged back,

What for?

Straightaway, the phone vibrated again.

Because you have to eat, because it's a nice thing to do, and because it's what friends do when they both have some time to spare XX

While I was still trying to figure out if he had a hidden agenda, another text came in.

And because I want to make sure there's no hard feelings (on either side) XX

That seemed reasonable to me and the prospect of a weekend alone, wallowing in my self-pity, wasn't appealing.

Okay. When and where?

Now we had established ground rules, albeit tacitly, lunch turned out to be surprisingly fun. As a friend, Seth was amusing company. We discovered that we thought alike on any number of subjects and both had a love/hate relationship with the Guardian crossword. We completed it over a couple of glasses of wine in the garden of a riverside pub.

*

Over the next couple of years – to my surprise – Seth and I did become friends. He would often text me or message me on my laptop while I was working at home in the evenings and he was trapped in his study while Roz was 'on the rampage'. I still wasn't comfortable with the image Seth painted of his home life and I wasn't always able to square the mental picture of the wild-eyed drunk woman screaming and ranting around the house, with the quiet, gentle woman I had met at the launch. And still saw occasionally at various functions and social occasions.

At work, we were busier than ever. Schools seemed to be falling over themselves to book us. There, Fergus, Ollie and I made quite a team. Marjorie, however, was a different story. Always protective of Seth, she now seemed to be at his side constantly and she seemed determined to make sure that we wouldn't have any time together.

"I don't think she likes me," I said to Seth as we were packing up my car one day. "In fact, I know she doesn't."

"It's not like that," Seth replied. "It's complicated, too complicated to go into now. I'll pop over tonight."

"Okay, if you think she'll let you." I rolled my eyes.

When he arrived at my door that night he was clutching a bottle of wine. "This may be a two-bottle job," he said. "But I'm thinking you've probably got spares."

"What exactly are you trying to say, Mr Peterson?" I clutched at my throat in mock indignation.

"Why don't you go get a couple of glasses and I will tell you the story of Marjorie and me." He didn't even crack a smile.

"Is this going to give me nightmares?" I grabbed a couple of glasses and a corkscrew and then flopped down on my sofa.

Seth remained standing. "I met Marjorie at a charity event. She was on her own and she seemed to take a shine to me. I didn't think much of it at the time but I've since learned why, and it's why I cut her a bit of slack now and then."

"Don't tell me the Concrete-haired Witch has a heart?"

"Is that what you call her? That's a bit mean. Accurate but mean. But, yes, she does have a heart—"

"—Very deeply buried, I think."

"Are you going to let me tell this story, or not?"

*

"I can't tell you what Seth told me about Marjorie."

"Why not?" DS Wood looked surprised.

"Because it's Marjorie's secret. Seth shouldn't have told me and I'm certainly not going to tell anyone else. I'm pretty sure it has nothing to do with his death, though, but if you want to know you'll have to ask her yourself."

"This is potentially a murder enquiry—"

"— And I believe we know the story already," DI Nixon said, cocking an eyebrow at her DS. "What were your thoughts on it, Eleanor, when he told you?"

"That it was a sad story. I felt sorry for her."

"Anything else?"

"Such as?"

"Anything. Did it change your opinion of Marjorie? Or Seth?"

"Yes, in fact it did. I thought Seth was wrong to have told me, no matter that on the face of it he did it for good reasons. I thought Marjorie would hate that I knew, particularly that I felt sorry for her. And…"

"And?"

"And I felt uneasy. It was how Seth told me, the way he professed concern and said that it was up to him to take her into his family, that he was going to look after her into her old age…"

DI Nixon frowned. "But surely that's a good thing?"

"You'd think so, wouldn't you? That's what I told myself, but I just had an uneasy feeling at the back of my mind."

"Eleanor, I feel you have something else to say. Just come out and say it."

"Okay, it's not like I owe him any loyalty. He was banging on about responsibility, and taking the place of her long-lost son, and I couldn't help feeling… wondering… if he would be quite so ready to do all of that if she wasn't such a very rich old lady. Seth had never struck me as the altruistic type, but then I can be very cynical."

"Did you do anything about it? Did you say anything to Marjorie?" DS Wood chipped in.

"Of course not! I wasn't going to tell her that Seth had broken her trust, to me of all people. I told myself that I was just being cynical and I put it to the back of my mind. Marjorie is grown-up enough to take care of herself and I really couldn't see anyone – even Seth – pulling the wool over her eyes. But I did try to cut her a bit more slack after that."

"Fair enough, go on with your story."

*

One Friday evening, a few months after his revelations about Marjorie, I was at home working on my lesson plans for the following week when my phone rang. I'd told Seth I was going to be busy for the evening but he had a tendency to ring me for a chat when he got bored – which was quite often – and so I nearly didn't answer. I checked the caller ID and was quite surprised when Fergus's name came up.

Ellie, it's Fergus. I'm sorry to disturb you.

"Hi, Fergus. How are you? Is everything okay?"

Not really. I'm outside your house and I've got Roz and Toby with me. Can we come in?

I went to the door and threw it open. Fergus's van was pulled up at an angle to my car. He was trying to persuade Roz to get out. She was crying. Toby stood to one side, white faced.

"Oh my God, Fergus, what's happened?" I ran to Toby and put my arms around him. "Come on, Toby, let's get you inside and put the kettle on for Mummy."

As I walked him inside, Toby also began to cry. I got inside, sat him down on the sofa and knelt in front of him. "Toby, sweetie, you need to tell me slowly what has happened. So I can see what you're saying, remember?"

He nodded, and then took a deep breath and spoke slowly. "Mum and Dad had an argument and Dad was shouting a lot. Mum sent me up to my room, but I could still hear them. I don't know what happened but Mum came and got me and then we went to the phone box and Mum called Fergus."

"Where's your dad now?"

"I don't know," Toby cried. "Is Mum all right?"

"Yes, darling, I'm fine." Roz came into the room with Fergus, sat beside Toby and put her arms around him. "I just got a bit silly when Daddy started shouting. It's going to be fine." She was pale, but was obviously making an effort – presumably for Toby's sake – to appear calm. I could see, though, that she was rigid with the struggle to keep control and her hands were shaking as she cuddled her son.

I stood up. "Come on, Fergus, let's go and put that kettle on." We went out to the kitchen and left Roz and Toby curled up together on the sofa.

What on earth happened? I gave Fergus a hug and then stood back to look at him. He looked worn out.

I don't know. When she phoned me, she was almost hysterical. I'm sorry to bring them here, mate, but I've got a gig in an hour. I didn't know who else to call. And I was worried about Toby.

That's okay. Does Seth know they're here? I busied myself with hot chocolate for Toby and tea for Roz, Fergus and me.

No, and I don't think he knows she called me. Probably best to keep it that way until we know what's going on. The thing is Ellie... This isn't the first time. But it's not been this bad for a while. And I've never known it kick off so badly in front of Toby.

Oh, okay. Let's take them their drinks and try to piece together what's gone on.

That's easy. She's married to a total, mind-fucking control freak. That's what's gone on.

We took the drinks into them and by the time he had drunk his hot chocolate, Toby's eyes were drooping.

"I'll tell you what, Tobes," I said. "Fergus has to go now, but why don't I get him to carry you up to my incredibly comfortable spare bed and then you can have a little sleep. I'll have a chat with Mum, and then either you two can stay here tonight or I'll drive you home." He nodded sleepily but insisted on walking up the stairs on his own.

By the time I'd said goodbye to Fergus and come back into the sitting room, Roz had found an opened bottle of wine and was halfway through a large glass. She indicated a second glass. "If it's all right with you, we'll take you up on the offer of staying, so you might as well join me."

I poured myself a glass and settled on the other sofa, opposite her. "Do you want to talk about it?"

She heaved a huge sigh. "I'm not sure that I do. At least, not right now. Would you mind awfully if I had a bath? I feel the need to get myself clean."

*

I was just putting the finishing touches to what I had been working on, while I waited for Roz, when my mobile lit up.

Are you busy? X

  Very

Fancy some company? X

                                                                                     Absolutely not

I'm just down the road X

                                                                Don't come round. I'm having
                                                                a bath and an early night once
                                                                I've finished the lesson plans

I could always come and join you ;-)
(not for the lesson plans, obv) X

                                                                         Not a chance. Go home

The fucking bitch is on one of her
rampages. Home is not a great
place to be at the moment.

                                                                    Sorry about that. You're still
                                                                            not coming round.

You've got someone there
haven't you?

                                                                        None of your business

Fuck you then

"Charming," I said, and drank my wine. When I thought of Roz's and Toby's shocked and tearstained faces as they sat huddled together earlier, I couldn't imagine anyone less likely to be on a 'drunken rampage'. And I certainly couldn't dredge up any sympathy for the man who seemed to be the cause of their distress. I deleted the conversation from my phone just as Roz came in.

"Thanks for the loan of the pyjamas."

"Sometimes, only a pair of jim-jams and a snuggly dressing gown will do. That, and toast and chocolate spread. Want some? We could make it a proper sleepover."

"Yuck, I can't stand chocolate. You haven't got any Marmite, have you?"

And so we sat in front of the fire, making toast and drinking huge mugs of tea. Slowly, Roz started to open up. "I had to have a bath, I felt so dirty. He spat at me, right in my face—"

"What?"

"— And when I said 'What did you do that for? It's disgusting.' he replied, 'Because it seems I'm not allowed to hit you anymore.'"

"Anymore? Christ! Has he hit you before, then?"

"Loads of times. I've lost count. Never where anyone would see it, though."

"My God, Roz! Why are you still with him?"

"Where else would I go? And I couldn't leave Toby with him."

"You wouldn't have to – you could throw him out and keep Toby."

"Oh Ellie, don't be naïve. I'm an alcoholic. By the time he had finished with me, no judge in the land would let Toby anywhere near me. He is too good at winding me up; too many people have seen me when I reached the end of my rope with him and lost my rag, shouting and ranting. But that's all I've ever done, Ellie, and that only two or three times. They'd be lining up to badmouth me and support poor, henpecked Seth. Surely he's done that routine with you?"

"I... er..."

"Of course he has! It's his fast track into the knickers of his latest target. His version on the 'My wife doesn't understand me' theme: 'My wife is a drunken bitch who beats me up.'"

"Not into my knickers, honey. But, yes, I've heard something along those lines."

"I got the impression you were a bit different. He talks differently about you." She regarded me with a thoughtful expression.

"Maybe because he hasn't got into these knickers of mine? Which I promise you, Roz, he will never do."

"Oh, he will, Ellie," she said with a hollow laugh. "If he really wants to, he will. You haven't seen him when he's in full charm offensive mode." She shook her head slowly, her face a picture of abject misery.

I reached across and took her hand. "Roz, I have seen him and he can charm me all he likes, it won't happen. Not only is he not my type, he isn't even my preferred gender. Do you understand?"

She stared at me for a moment, confused. Then I saw realisation dawn on her face. Her mouth formed an 'O' shape and then she started to laugh. "Oh my God," she said, although it was hard to read as she was still laughing. "Does he know?"

"No," I said, also laughing now. "None of them do."

She stopped laughing and became serious. "Sorry," she said, looking at me intently. "Is it a secret?"

"Not particularly, no." I leaned back against the sofa cushions. "But I don't want to know about anyone else's sex life and mine is my own business. Simple as that."

"Well, good for you." And we toasted each other with tea.

*

I drove Roz and Toby home the next morning, although I didn't want to. Seth's car wasn't outside when we got there. Roz wasn't surprised.

"Probably gone to one of his floozies," she said grimly. "At least it means we'll have the house to ourselves for a while. Tell you what, Tobes," she went on, turning in her seat to look at him. "Let's go and get sorted, then we can go and find Trev and Dolly for a while."

"Cool," said Toby. "Is Ellie coming too?"

Roz smiled at me. "I should think Ellie's had enough of us by now."

"Not at all, and I'd like to meet the famous Trev and Dolly. I've heard so much about them."

"I'll bet you have," Roz said dryly. "And I bet none of it's good."

"Actually, the more I heard about them the keener I was to meet them." I winked at Toby. "I always think that the people everyone else disapproves of are usually the most fun, don't you?"

He grinned and nodded, then jumped out of the car and ran to the house.

"I'll wait here," I told Roz. "Just in case. And Roz, honey, you might want to give Fergus a ring while you're in there. He was very worried about you last night."

She nodded and went to join Toby, then they disappeared into the house.

Trev and Dolly lived in a shelter on the promenade, which Dolly referred to as their 'summer residence'. I liked them enormously and even persuaded them to sit for a couple of sketches. Fergus came down to join us and we all spent the day relaxing and chatting. It was exactly what Roz needed – a normal, happy, family day.

*

My first instinct, after that night, was to tell Seth exactly what I thought of him and get the hell out of Dodge, but I very quickly realised I couldn't do that. At some point that night, over the tea and toast, I had started to have feelings for Roz – this funny, vulnerable yet incredibly strong woman. They were vague and confusing, and they would never be reciprocated, but they were there.

So Seth absolutely couldn't know that I had given Roz and Toby shelter that night – she would never be able to come to me again and I was determined to be around for her when things got tough. I had no doubt that they would. I figured that, between Fergus and me, we could keep an eye out and make sure she and Toby were both safe.

Of course, this meant I had to maintain a semblance of friendship with Seth, even though the thought of it made my skin crawl. I resolved to spend as little time as possible in his company. I invented a couple of private commissions, which would keep me busy in the evenings and at weekends. And Marjorie became an unwitting ally in this. She had always been suspicious of our friendship, and previously I had delighted in finding ways to foil her attempts to keep us apart. Now I was more than happy to let her 'win', I managed to distance myself from him quite effectively.

Or so I thought. After a couple of months, I was at home one Friday evening, relaxing with a glass of wine when the lights flashed – indicating someone was ringing the doorbell. I opened the door to find Seth, clutching a bottle of wine. "I thought we needed a chat. I get the impression you've been avoiding me recently and yet you appear to have time to hang out with my wife. Have I done something to offend you?"

"No," I lied. "I'm just really busy and I don't have time for anyone at the moment. I've bumped into Roz a few times, that's all. Sorry."

"Can I come in?"

"Do you mind if you don't? It's been a long old week and I'm so tired. I'm just about to head for a bath and an early night."

"But I've brought wine and chocolate." He flashed his best endearing little-boy smile.

"No." I put my hand gently on his chest to stop him coming in and smiled wearily. "I'm sorry, Seth. I really am knackered, but I'll give you a ring tomorrow, okay?"

I thought for a moment he was going to argue but then he shrugged. "Suit yourself, it's your loss. I'll drink the wine myself, then."

"Yeah, you do that." I smiled what I hoped was an apologetic smile. "Good night then."

"Yeah, good night." He turned and walked away down the path.

137

I shut the door behind him and locked it. It had only been half a lie – I really was tired – and suddenly that bath and early night seemed like a great idea, so I locked up everywhere else. Then I switched off all the lights and headed upstairs.

*

I never close my curtains at night – there are no neighbours to overlook me, so why bother? – and so I woke at first light the next morning. For some reason I felt uneasy. *Something's not right, you need to wake up.* Groaning, I pulled the covers up higher and tried to will myself back to sleep, but the thought wasn't going to go away. *Wake up, Ellie. You need to wake up NOW.*

I sat up and scratched my head vigorously, no doubt adding to the messy bed hair I would be confronting in the mirror shortly. As I did so, I caught a slight movement out of the corner of my eye. Squinting, I looked across the bedroom. Seth was sitting in the chair in the corner.

"Seth?" I rubbed my hands over my face and tried to focus. "What are you doing here? How did you get in?"

He was sitting, leaning forward, elbows on his knees with his hands clasped under his chin. His eyes were dark. "I have a key."

"What? I've never given you a—"

"I had it cut when you left your keys in the office one time. I thought it might come in useful."

"What the hell?" I was waking up rapidly, but having trouble processing what he was doing there and why. I pulled my pyjama top straight and reached for the cardigan I keep on the end of my bed.

"Details," he said. "Trivial details. We have more important matters to discuss. Like how you are a lying bitch."

Did he just call me a lying bitch? "What? I couldn't read that properly. What did you say? And, no, it isn't trivial that you have stolen the key to my house." How dare he?

"Forget about that. Is it true?" He stared at me, his eyes glittering and dark.

"No, I won't forget about it. This is my home, you have violated it, as well as my trust." I tried to keep my voice calm. "Is what true? What is this all about? Why don't you go downstairs and put the kettle on while I get dressed? We can talk down there." I swung my legs out of bed, but kept watching him. *I don't know what's going on, but I am not going to turn my back on him.*

138

"Stay where you are." He made a move towards the bed, but stopped when I shrank away from him. "Is it true that you've been stringing me along all this time?"

What the hell? "Stringing you along? I don't understand."

"You let me think that we could have something going. That if I ditched Roz I could move in here and we could live together."

This is getting weirder and weirder. "No! No, I certainly didn't. I would never—"

"Shut up. For once in your life, just shut the fuck up."

"Seth, I don't know what's upset you but I'm sure if we talk about it, we can sort it out." *I've got to get him out of the bedroom.* "Let me get dressed." I went to stand up, but he crossed the bedroom before I could get to my feet and pushed me back onto the bed.

"So, according to my beloved wife, you're a dyke." He sneered. "She says you're only interested in fucking other women. She laughed at me when she told me." I opened my mouth to speak. "I told you, keep your fucking mouth shut. I don't see how you can be a lezzie. You told me you were married."

"I did say I didn't come out of the story very well," I said quietly. *Oh God, I'm in trouble here.*

"And what about Mark?" He was standing over me, an expression of contempt on his face. "What was that all about? You were fucking him, weren't you?"

"No! We were just friends, Mark's gay as well. Seth, you're scaring me. Please, let's go downstairs and talk about this."

"I always thought he was a faggot. You know what your problem is? You've obviously never had a real man. Bet your husband was a faggot, too, was he?"

"No, he wasn't." The thought of Steve brought tears to my eyes. *Don't do that, Ellie. Don't cry, don't give him that power.* "He was a kind, lovely man. And I treated him so very badly. That's why I would never have led—"

"Shut up, bitch." Seth's hand came from nowhere and cracked against the side of my head, making my ears ring, and my teeth clamped down on my tongue. Immediately, I felt the metallic taste of blood in my mouth.

Yeah, you really are in trouble, Ellie. You need to calm him down. "I'm sorry, Seth," I said as quietly and calmly as I could. "Please don't hurt me, I thought we were friends."

"Yeah, so did I." His face was sneering above me. "But you've been lying to me all along."

"I didn't lie. I didn't realise… I didn't realise that you felt that way." I tried putting my hand on his arm as a placatory gesture. He shook it off, but not before I could feel him trembling with anger.

"You've been leading me on, how can you not have realised? You stupid bitch." He pushed me backwards so I was lying on the bed. "Your problem, as I was saying, is that you've obviously never had a real man. So I'm going to show you what you've been missing." He got onto the bed so that he was kneeling over me, one knee on each side of my body. He sat back on my legs, so I couldn't move, and started to undo his jeans.

No! I will not let him do this! "Seth, please don't do this," I pleaded. He wasn't listening to me now and I couldn't see his lips so I didn't know if he was saying anything.

Oh God, think, Ellie! Buy some time. I started talking. I have no idea what I said, just a steady stream of placating phrases; reminding him that we'd been friends; talking about Toby – what would he think if he could see him? All the time my mind was racing. *What can I use as a weapon? How can I escape?* I couldn't – I wouldn't – let myself think about what he was trying to do.

He stood back to pull his jeans down, then got hold of my legs to shove me further back across the bed. I scrambled over onto my hands and knees as soon as he let go and tried to crawl off the other side of the bed. He pushed down on the small of my back, making me sprawl face down. My arms were outstretched and as I tried to get a grip on something, anything, my fingers found the shoes I had abandoned the night before. I scrabbled at them with my fingers and managed to get hold of one of them. I tightened my grip, and Seth flipped me over onto my back again. He lunged towards me and as his head came closer I hit him as hard as I could with the heel of the shoe. I caught his ear and he rolled over to my left, clutching at the side of his head. I could see blood seeping through his fingers as I drew back my arm and hit him again near the nape of his neck. He slumped down, his face in the pillows. I didn't wait to see if he would move again. I threw myself off the bed, grabbed my phone from the bedside table and ran for the door.

*

I stopped talking and looked at the two detectives across the desk. "I'm quite sure I must have earned myself a cup of tea by now." I sat up in the chair and stretched my arms above my head. "More importantly, I think Fitch needs a comfort break and I deserve a smoke break. You did say I was free to leave at any time. Does that include wandering outside for a smoke?"

"I don't think—" Sergeant Wood began.

"I'll take you." Inspector Nixon stood up from the table. "Alex, perhaps you could organise the teas?"

We walked through the Police Station in silence. Outside and round the corner, out of sight, I let Fitch off her lead and then sat down on a bench and rolled a cigarette. DI Nixon leaned against a wall and watched me. I finished rolling and offered her the tobacco. She took it and expertly rolled a cigarette of her own and we smoked together in silence for a few minutes.

"I don't think we have a record of you reporting that incident," she said.

"No, I didn't report it."

"Why not?"

"Because... Roz asked me not to. And then because I couldn't face the thought of reliving it over and over again, when it would only ever be his word against mine."

"Why on earth did Roz ask you not to?" She looked genuinely mystified and sat down beside me.

"Why do you think? Because of Toby. It was bad enough that he was seeing the way his father treated her, without adding a court case for attempted rape into the mix." I stood up and started to pace around the bench.

She gently stopped me by putting her hand out. "Okay, I can understand that. But surely you wanted to see him punished? Get some justice?"

"Are you still interviewing me? Because I'm pretty sure you shouldn't be doing that without your little friend." Suddenly I seemed to be full of nervous energy. I threw down the cigarette and ground it out with my heel. Immediately I took out the tobacco tin and started to roll another one. I fumbled it and dropped the tobacco on the ground. "Shit!"

DI Nixon stood and gently guided me back so I was sitting on the bench. Then she crouched down in front of me to pick up the tobacco. She handed it to me, but remained where she was, putting her hands on my knees and looking straight up at me.

141

"Eleanor, right now I'm not being a Police officer. Right now I am trying to be a friend. You've just told me about a horrible and terrifying experience, and I am trying to understand."

"Well, forgive my cynicism, Detective Inspector Nixon, but a friend wouldn't expect me to have to go through all of that again. I'd put it in that box marked 'Don't Go There' in my head."

"If we're going to be friends, then you should call me Billie. And I would like to be a friend to you, because I'm not entirely sure that you actually have many real friends. And that's a shame." She looked up at me and smiled. "And now you're going to have to help me up, because my knees aren't as young as they used to be." She held out her hands and I stood and took them and pulled her to her feet. We were inches away from each other and I had the urge to bury my head in her shoulder and sob.

I dropped her hands and stepped sideways. "Might as well get back inside before the tea goes cold. Fitch, here!" I strode back to the station without looking round to see if she was behind me.

We were buzzed through by the officer on duty and reached the interview room just as Sergeant Wood was coming up the corridor with three mugs in her hands.

Once we had settled down, the interview restarted. "Eleanor—" DI Nixon began.

"I thought we'd agreed to Ms Chandler and Inspector Nixon." I jumped in. My tone was cutting, but – professional as ever – her face showed no reaction.

"You're right, we did. I apologise. Although I don't want to distress you any further, we do have to get back to where we were when the interview was paused. Are you prepared to do that?"

"I don't suppose I have much choice."

"We'll have to do it at some point. If we do it now, we get it over and done with. What happened after you left Seth in the bedroom?"

"I thought I'd killed him."

*

Oh God oh God oh God... I've got to get out of here... He's bleeding... Did I kill him? ... I should call the Police... I can't call the Police... What if I have killed him? ... Should I call an ambulance? ... But if he's dead they'll call the Police anyway... Oh God oh God oh God...

With all these thoughts running through my head I fled from the house. I reached my car, threw myself in and locked all the doors.

What if he isn't dead? ... He might be coming after me... I have to get out of here... Where can I go? ... I can't go to Roz... Oh God what am I going to tell Roz? ... For God's sake, calm down Ellie and THINK...

I fumbled around in the glove box and found my emergency supply of tobacco. My hands were trembling and it took me three attempts to roll a cigarette. Then I had to hunt around again for a lighter. I finally found one in the passenger foot well. I lit up and took a couple of deep drags.

Fergus... I'll go to Fergus... He'll help me... At the very least he can help me tell the Police...

Now I had a plan of sorts, I felt a little calmer. I finished the cigarette, keeping a close eye on the door of the cottage. There was no sign of movement. I chucked the butt on the ground and rolled two more which I placed on the passenger seat, knowing that I would probably smoke them during the twenty-minute journey to Fergus's house. I had grabbed my keys on my flight through the cottage so at least I didn't have to go back inside to get them. I put my key into the ignition and turned it. *If this were a movie, this is the point where the car wouldn't start.* Sometimes my inappropriate sense of humour even caught me unawares. Thankfully, it did start and I was on my way.

*

I thought I had done a good job of holding myself together until I was standing on Fergus's doorstep and found myself pounding on his door. When he opened it his face, still bleary from sleep, turned to shock at the sight of me.

"Ellie? What the hell?" I stormed past him into his sitting room, accidentally kicking a guitar off its stand as I did so. He followed me in, replacing the guitar, put his hands on my shoulders as I turned toward him. "My God, you're shaking. What's happened?"

"I've killed him." The tears that I had been holding in since I left my bedroom exploded out of me. "I've killed Seth. Oh my God, I've killed him. What am I going to do?" Suddenly, all my strength drained away and I sank to the floor. Fergus crouched down and put his arms around me while all the emotion that had been building up inside since I woke up this morning was released.

Finally, when I was calm enough to be reasonably coherent, he made us both tea and I sat on the floor and related the events of the morning. I was amazed to discover that what had seemed like hours had, in fact, been less than two and it was still not yet 8 o'clock.

"Christ, I knew he was a bastard but I would never have thought that he would do something like this." Fergus shook his head. "But the first thing we have to do, Ellie, is to go back to the cottage and find out exactly what the score is."

"I can't go back there! In fact, I don't think I'll ever be able to go there again."

"Yes you will, you have to. But I'll be with you, so you will be safe. Finish your tea, have another smoke, I'll get dressed and will go together."

We left my car at Fergus's and he drove us back in his van. The first thing I noticed when we got to the cottage was that Seth's car was no longer outside. The front door was still open as I had left it, and I stayed in the van while Fergus went to investigate. After five minutes he appeared in the front doorway and gestured for me to come inside.

"He's not here and there is no sign of him. There's no sign of anything. You'd better come and look."

Upstairs, not only was there no sign of Seth but my bed had been stripped bare – even the duvet and pillows were missing. The shoe with which I had hit him, and its partner, were also gone.

"I think it's safe to say he's not dead," Fergus said grimly. "And he's removed anything that might be used as evidence."

"So what do I do now?"

"That's up to you. I'll come with you to report it to the Police."

"No." I shuddered. "But what if he decides to report me?"

"To do that, he'd have to explain what he was doing in your bedroom in the first place," Fergus said. "And I think it's unlikely he'll be wanting to do that. But I think what you need to do now, for sure, is to talk to Roz."

"No, what I need to do now is to get some space between me and here. I'm going to go to the boat. Will you look after things here for me, please?"

*

I spent the rest of the weekend licking my wounds on the boat. By Sunday night I had a plan of sorts. Fergus agreed to tell Marjorie I was going to be off sick for a couple of days and to cover for me at work. We agreed as well that he wouldn't say anything to Seth – "although it will probably kill me not to be able to lamp him one." – and to let him stew until I had been able to speak to Roz.

144

God, that was hard! I drove back to the coast on Monday evening and stayed at Fergus's, arranging to meet Roz after she had dropped Toby at school the next morning.

"Come round for coffee!" She suggested when I phoned her, but I couldn't face going into Seth's house. And if she let slip that I was coming would he be there waiting for me? Eventually, we agreed to meet at a little café not far from the house.

"Go easy on her," Fergus said that evening as we shared a bottle of wine. "She's fragile, you know. She knows he's a grade A shit – should do, the stuff he's done to her – but she takes it all on herself, feels guilty for the misery he causes other people. And her priority is Toby. That's why she puts up with all the rubbish, because she wants to protect Toby."

"Why doesn't she leave him?"

"Because she's terrified that if she did so, Seth would fight her for custody. And win. Then Toby would be under Seth's influence and she'd have little or no say."

"Why would Seth get custody?" But even as I asked, I remembered the night Fergus brought her to me after a fight with Seth, when she explained her predicament. There was no doubt in my mind that Roz's drinking was caused by Seth, was probably her only way of coping. But now she was trapped in a vicious circle – the only way she could get a handle on it was to leave Seth. But if she did that he would use it against her to keep her precious boy. "Oh my God, poor Roz."

"If I thought I could get away with it, I'd kill that man tomorrow for what he's done to her. And now to you, that bastard." Fergus's eyes were shining with unshed tears. "How many lives does he have to ruin?"

"You're in love with her." It was a statement, not a question. I couldn't believe I hadn't seen it before. Probably because I had been blinded by my own mixed feelings for Roz.

"Oh, only since I've known her." Fergus replied with a bitter laugh. "Why do you think I agreed to work with him? After all the crap he put me and my friends through? Because it was the only way to keep her and the little fella close, and to keep an eye on them. Not that I've been much help to her." His fists were clenched and I could see the angry tension in his body.

"You've been a friend and you've cared for her," I said determinedly. "Given her situation, that's all you can do at the moment. I'll talk to her tomorrow about whether she wants me to go to the Police, bearing in mind he's removed all the evidence, I will take it from there."

*

145

Roz was so happy to see me the next morning. After I'd ordered our coffees and sat down, I felt sick as I told her about the events of Saturday morning. Her face was as eloquent as any words as I told the story. At first it hardened at the thought of Seth being 'up to his old tricks', I guess. But as I went on, she paled and grabbed my hand.

"Oh my God, Ellie," she gasped. "Are you okay? No, of course you're not okay. I mean, did he hurt you?"

"He didn't hurt me – not physically, anyway. I think I probably did more damage to him than he to me. I thought I'd killed him."

"I wish you had," she said grimly. "Unfortunately, he was alive and kicking this morning. Oh God, I feel so bad. I should never have said anything about you to him, but he just kept pushing me and pushing me. Did you go to the Police? What did they say?"

"No, I haven't been to the Police." I told her what Fergus and I had found when we returned to my cottage. "I don't think they'd have much of a case, after he removed everything from my room. It would be my word against his." I slumped back in my seat. "I'm so sorry to dump all this on you, honey, but Fergus and I felt we should warn you… And also see what you would want me to do."

She sat and stared out of the window for a few minutes. "I need time to think. And space. Will your funny little car make it to Norfolk, do you think?"

"Of course."

"Good. Take me home, then, please. I need to pack some things and ring the school. Then we'll pick up Toby. Oh! I should ask if you mind driving us to Norfolk?"

"As far as work is concerned I'm 'off sick', so no worries there. What's the plan?"

*

The way in which Roz swung into action made me think that this plan had been in the back of her mind for some time. She collected her stuff from the house while I went and filled up with petrol etc. Then we collected a slightly bewildered Toby from school, citing a family emergency, and drove the three and a half hours to Roz's old school friend Rosie's house, not far from Great Yarmouth.

"It's known as World's End," Roz laughed as we picked our way up the bumpy lane to the house. "Which always struck me as an appropriate name for somewhere to escape to."

I stayed over on Rosie's sofa, and they spent the evening regaling Toby and me with tales of how to be rebellious teenagers when growing up in the middle of nowhere. They had lost touch for a while but been reunited through social media and as I

146

watched Roz relax in the company of her old friend, I could see the vibrant young woman she had once been re-emerging.

Seth wasn't even aware that Rosie existed, Roz told me, and so would have no chance of finding her. We arranged that I would go back and spend the week on my boat and we would be in touch the following weekend when she had had time to think.

As I drove down to Oxford, the following morning, I reflected that Rosie would be good for Roz right now. She struck me as sensible, level-headed and caring and I was sure that a few days of long walks and common sense would be just what Roz needed.

And it seemed it was. She phoned me on the Saturday night to say that she had decided to stay for another week. "But I think we should talk about what you're going to do. About Seth, I mean. I've been thinking about it a lot."

"Me too. I don't want to do anything that would make your life worse than it already is. What do you want me to do?"

"It's your choice, of course," she replied. "I can't tell you what to do, but if I did have a choice then I'd ask you not to go to the Police." When I didn't respond, she went on. "First of all, I want you to know that I absolutely believe you, without question—"

"I didn't doubt you would, honey."

"— But, as you say, it's a flimsy case at best. Seth is world-class at talking his way out of any situation and there's no doubt that Marjorie would say anything to protect him. But, because of the Foundation and how well-known it's become locally, there would be publicity. Seth would no doubt be named. And while I would love to see his name dragged through the mire, I couldn't do that to Toby. If I thought we could get a conviction, I wouldn't hesitate but – as you say – that's highly unlikely. So the Project would probably crash and burn which means Seth would lose his job, and unemployed Seth is a thousand times worse than Seth as he is at the moment, believe me. And Toby would become known as the son of a potential rapist. Can you imagine how that would go down at school, if he even managed to remain at that school?" She choked down a sob.

"So you'd be okay with him getting away with it?" I wanted to be sure.

"No, of course not! But in this scenario the only person I can see being punished is my little boy, who has a crappy enough life with Seth as his father as it is." I could hear that she was crying, even though she tried to sound as if she wasn't. "He's happy at that school and he has friends and even that would be taken away from him. It's a lot to ask you, Ellie, but..." She trailed off, as if she just couldn't bring herself to say the words. "And I honestly don't think he's ever done anything like this before, nor would I imagine he'll do it again. All of this – you, the threat of the Police, me going AWOL with Toby for a couple of weeks – will have scared him shitless..."

"It's okay," I said. "I get it. Fergus told me how things are at home and I've seen some of it for myself. I'm so sorry, honey. I wish I could make it right for you."

"So do I, but no-one can. By my reckoning, I only have to live like this for another seven years or so until Toby is eighteen. I've done eleven already, so I'm well over halfway through my sentence."

"Well, if you have to do seven years, then I'll do them with you. I won't leave the Project. Deal?"

"He won't let you stay," she said sadly. "You've got something on him now and he won't tolerate that. Your life is about to become one big shit storm, Ellie my love. I'd get out while you can. I wouldn't even bother to go back to work."

"No way am I going to let him think he's beaten me, or that I'm scared of him, or that I condone what he did in any way. I'm going back to work on Monday." Although my stomach clenched at the thought of facing Seth I knew I had to do it. Not only for me, but for this woman who, I realised this sudden pang of self-knowledge, I loved. She would never love me, not in the same way, but that was okay. I felt a flash of sympathy for Fergus.

"Ellie, believe me, I know what I'm talking about," she said fervently. "He will make your life hell."

*

He did. As soon as I arrived in the office it started. I'm not prepared to bore you with the details, Inspector Nixon – I'm sure you can guess the sort of thing – and he revelled in it. It was an office day, no schools, so we were all in except Olly who had a couple of days leave. Fergus looked as though he was going to say something, when Seth had spoken over me for the umpteenth time that morning, but I raised a hand to stop him.

Don't. Don't give him the pleasure, I'm fine.

"I thought I told you two about signing at work," Seth said with a sneer. "It won't be tolerated."

"Really?" I replied. "I'm not entirely sure how you can stop it, but if it's annoying you so much then we can go outside and have our conversation over a cigarette. Coming, Fergus?" Without waiting for a response, I gathered my bag and walked out.

I don't know how you're managing to keep your temper, Fergus signed when we got outside. *It's all I can do not to lay him out. And have you seen how much Marjorie is enjoying it?*

Of course she is. It's her dream come true. Don't worry about me, I'm made of pretty strong stuff. And don't you go doing anything that could jeopardise your job here.

What about you? I'm amazed you came back at all. Surely you're not going to stay?

He had a point. I had been so focused on facing Seth down that I hadn't considered the long-term. At the moment, my fury was buoying me up, but that wouldn't last and this atmosphere made things hard for Fergus as much as anything. Seth didn't know that Fergus knew what had happened, and that was for the best. Roz needed Fergus around and the best way for him to watch out for her was to keep his job.

No, it's three weeks until the end of this term, so I'll hand in my notice at the end of the week. I could go now, but I'm actually enjoying watching his pathetic attempts to bully me. I learned how to deal with bullies a long time ago.

*

I ended up not working my notice. Marjorie seemed pleased to be rid of me, as I knew Seth would be. As soon as they had read my letter of resignation, which I'd placed on Marjorie's desk for her to read first thing on Friday, she informed me – with a barely suppressed smile – that I could clear my desk there and then.

"Happy to," I said breezily. "And obviously I'll be taking all my artwork with me, as of course you won't be able to use it in your presentations anymore."

"But—" Seth began, but Marjorie placed a warning hand on his arm.

"Fine," she said with an icy smile. "I don't think we'll be bothering so much with the art side from now on, anyway. I think it's best to keep things to the core team. And we paid you for the promotional stuff you did at the beginning so we own that, don't we?"

If she was expecting an argument from me she would be bitterly disappointed. "Yup," I replied, and my tone was equally glacial. "And you are most welcome to it."

Fergus, Olly and I spent the day clearing my gear out of the offices. At first, Seth tried to stop them helping me but they ignored him, and I think he soon realised that he was in danger of making himself look pathetic and petty – particularly as neither they nor Marjorie were aware of the background to my decision, as far as he knew.

Around 4 o'clock we loaded the last of my boxes into Fergus's van. "Are we going to the pub?" Olly asked. "Surely we're buying Ellie a goodbye drink?" If Seth or Marjorie heard him, they gave no sign.

"Of course we are," said Fergus, smiling at me. "It's the least we can do to say thank you for all your hard work." Seth and Marjorie still appeared to be engrossed in the timetables they were preparing for the following week. Fergus winked at me and grinned.

"That's very kind of you gentlemen," I said, also grinning. "It's nice to know when one is appreciated." And I left the office, still smiling, without a backward glance.

*

DI Nixon broke in. "The way you're telling this, it seems like it didn't bother you at all but I can't believe that's the case. And I already know there was more trouble after you left the Project."

"You could say that. It was unpleasant. He'd wanted to humiliate me, he'd wanted me to suffer and I wouldn't let him. Work became a battleground in a war of attrition. Of course it couldn't last, but neither of us wanted to be the one to back down. In resigning, I felt I'd made a tactical withdrawal. My only problem was how uneasy I felt that he was working with children." Fitch jumped up and placed a paw on my knee. "This dog needs a pee and I need a cigarette."

Outside, while I rolled a cigarette and Fitch busied herself beating the bounds of the car park and marking it as hers, DI Nixon sat down on the bench beside me. I offered her my tobacco tin and she took it and rolled herself a cigarette.

"That's when I got Fitch." I nodded towards her. "Roz's friend Rosie breeds Jack Russells, and when Roz told her what had happened with Seth she trained her especially for me. As an assistance dog, but also for protection. I'll never be alone and vulnerable like that again."

"I can see how she would make you feel safe. They are loyal little dogs and can be fierce when they need to be."

"Don't tell anyone, but she's more likely to distract an intruder by rolling over and getting them to scratch her tummy than she is to attack them." I grinned and we smoked in silence for a few minutes. Then I became aware that she was saying something to me.

"Sorry?"

"I was saying, you had obviously realised that he had violent tendencies as well as being a sexual predator. You're an intelligent woman, Eleanor. You must have realised that this would raise safeguarding issues." She took a drag of her cigarette and looked at me intently.

"Wouldn't this be better being discussed inside?" I asked. "I find it so boring when I have to repeat myself."

"You're right, so tell me about your boat. I've often thought I would like to live like that once I've retired."

"Retired? You're about the same age as me, aren't you?"

"Yes, but my thirty years is up next month. And I haven't given as much thought as I should to how I'm going to fill up all that spare time. This job has been my life for thirty years." She visibly shook herself. "Have you finished your cigarette? I'm pretty sure that dog is all peed out."

Back inside the interview room, she asked the question again. "Before the break, you were saying you were uncomfortable knowing that Seth was working with children. What did you do about that?"

"I went to Mark. After all, the Council were providing a lot of their funding and support. They were also in charge of the schools. Unless I made an official allegation, it was my word against his and, without proof, he would have grounds to sue me for slander. But Mark made sure that they were quietly squeezed out of working in the schools. That's why they moved into workplace disability awareness training."

"I see. Unfortunately, Mark had a point."

"I also tried to talk to Marjorie, but I guess I already knew that would be dead in the water before I even started."

"You raised it with Marjorie? How did that go?"

"Oh, about as well as you think it might have done…"

*

Marjorie put down her coffee cup and stared at me. "Well, that's quite a story, Eleanor. Quite a lot for me to take in."

"It's not a story, Marjorie, it's the truth."

"So why haven't you gone to the Police?"

"I've told you – Roz has asked me not to, because of Toby. And I have no proof. But I thought you ought to know, as he is working for you and because he's working with children. Not that I think he's a threat to the children, to be fair."

"And that's the problem I have believing your story, Eleanor: You have no proof. I have only ever seen Seth as a loving and devoted father. I know his marriage to Roz is not the easiest, but I think he copes with her and her drinking marvellously well. And as far as the children we work with go, he couldn't be more understanding or dedicated."

"But I—"

"Please allow me to finish." She held up her hand to stop me. "Seth has already told me that you developed feelings for him, which he tried to discourage, but that you wouldn't take no for an answer—"

"That's a complete lie!"

"Eleanor, I allowed you to speak without interruption. Please accord me the same respect. Seth did warn me that you might try to stir up trouble. Let me warn you now that I will not allow a silly girl like you to destroy what he and I are building up. If you want a fight, I will give you one, but for both our sakes I think you should just walk away." She smiled triumphantly and sat back, her expression challenging me to say more.

"You know, Marjorie, I was trying to warn you but actually I think you and Seth deserve each other. If you're not careful he will bring you both down, but at least I won't have to watch it." I stood, gathered my bag, turned and walked out of the café.

*

"Did she say anything?" DI Nixon asked.

"I have no idea. That's one of the good things about being deaf. I can always have the last word, I simply stop looking at the other person."

"Good point, I'll have to remember that." She held my gaze for just a little bit longer than was entirely necessary.

"Make sure you do, Detective Inspector Nixon." *Right back at you, Beatrice-Call-Me-Billie. Is it really appropriate to be flirting with a suspect?* "Anyway, that's the last time I saw Marjorie, and if I never see her again it will be no loss to me."

"So what about Mrs Barnes-Colon? Where does she fit in all of this?"

"Imogen? She doesn't really, not as far as I'm concerned. I'd met her, obviously, when she started liaising with the Project. And I knew her vaguely, through Mark, because she worked at the Council. Then there was that scene when she found out about what he'd done to me, silly bint."

"Scene?"

"Oh, it was too ridiculous to talk about. Didn't Roz tell you? You'll have to ask her. I don't know why – or how – she's put up with Immy for all these years. Now, is that me done? Can I go?"

"For now, yes, but I may need to talk to you again. Don't disappear, will you? I can contact you on your mobile number, I take it?"

"Any time." *No, really, any time.* I smiled and stood up. Fitch also stood and stretched herself out. "I'm staying at the cottage, as it happens. I'm between tenants so I'm going to stick around for a while – do some decorating, be around for Roz and Toby if they need me, that sort of thing."

"Good. Well, I'll be in touch. Come on, I'll show you out."

* * *

Beatrice

I stood outside the station for a while after I had seen Eleanor off in her taxi. Alex came out to bring me a coffee and we strolled around the corner to the bench where I had sat with Eleanor not so long ago. I rolled a cigarette.

"You know, Guv, if you like her you should say something," Alex said offhandedly, gazing off into the distance.

"What?"

"I realise I may be stepping over the line here, but I hope you'll take it as I intend it. The chemistry between you is quite obvious."

"She's a witness, if not a suspect, in a possible murder enquiry. If we're talking line crossing then I think that would score pretty highly, don't you?" I said, trying to shut the conversation down.

Alex was having none of it. "I think it's pretty obvious it wasn't her, if it was anyone at all. And, anyway, it's your last case. Even if anyone found out or raised objections, what could they do? It's not like they could sack you, could they?"

It was almost as if she was reading my thoughts aloud. "When I need your help with my love life, Detective Sergeant Wood, I will ask for it," I said firmly. "In the meantime, I suggest we go and prepare to interview Imogen Barnes-Colon tomorrow. I'll follow you in when I've finished here."

"Of course, Detective Inspector Nixon." She stood up and turned to go inside. "But you know I'm right." She smiled and winked, then walked away.

I shook my head, suppressing a smile until she was out of sight. *You're a good friend, Alex, and of course I know you're right. But, whether I'm leaving or not, it would still be unprofessional and in thirty years I have always toed the line. Am I prepared to break the habits of a lifetime?* I sighed, stubbed out my cigarette and put it in the bin before going inside.

* * *

IMOGEN

I've never been interviewed by the Police before, but I wasn't going to take any chances. I made sure that I met my solicitor beforehand and we went into the Police Station together. I spent ages choosing my outfit that morning – it's important to always look the part – and I had finally settled on a sombre navy business suit, with a high-necked blouse and low-heeled navy court shoes. I'd gone for a natural look with my make-up and wore my hair in a low ponytail, wanting to appear as innocent and nonthreatening as possible. Eleanor likes to use her height to intimidate people; I use my lack of it to do the opposite and make them feel protective. Time enough for them to learn that crossing me is not a good idea.

The female Detective Sergeant showed us into the interview room, where the Detective Inspector joined us. I was a little surprised that they would allow two women to run the investigation, but I suppose the Police – like everyone else – have to be seen to be politically correct. And it's not like I haven't used the sexism card to my advantage to get on in my job.

Once we had gone through the formalities, the Detective Inspector started. "Mrs Barnes-Colon, thank you for coming in. And for bringing your solicitor. You are aware that you are under caution?"

Matthew – my solicitor – had explained what this meant to me before we came in. "Yes," I replied in a low, steady voice.

"Now, Imogen… May I call you Imogen?" She smiled in an encouraging manner.

You might think you're playing me by making me think you're my friend, lady, but I'm on to you. "Please do."

"You seemed very upset when I saw you at Mr Peterson's grave side. What was the nature of your relationship with Mr Peterson?"

"We had been work colleagues. And friends."

The Inspector raised an eyebrow. "Nothing more than that?"

And so the games begin. I turned to Matthew. "Do I have to answer that?"

Matthew made a note on the pad in front of him. "Inspector Nixon, is this relevant?"

She was unfazed by his interruption. "I'm trying to establish the circumstances of Mr Peterson's death. Certain allegations have been made about the nature of Imogen's relationship with the deceased. So, yes, I think it's relevant." She looked at me expectantly.

"We were close friends. Our sons were the same age, so we often took them out together." *Although Ben couldn't stand Toby, used to call him a prissy little sissy.* Thinking of Ben made me smile. "We had some fun times," I said.

"So the families were friends?"

"In a way, but more often than not it was just me and Seth and the boys."

"Oh." She sounded surprised. "These outings didn't include Mrs Peterson – Roz – or your husband, ah…" She glanced down at the file in front of her and appeared to be looking for something.

"Adrian. My husband's name is Adrian." My voice sounded flatter than I intended. "No, it was usually just me and Seth. Adrian's work keeps him busy and Roz… Well, let's just say that Roz had usually found a bottle to climb into." *Or Seth had left one conveniently placed.*

"I thought you and Roz were friends?"

"We were… I mean, we are. But that doesn't mean I can't recognise her faults. She made Seth's life a total misery with her drinking. She would get drunk and then harangue him. Sometimes she even got violent." *He would shake and his voice would crack when he was telling me about these episodes. My heart would break for him.*

"Did you witness her being violent?" the Detective Sergeant asked, pausing in her writing and looking directly at me.

"Of course I didn't, she was cleverer than that. But he would call me from his study when she was on one of her tirades. He would have to lock himself in."

"Really?" The Detective Sergeant sounded sceptical.

"You don't believe me, Detective Sergeant? I can assure you that it's true. Seth told me that their house was like a battlefield." *I really don't like you, madam.* "I get the impression, Detective Inspector, that you two have already made your mind up about Seth. Roz and Eleanor have obviously told you all sorts of lies. Well, I'm about to give you the true story. And I got it from Seth himself.

"I met Seth at a Council meeting…"

*

157

I can't tell you how much I hate 'progress update' meetings. My job – one I had recently been promoted into – could loosely be described as monitoring and mentoring. Once the Council decided to support a project I was to be brought in to advise on the way forward and how to access further money from other sources. Today, we had two or three of the previous lucky winners giving presentations to the Councillors. Which meant I was going to be spending the afternoon listening to a load of do-gooding hippies waffling on about social responsibility etc.

I spotted Mark, the Policy Director, pouring himself a coffee as we all milled about waiting to go in. "God, I hope that's strong," I said as I joined him and poured one for myself. "I'm going to need something to help me stay awake."

"Really?" He raised an eyebrow. "Isn't this sort of thing your raison d'être, you being the Community Inclusion Officer and all?"

"As long as I can tick those boxes on the endless forms they send down from the government that say we're working with community groups and 'utilising them to fulfil our inclusion obligations', then that's my job done. Well, that and a couple of phone calls and some emails about the usual funding sources. I could do without actually having to engage with them." I added two sugars to my coffee and grabbed a couple of biscuits. Maybe a sugar rush would help me get through the afternoon.

"That's a shame," said a velvety voice behind me. "I'm rather proud of the presentation I've put together for today."

I spun around to find a pair of dark eyes boring into mine, although I could see a crinkle of amusement at their edges. "I… Er…" I stammered, as I felt a familiar lurch somewhere slightly south of my stomach.

Thankfully, Mark stepped in to spare my blushes. "Imogen, this is Seth Peterson from WE CAN. Seth, let me introduce you to Imogen Barnes-Colon, the Council's newly appointed Community Inclusion Officer."

Seth held out his hand and, as I took it, I felt a frisson – almost like an electric shock – pass through me. "Pleased to meet you, Imogen, I do hope I'm not going to send you to sleep today." He smiled and I felt my body flood with desire.

This is interesting, I haven't felt like this in a while. "I'm quite sure that you don't often have that effect on women, Seth. I'm sure you have them hanging on your every word." I gave him a knowing smile, dressed up as polite professionalism.

"We'll just have to wait and see, won't we?" Seth's smile reflected my own. "Maybe I'll catch you after the meeting and you can tell me what you thought."

At that moment we were called in to take our seats. I sat down next to Mark and busied myself arranging notepads and pens. "I'll pour you a glass of water, Imogen," Mark said with a grin. "You're looking a little overheated."

"Oh, funny," I replied. "I'll have you know I'm a respectable married woman."

"Just because you've bought a book, it doesn't mean you can't browse the library, darling. And besides, he's married too. Just to warn you though, Ellie's been working with them and she thinks he's a creep. She does Art Therapy classes for them."

"Because Eleanor is such a good judge of men." I'd never really had much time for Mark's BFF, who seemed to have a very high and completely unjustified opinion of herself.

"Actually, I put a lot of store by Ellie's judgement," he said, serious now. "She's a good reader of body language. She kind of has to be. Mind you, the one she's really wary of is his partner in the Project, Marjorie. She doesn't seem to be here today but she's the money, and she's the one who wears the pants."

"Is that his wife?" I tried to sound casual.

"Oh no, by all accounts he's married to a drunk. Shame, because I believe there's a kiddie. No, Marjorie is quite a bit older than him but she keeps him on a very tight leash, according to Ellie. It all sounds a bit odd to me."

"You're such a gossip, like it's of any interest to me."

"I'll tell you one thing, though: that man knows how to spend money – especially other people's. I'll be interested to see his progress report and whether it justifies the money we've paid out to him and his Project so far."

"Ooh, is this you being all masterful and wielding your mighty abacus?" I teased. "Come off it, Mark, we all know you're really a fluffy-wuffy pussycat... Especially where sexy, handsome men are concerned."

He frowned. "Immy, you're on your own in thinking Seth Peterson is sexy and handsome. He makes my skin crawl."

I shrugged. "Each to their own, I guess."

The afternoon passed every bit as slowly as I had expected, although having Mark there did at least brighten it a bit. I'm not what you'd call a fag hag, but gay men always amuse me. And Seth's presentation was very polished – even Mark grudgingly acknowledged that he did seem to be doing a good job.

As the meeting wound up, I took my time gathering my belongings together. As I had expected, Seth came over to me as I was just about ready to leave. "So, Imogen, I haven't sent you to sleep then."

"Not at all," I replied coolly. "I'm wide awake and ready to go." I looked up at him from under my eyelashes, a look I've perfected over the years as men seem to like it.

"Yes, I'm quite sure you are." His gaze wandered up and down my body, then he smiled. "Do you have to rush away? I thought we could spend some time getting to know each other a little better."

"I have some time, I just have to collect a couple of things."

"I'll walk with you. I'd be interested to see your office."

We didn't actually speak as I led the way back to the office I share with the rest of the community liaison team. I collected my coat and briefcase after briefly introducing Seth to the couple of people still at their desks, then we headed out towards the lifts. As we passed the door to the disabled toilet he opened it and pulled me inside. We still didn't speak until, panting and exhausted, I slid down the wall to sit on the floor. He stood over me, pulling himself back together and fastening his belt. Then he silently tore off a handful of loo paper and handed it to me with a wry smile.

"Well, that's certainly not how I expected the afternoon to end," he said smoothly. "You are quite a surprising lady, Ms Barnes Colon."

Me neither," I said, standing up and disposing of the paper. "You're quite a surprise yourself, Mr Peterson. Shit, why do they never put mirrors in disabled toilets?" I fished around in my bag and found my compact. "Do the designers think disabled people are so hideous they don't want to look at themselves?"

"Probably, and a lot of the time they've got a point. You look fine, a little tousled perhaps, but no-one would guess that you'd just had your brains fucked out on the sink of the disabled toilet."

"Oh, that's a little presumptuous, I feel," I said, looking up at him out of the corner of my eye. "I think I'm still in full possession of my brains."

"Really? Am I to take that as a challenge?"

"You can take it any way you like. Now, I suggest you wait a good few minutes after I've left before you make your own exit. We don't want to be seen leaving together." And without looking back, I left.

I didn't actually go very far, just into the Ladies next door. I wasn't quite as cool and composed as I had pretended to be, that was just an act for Seth. I locked myself into a cubicle and sat down, waiting for my heart to slow to its regular rate. *What the hell? Imogen, what have you done? Flirting is one thing, but this is what happens when you play with the grown-ups.* I heard Seth leave and automatically checked my watch. I decided to take ten minutes to clear my head and work out what I was going to do. I suppose I should have been thinking about Adrian – good, sweet Adrian – but I knew that he was the least of my problems. He would always believe everything and anything I told him and, in this case, there was nothing to tell. I would be home from work at the usual time and there was no need for him to think there was anything amiss.

I suppose if this were a novel, or that dreary film with the trains, I would have spent the evening wracked with guilt and recriminations. But Seth was no Trevor Howard, thank God, and I didn't. My overwhelming feeling was that I wanted more… And I didn't care what I had to do to get it.

*

I heard nothing from Seth the next day and, although I looked up his contact details on the Council's database, I was determined to play it cool and let him make the next move.

By day three I was desperate to hear from him. Tomorrow was Friday, then there would be a weekend to get through and I didn't think I could. Late in the afternoon, I picked up the phone and called his office. He answered and I stammered out my pretext for calling him.

"Well, Imogen, if indeed there is a problem with our grant application, it needs to be sorted straightaway." The amusement in his voice was clear. "It sounds like we have to have a meeting."

"Yes, as soon as possible." I abandoned all hope of playing this cool. "We obviously don't want your grant application to be held up."

"No, we definitely don't want that." He was laughing at me, I could hear it in his voice. "Unfortunately, I'm completely tied up tomorrow, and I'm in schools for most of next week…" There was a sound of him tapping on computer keys. "I'm in the office now, for a couple of hours, if you could make that?"

I took a deep breath, knowing that I was about to blow all pretence of maintaining the upper hand. "That would be fine, I can come to you."

"Of course." He wasn't even bothering to hide his amusement now, and I was beyond feeling any embarrassment. He gave me the details of how to get to the office and within five minutes I was in my car and on my way.

Although their office was in a pretty remote location, I found it quite easily. Seth met me at the door. "How nice to see you again, Imogen," he said smoothly. "We're just winding up for the day. Come in and meet the team, I'll give you the grand tour before we start our meeting."

Meet the team? I hadn't actually given any thought to the details of how this was going to go. It hadn't occurred to me that there would be other people around in his office. The WE headquarters were in a huge old farmhouse and he showed me into what must once have been the kitchen – a big room at the centre of the house.

At the back of the room was a large, wooden, leather-topped desk. This was opposite a big fireplace which contained an old-fashioned range and was flanked on either side by two old Chesterfield-style sofas. Mark's friend, Eleanor, was sitting on one of the sofas and there were two young men sitting on the other, with their feet on a low table in front of them. In the corner, I could see a couple of kitchen units and a fridge.

"Feet," Seth barked as we entered the room. The young men casually lowered their feet to the floor. "Fergus, Ollie, this is Imogen Barnes-Colon, the Council's inclusion Officer. She's here to talk about our grant application, so try to behave yourselves." He waved his hand to attract Eleanor's attention. "Ellie, this is—"

"I know Eleanor," I said. "How are you?" I enunciated the words slowly, so that she could read my lips.

"I'm fine thank you, Imogen," she said with an amused smile. I always got the feeling that Eleanor was secretly laughing at me, but I didn't know why. I had always gone out of my way to make sure that she could understand what I was saying, but she didn't seem to appreciate my efforts at all. It had crossed my mind on previous occasions that maybe she was attracted to me and trying not to show it. I've never liked ginger hair, though, so she would have had no chance – even if I did like women.

Just then, an elegant, older woman entered the room through a door behind the reception desk. She was wearing a coat and had a set of keys in her hand. "Oh," she said, apparently surprised to see a stranger in their midst.

"Marjorie, this is Imogen – from the Council," said Seth. "We have a meeting."

She looked confused momentarily, but covered it well. "There's nothing in the calendar and I have plans for this evening."

"I know," Seth replied. "It was a bit last minute, just a minor hitch with the grant application, but nothing for you to worry about. You go on, I can handle this."

She looked put out, and I saw Eleanor and the boys exchange amused glances. "Well, if you're sure? But how will you get home?"

"Oh, I'm sure Imogen won't mind dropping me off," Seth said smoothly and looked down at me. I nodded.

"Very well," she said, her voice clipped. "I'll be off then." She nodded in the general direction of the sofas and moved behind us to the door, giving me a sidelong glance as she did.

Eleanor stood up. "Time I was off, as well. Are you guys coming?"

Seth waited until we heard the outer door close behind them, then he turned to me. "I'll make you a coffee. Ellie and the boys will stop and have a cigarette before they leave, so we'll wait until we know they've gone." He moved over to the kitchen area and filled the kettle.

Apart from speaking to Eleanor, I hadn't yet said a word. I cleared my throat. "What if I really am here to discuss a problem with your application?"

He turned to face me. "Are you?"

I felt my face flood with colour. I opened my mouth to speak but he interrupted me.

"Imogen, I dislike playing games, we both know why you're here. I will tell you this, though: if you ever walk out on me again, like you did on Monday, it will be the last time you see me. Do I make myself clear?"

I felt like a schoolgirl being taken to task by the headmaster and I hung my head. "I'm sorry," I mumbled. I was beginning to wonder if I'd made a mistake.

He was leaning back against the worktop, waiting for the kettle to boil, and he held out his hands towards me. I walked forwards to take them but as I reached him, he took hold of my shoulders and spun me so I was facing the sink.

"Bend over that sink," he growled. With one hand he gripped my shoulder, pushing me down, and with the other he lifted my skirt. I had removed my underwear on my way over and he grunted when he realised this.

It was fast and hard. As he finished, he took hold of my hair and pulled my head up so that his mouth was next to my ear as he said, "I just want you to remember who's in charge here, Imogen, and it isn't you."

He stepped back, tucked himself in, then continued to make the coffee while I hung over the sink, panting. He left a mug on the worktop, saying "I'll leave you to put your own sugar and milk in." Then he strolled over and sat down on one of the sofas, placing his coffee on the table in front of him.

I pulled myself together, added sugar to my coffee, then carried it over to the sofas. He indicated I should sit on the one opposite his. "I like you being ready for me," he said. "From now on, I want you to be like that every time you see me."

Relief flooded through me as I took in his words. That meant he did want to keep seeing me. I smiled at him. "Okay, if that's what you want."

He checked his watch. "I haven't got long. Let me show you around. Bring your coffee if you like."

It was a good setup. Seth told me that the farmhouse had been converted, some years before, as a recording studio. As well as the studio itself, with a fully working engineer's booth, there was a soundproofed rehearsal room – currently full of guitars and other musical instruments – and an office with two desks, all on the ground floor.

Upstairs, there were two former bedrooms – both containing Eleanor's art stuff – and a bathroom.

It amused me, when Seth took me again on Eleanor's desk, to think of my theory that she secretly fancied me. It seemed to occur to him as well, as he said, "This would be even more fun with the two of you," before slipping out of me.

I raised my eyebrows.

"Just think about it," he said.

"I will, but probably not as much as I suspect you will." I gave him a knowing smile and it felt good to have regained a little more semblance of control.

I drove him home and dropped him off on the seafront at Suniton.

"I live up there," he said vaguely when I enquired. "You don't need to know exactly where, it's not like you'll be visiting." I decided to let that go for the moment. I wasn't interested in his home life, anyway. At least, not at that stage.

*

Matthew gave a little cough. "I think this would be an appropriate time to take a break," he said. "I'd like some time with my client."

The Detective Inspector and her Sergeant exchanged glances. "Of course," she said. "I think we could all do with a break." They gathered up their papers and left the room.

"I'm, ah, unsure why you're going into quite so much detail…" Matthew began, his face flaming red.

"Oh? You said not to hold anything back. And aren't you enjoying it?" I smiled, enjoying his discomfort.

"To be frank, I find it quite distasteful. And so far I don't think it has any relevance. I'm not sure of your motives for being quite so, ah, graphic."

"I thought we were aiming for full disclosure," I said innocently. "Isn't that the case?" *And when this goes to court, as I'm hoping it will, then Roz and Eleanor will have to listen to this interview, as well as that bitch Marjorie. Then they'll all know the truth, that I was the one he really loved, he really wanted. That I was the one who knew how to satisfy him.*

"Mrs Barnes-Colon—"

"Imogen," I said with a coy smile.

"Mrs Barnes-Colon," he repeated more forcefully. "You chose me as your solicitor because I act for, am friends with, your husband. I feel that there would be a conflict of interest for me to continue acting you in this matter. We are bound by attorney client privilege, so I could not tell Mr Barnes of anything that has been said today, but I'm not prepared to listen to any more of it." He opened his briefcase and placed his pad and pen inside it. Slamming it shut, he stood and looked down at me.

"I don't know what game you're playing, Imogen," he said. "But I want no part of it." He left the room.

I shrugged. *Suit yourself, who needs you anyway? You're obviously as weak and pathetic as your little friend Adrian.*

* * *

165

Beatrice

Alex and I grabbed a couple of coffees and took them into my office. We sat down on either side of the desk and it was some minutes before either of us spoke. It was Alex who cracked first.

"Oh. My. God." She laughed uneasily. "What the hell was that?"

"I have no idea," I said slowly, shaking my head.

"You know, if this does turn out to be murder I really, really hope she did it. Those two definitely deserved each other. But why the hell is she telling us all this?"

I had been wondering the same thing. "And we're only onto their second meeting, this could get really pornographic."

"I was beginning to think her solicitor would never intervene. Poor Matthew, I've never seen him look so uncomfortable."

"My dad always said you should never interrupt the flow of a confession, if that's what this is, but I bet he never came up against anyone like this woman. Hopefully, Matthew's in there, putting the brakes on." I took a sip of my coffee. "I hope he takes his time, I don't think I'm ready for round two yet."

No such luck. At that moment, a uniform PC knocked and stuck his head round the door to say that Imogen Barnes-Colon's solicitor had apparently removed himself from the case, but that she had announced she would carry on without him. Alex and I both groaned at the news.

"Take her a cup of coffee," I said to the PC. "And if you could find some bromide to put in it, that would be good. And tell her we'll be about half an hour if she wants to go out and get some fresh air. She's not under arrest."

"Yeah, maybe she'll cool down a bit," Alex said. "We can only hope."

* * *

166

IMOGEN

I was disappointed at Matthew's chickening out, but determined to carry on. I have never had a chance to tell anyone the full story of me and Seth, and this was my opportunity to put everyone straight. At the time it all blew up Roz and, to a certain extent Eleanor, took centre stage and I was left on the side-lines. I was as much a victim as either of them, more so probably, but they had written me out of their lives like I never existed. Even though I kept in touch with Roz regularly, mainly in order to remind Seth that I was still waiting for him, I never felt that I was welcome. And as for Marjorie, all she cared about was her precious little Project.

I sipped my coffee and sat demurely in the interview room. I'd seen plenty of TV cop shows and I knew that somewhere in another room my every move was being watched. I knew that I couldn't let my act slip for a moment. I knew that this waiting was probably a ploy to put me under pressure, but I knew their games and I wasn't going to be tricked.

The Detective Inspector and her Sergeant came back into the room and took their seats opposite me. "Imogen," she said. "You've been very frank about the nature of your relationship with Mr Peterson, thank you. How long did it go on for?"

Not long enough. Not nearly long enough and it was all Eleanor's fault when it finished. Her, that bloody Audrey woman and Marjorie. "Three years."

"What happened?" The Sergeant asked.

"First of all, you have to understand that he loved me. He was the love of my life and I, his." I allowed my voice to break a little as I said this. It wouldn't hurt to show I could be vulnerable, that I was as much a victim of Seth Peterson as anyone. "We had plans to be together…"

*

167

The day after our meeting at his office, I sent Seth a text to ask if he wanted to meet for lunch over the weekend. He replied that he liked to spend the weekends with his son.

How old is your son? X

7

Really? Mine's 7! We should get them together X

We have stuff on this weekend

Okay, another time? Have a good one X

I didn't want to appear too keen so I left it at that. I knew that he would contact me again. I knew that I had as much of an effect on him as he did on me. It just meant that I would have to spend the weekend doing boring family stuff with Adrian and Ben.

The next time I saw Seth was on a school visit. He had invited me along 'to see community inclusion at work', as he put it. I arrived, as he had suggested, in time for the morning assembly and I took my seat beside him to watch his team perform. I hadn't realised he had so many volunteers from the disabled community working with him. The assembly was quite good but I was more aware of his thigh pressing against mine as we sat on a bench at the back of the hall. Afterwards, we toured the different classrooms where his team were working with the children, even Marjorie.

We stopped for a while in the classroom where Eleanor was working, talking to the children in a basic sign language and helping them to create posters and drawings around the theme of inclusion.

"Aren't you worried about leaving her on her own with the children like that?" I asked as we quietly left the room. "What happens if she loses control of them?"

He looked down at me, surprised. "Of course not, she's really good. She's one of the best." I felt jealousy churn in my stomach at the admiration in his voice. "Where would you like to go next?" he asked, checking his watch. "We have about twenty minutes till break time."

I looked around the corridor and spotted the familiar wheelchair sign on a door. I smiled. "In there," I said, indicating it with my head.

"I don't think that would be very appropriate," he replied, although I thought I caught a glint in his eye.

"Who cares about appropriate?" I opened the door and pushed him inside. There was a low padded bench in one corner of the room, presumably some sort of changing table, and I propelled him back towards it, undoing his belt and trousers as I did so. "For once, I'm in charge," I growled as I pulled down his trousers. I had obeyed his instructions and was wearing no underwear and I lowered myself onto him in one move.

We exited the toilet a couple of minutes before the bell rang for break time and arrived in the staff room at the same time as the rest of the team. I drank my coffee and chatted to some of the teachers, explaining who I was and what my role was within the Council. At the end of break I went over to Seth and Marjorie.

"I should get back to the office," I said. "But I've been really impressed and I look forward to working more closely with you in the future."

Seth didn't miss a beat. "That would be great, Imogen. You can find your own way back to your car, can you?" He turned back to Marjorie.

I walked back to my car fuming. How dare he just dismiss me like I didn't matter? Hadn't I just proved to him that I was at least his equal when it came to taking the lead sexually? I lit a cigarette to calm myself down. Then it occurred to me – Eleanor. I remembered the admiration in his voice as we watched her taking the class. Seth was obviously in thrall to Eleanor. Surely he knew that she was into women? I allowed myself a laugh at his expense, threw the cigarette end out of the window and drove out of the school gates.

By the time I got to the office I had calmed down and decided I just didn't need to be playing games. I had a husband who adored me, a beautiful son and a nice house. Why did I need to go looking for cheap thrills? Seth wasn't all that, I told myself, and if he wanted to go chasing after a dyke like Eleanor he was welcome to her.

*

I spent the rest of the morning catching up on emails. Towards lunchtime, I headed to Mark's office. "Fancy accompanying me to the sandwich bar?" I asked casually and he agreed readily.

It was a lovely day and so we took our sandwiches down to the prom and sat on a bench looking out to sea. "I saw Eleanor this morning," I said as I kicked out at a seagull who clearly thought he could psych me into giving him part of my sandwich. "I was checking on that charity she works for. She looked well."

"Checking on the charity? Really?" Mark didn't bother to hide the cynicism in his voice, although he was smiling. "Nothing to do with a certain CEO, of course."

I gave him a 'who, me?' look.

"Seriously though," he went on. "How is she? I feel really bad, since I met David I've hardly spent any time with her, or even really spoken to her."

"I didn't get to speak to her because she was taking a class, but she looked well. Is she with anyone at the moment?"

"I wouldn't know. The last I heard from her, her divorce had finally come through." He threw the rest of his sandwich some distance away and we watched the seagulls pounce on it.

"Divorce? I thought she batted for your team, so to speak?"

"I get the impression it was a misguided experiment, but who's to say where Cupid's arrow might fall? I might even fancy a woman myself one of these days." He roared with laughter. "God forbid!"

*

The following weekend I decided we were due for some quality family time. Adrian works nights at a local factory so I can pursue my career during the day. I sent Ben to wake him up in the late morning, then I dragged us all out for a long walk to our favourite family pub for lunch. As soon as we arrived and started looking for seats in the garden some movement in the corner caught my eye. My chest tightened and I stopped dead, staring over to the table where Seth and Eleanor sat, heads together, apparently working on a crossword.

"It looks too busy," I said to Adrian. "Let's go and look inside, or we could just go home." But going home would have meant another hour's walk back on empty stomachs and, while I was now feeling too sick to eat, I knew that Ben would kick off and probably cause a scene if we didn't feed him soon and I didn't want to attract any attention. We went inside and found a table, away from the door but near a window that gave me a view out to the garden. I pleaded a headache and let Adrian and Ben prattle on while I sat quietly, keeping my sunglasses on and not taking my eyes off Seth and Eleanor. I watched them walk to the car park and actually let out a whimpered moan as Seth got into his car – on his own – and drove away.

Adrian took this as a sign that my headache was getting worse. "Poor old you," he said sympathetically. "What rotten luck. Tell you what, Ben, let's finish here and then splash out on a taxi and take Mummy home." He squeezed my hand. "Then Ben and I will go out for the afternoon and let you have some peace and quiet and a nice sleep."

Of course, I didn't sleep. How could I? I paced around the house, fuming. All my resolutions from the day of the school visit were forgotten. I was not going to let Eleanor win. I had never liked her much – she was always so together, so damned confident, with her arty clothes and everyone making so much fuss of her just because she was deaf – and I had always had that nagging feeling that she was laughing at me. Seth was mine and she was not going to have him.

170

2010, Suniton Police Station

The Detective Sergeant interrupted, looking confused. "I don't understand," she said. "You'd known Seth, what, less than a fortnight? Admittedly it was a pretty intense fortnight." She frowned. "But you had no proof that there was anything going on between him and Eleanor, and anyway he was married. As were, are…" she emphasised 'are'. "… you. You'd already decided not to pursue the relationship with Seth. Why were you so upset?"

I saw a look of irritation flash across the Inspector's face. *Aha, you don't want her to interrupt me. You understand me.*

"Obviously, you have never experienced love at first sight, Sergeant. Never felt such overwhelming passion, like a drug. When you would do anything, absolutely anything, for just one more taste." I smiled knowingly at the Inspector. *You know what I'm talking about.* "And of course," I went on. "You never knew Seth. If you'd met him, you'd understand."

"I'm sure we would," said the Inspector and I could tell she was trying to keep her voice disinterested. "Please go on."

I knew I had to have a plan. I knew I had to make Seth fall in love with me and forget about Eleanor. And the best weapon I had in my arsenal, apart from the sex, was our boys. It was almost like Fate was on my side – the fact that our boys were practically the same age. I needed to show him what a cute little family we could be. And I needed to start straight away, before he could get too cosy with Eleanor. I grabbed my mobile and texted him.

Hi – good day? X

Hi. Average, been at home with family.

I swallowed my surge of rage at the lie.

Much the same. We're thinking of going to the new Fun Park tomorrow and I wondered if you and your son would like to join us? We're going to make a day of it. X

Should be OK. I doubt his mother has anything planned.

It'll just be me and Ben. His dad's busy. X

He picked up the hint and we made our arrangements. I got the feeling that he would be quite pleased to leave his wife behind.

Adrian and Ben came home later, bringing fish and chips so I wouldn't have to cook. Adrian was full of sympathy about my headache and brought me a blanket, so I could 'snuggle on the sofa', and a hot water bottle.

"You're so good to me." I said to him sweetly, while Ben went upstairs to get ready for bed. "And I feel so bad that you didn't get to sleep much today, after your shift. I'm going to take Ben out all day tomorrow so you can sleep as long as you want. I thought I'd take him to the new Fun Park for the day."

He frowned slightly. "Can we afford it? After all, we spent quite a lot on lunch today. And then there was the taxi home."

I sighed inwardly. Adrian could be so boring about money. "Oh, I got freebies through work," I said airily. "And we'll take a picnic. You'd like to go to the Fun Park, wouldn't you darling?" I said, as Ben came in wearing his pyjamas.

"I suppose so," he said. "Can I take my Nintendo?"

"Of course," I said. "Great! So we're all set."

*

I dressed very carefully the next day, nothing overtly sexual. I wanted Seth to see what a good mother I was, how I could be a good stepmother for his son. I remembered what Mark had said about his wife being a drunk and decided to be a paragon of maternal virtue. No matter how tempting, there would be no illicit sexual encounters today. Today he needed to see me as a Madonna, not a whore.

It was just a shame that the boys had different ideas. I hadn't counted on them not liking each other. "Mum, he's so boring," Ben complained when he and I went off to buy ice creams for the four of us. "He's such a little sissy," he grumbled.

"I know," I replied. "But his father is a really important business contact, darling. If you could just pretend to like him, for my sake, it would be so good. I'll get you that new game for your Nintendo," I wheedled.

"Zelda? Oh-Kay," he said, rolling his eyes. "But I want the game tomorrow. As soon as I get home from school."

"I'll see what I can do, darling," I said, ruffling his hair. "Thank you."

He wasn't wrong, Toby was a little sissy. Perhaps it was that posh school that Seth sent him to, or perhaps he was psychologically damaged by having a drunk for a mother. He was so quiet and overly polite, like he didn't dare say boo to a goose. Ben could be a handful, but that was because he ran full tilt at life. He wasn't scared of anything, like me. Toby seemed fearful of his own shadow, but Seth didn't seem to notice. I did my best to encourage Toby to talk, but in the end I gave up. Seth had told me he liked Doctor Who so I tried talking to him about that, but I couldn't get beyond monosyllabic answers to any of my questions.

"He's just shy," Seth said as Toby went off to see the animals in the petting zoo.

"Poor thing." I tried to sound as sympathetic as possible. "Has he always been so shy?"

"I don't suppose it helps that his mother's a drunk, who seems to think that tramps and vagrants are suitable companions for a young boy," he snarled.

"Really?" I said in a shocked voice. *This could be useful.*

"Oh yes, that's not the half of it. She gets drunk and gets into these terrible rages and just shouts all the time. There's nothing I can do to stop her."

I reached over and took his hand. "That must be terrible for you, for both of you."

"Well, she doesn't shout at him, just me." I could hear a catch in his voice. "I have to give her her due, she's a good mother. But he hears her raging at me and it can't be good for him."

I suppressed a small smile of satisfaction. Although I hadn't even considered the wife before, it was clear she was going to be no threat. So Eleanor was my only problem. "Can't you leave her? Surely you'd have grounds?"

"Probably, but she owns half the house and it can't be sold without her agreement. I could never afford to buy somewhere on my own." He sat up and started packing up the picnic. "Anyway, you don't want to hear about my problems." He gave me a thin smile. "Are you wearing underwear today, Imogen?"

I gave a little shake of my head at the sudden change in the conversation. "Yes I am," I said primly, but with a coy smile. "I'm being a good mummy today and that means no sneaking off to do outrageously dirty things with you, Mr Peterson."

"That's a shame." He ran a finger up my arm. "Although I quite like seeing this side of you, knowing how easy it would be for me to reduce you to a quivering heap – right here, in front of all these nice families enjoying their Sunday afternoon." He let out a laugh as I removed his hand from my arm.

"I don't think we should put that boast to the test, do you?" I said, also smiling. "I don't think that's what they mean by a petting zoo."

"Speaking of which…" He stood up. "… I should go and find Toby and take him home. But thank you for today, Imogen, it's been a nice interlude."

Ben was scathing on the way home. "Toby spent most of the afternoon talking to the rabbits, Mum, and helping the keeper clean them out. He even told the keeper that he and his mum grow carrots and that he would bring some next time he came. How gay is that?"

"I know, darling, but as I said his father is an important business contact so please try to be nice to him whenever we see him. We may be seeing quite a bit of them in the future."

Ben groaned and spent the rest of the journey doing a wicked impression of Toby's conversation with the rabbits. By the time we reached home we were both laughing fit to burst. I explained to a startled Adrian that we had bumped into a business colleague at the park, then Ben told him about Toby and the rabbits and did his impression again. Adrian, of course, didn't find it funny and told Ben he was being cruel.

"Oh for God's sake, Adrian, it's not like the kid can hear him," I snapped, then sent Ben upstairs to get ready for his bath. "We've had a really nice day and it's so typical of you to put a downer on it. Well done." I trudged up the stairs after Ben, thinking how different things would be with Seth.

*

A couple of nights later I was at home working on my laptop. Adrian was at work and Ben was in bed. My mobile rang and I felt a momentary triumph when I saw it was Seth. "Hello Mr Peterson," I purred. "And how are you this evening?"

"Are you alone?"

"Yes, why?" I was a little startled by his abrupt tone.

"What are you wearing?"

"I just had a bath so I'm wearing my bath robe." *Why does he want to know what I'm wearing?*

"Really?" His tone became softer. "Anything underneath?"

Ah, now I see where this is going. "No, I'm too hot." I made my voice low and seductive. "And I was just about to put my body oil on." Actually, I was wearing my ratty trackie bottoms and an old Glastonbury T-shirt from the 90s that I had nicked from a boyfriend, but he wasn't to know that.

"Good." His voice was smooth as melted chocolate. "I'm going to tell you exactly what to do."

I'd never had phone sex before and, even though I wasn't starting exactly from where he thought I was, we certainly both finished in the same place. I lay back on my sofa, panting. "Well, that was an unexpected surprise."

"It certainly was. The bitch is on one of her drunken rampages and I've locked myself in my study. I was hoping you'd cheer me up."

"We aim to please," I said flirtatiously. "But seriously, are you okay?"

"Oh yeah." Now his voice was flat. "She'll wear herself out in a bit and then that will be her passed out till tomorrow morning. I'm used to it. How come you're on your own? Where's your husband?"

We talked for about an hour, exchanging information about our spouses and how each of us had been duped into marriages that were nothing like what we had expected. When we finally hung up I felt we had reached a new mutual understanding.

*

Seth's wife, Roz, seemed to have these drunken rampages two or three times a week, which was when he would phone me from his study. "I can't go out there." The despair in his voice would break my heart. "If she gets violent, I can't hit her back because I would probably kill her. All I can do is wait for her to pass out."

175

Quite often, she would already be drunk when he got home from work, so he would lock himself in without eating anything. "I've bought myself a mini fridge and I have a kettle in here, so I'm okay," he explained one time. "And my bed has been in here for months. We're basically living apart, but in the same house."

When I asked after Toby, he dismissed my concerns. "Oh no, she'd never hurt him. If nothing else, she's a good mother." I couldn't believe that he could be so generous towards a woman who made his life a living nightmare and told him so.

"It's the truth," he said simply. "I loved her once. I at least owe her that." And that just made me love him all the more.

*

"You see, Detective Inspector, whatever Roz and Eleanor have told you, it's not true. Seth Peterson was a caring, wonderful human being, who was victimised by a drunken wife and has been slandered outrageously by that bitch, Eleanor."

The Detective Inspector raised her eyebrows and leaned back in her chair. "But he was content to let this violent drunk 'rampage' around the house while his young son was alone and defenceless, and he himself was locked in his study? And neither of you thought to report this to the authorities?"

"I told you he knew that Roz wouldn't hurt Toby—"

"But you're a mother yourself, Imogen!" The Sergeant exclaimed. "Regardless of whether she would hurt him, surely you were concerned about the psychological effect on Toby? You've already said that you thought he was withdrawn. You work for the Council, didn't you even think to have a conversation with someone from Social Services?"

"It wasn't my place to call in Social Services. I did tell Seth that it would help his divorce if he reported her, but he explained that he couldn't. He worked with children. If his own child was known to them it might jeopardise the Project or his place in it."

"So he was more concerned with protecting his own arse than his child?"

"Of course not!" I reacted angrily. "He knew that Toby was perfectly safe, he knew that Roz would never harm him. It broke his heart that Toby had to witness his mother's drunken behaviour."

"I'm sure it did…" The Sergeant was about to say more, but the Inspector held up her hand to silence her.

"I think we could all do with a break at this stage," she said. "Why don't we all go and get some lunch and continue this in an hour. Imogen, you're not under arrest and I'm sure we can trust you to come back?"

"Of course, I want to make sure you get the whole truth about Seth."

"I'm aware of that." She stood and held the door open for me. "Sergeant Wood will show you out and we'll see you in an hour."

* * *

Beatrice

"That woman!" Alex burst into my room after showing Imogen out. "Is she for real?"

"I can't say I disagree with you," I said, measuring my words. "But that was completely unprofessional. If you can't control yourself in there I'll have to get someone else."

"I'm sorry, Guv, she just really got to me. She couldn't give a rat's arse about that little boy, neither of them could. I just kept imagining him, cowering in his room, absolutely terrified of his own mother—"

"Ah, so you believe that Seth was telling the truth about Roz?"

"Well no, of course not! From what Roz and Eleanor have told us, it was more likely to have been him doing the rampaging... Oh!"

"Exactly. I think Seth had his own reasons for telling Imogen all of that, just as she had her own reasons for believing it all. I think she has a lot more to tell us, but we're not going to get anywhere if you keep interrupting and antagonising her."

"Yeah, sorry Guv. I shouldn't have let her get to me."

"No, you shouldn't. But if you get me a latte and a sandwich, I'll let it go this time." I smiled and handed her a note from my wallet.

While she was gone I leaned back in my chair and closed my eyes, trying to piece my thoughts together. But all I could think of was Eleanor and her face as she told us what Seth had tried to do to her. A terrifying experience in anyone's book, but what must it have been like, not being able to hear what was happening? And Seth had known how much more vulnerable she was.

By contrast, Imogen seemed to like the rough side of Seth. A couple of the incidents she had described could easily have been rape in someone else's eyes. Did Seth know that she would be willing? Did he care?

I didn't believe the stories Seth had told Imogen about his home life, but I knew it was a dangerous game to start forming opinions before I had heard all sides. I was going to have to be very careful to avoid letting my bias affect my judgement. I sighed and picked up my mobile. It would be good to have a third party to bounce this one off.

"Hi Dad, it's me. Could I buy you dinner this weekend? I can do with the great DCI Bill Nixon's advice. Yes, it could well be a two-bottle job. Great, see you then. Love you, Dad." I smiled as I thought about what his reaction would have been to Imogen's statement this morning. 'Feck it lass, in my day we'd have been selling tickets to that one.' I shook my head and was still smiling when Alex came back with our lunch.

* * *

IMOGEN

I took the opportunity to go for a walk in the park while the police took their lunch break. I didn't get anything to eat myself, but I picked up a coffee and sat on a bench while I went over the story I had given them so far. I wondered how it had gone with Roz and Eleanor. Whether they had told the whole truth or had rehashed the old lies that they had been spouting back in the days when I had started pretending to be their friend. I couldn't bear to think of them trashing Seth's name all over again.

I finished my coffee and had a cigarette. There was a group of lads – students probably, from the local College, about the same age as Ben – playing football nearby and I sat and watched them for a while. A stray ball rolled to my feet and I picked it up. The boy who came to collect it reddened when I handed it back to him with a flirtatious smile. I don't think any of them could have guessed that I was old enough to be their mother and I stayed a bit longer watching them, amused at their boyish attempts to attract my attention. When I got up to go I gave them a little wave and heard their sheepish laughter behind me as I walked away.

Back at the Police Station, the Detective Inspector clearly wanted to push things along. "So, Imogen. You say the relationship with Seth lasted three years. What brought it to an end?"

"Eleanor," I said flatly. "It ended when Eleanor left."

"How come?" She looked puzzled. "What difference would that make?"

"I didn't know then what she had been saying about him. I only found out later, but that's when it started to go wrong. Poor Seth, didn't he have enough to cope with already? Without having to deal with her lies? And to have to face it all alone, not being able to tell anyone. He must have felt so lonely."

"That doesn't explain why the relationship ended. Surely he would've appreciated having you on his side?"

"Yes, but he had to be whiter than white, don't you see? As I say, I didn't know what was going on, I just knew that he was shutting me out..."

*

180

We had been seeing each other for about three years, two or three times a week, sometimes at the weekend with the boys. Sometimes meeting up at a motel near the airport where the manager was quite happy to accept some cash to let us use a room for a couple of hours. Most nights we spoke on the phone or chatted on the Internet. I loved him and we would often spend our time fantasising about a future where we were together, him free of Roz and her drunken rampages and me from dull-as-ditch-water Adrian.

The only issue for me was his inexplicable friendship with Eleanor. I made out that it didn't bother me but I just couldn't understand it. Surely he knew she was a lesbian – everyone did – and why would he want to spend time with a woman who couldn't give him what I did? Of course, I didn't want to seem like I was bitching or gossiping or – God forbid – jealous, so I never came out and said any of this to him.

"She's lonely," he said one day when I casually mentioned their friendship. "She's all on her own in that cottage and I felt sorry for her. Trouble is, she's become quite needy now. I think I might be her only friend. That Mark from your place used to sniff around her but he buggered off when he got that job upcountry."

"Doesn't she have any friends at work?"

"Well, she and Marjorie can't stand each other and I had to warn Fergus off. It's not a good idea for co-workers to get too close and, anyway, he can't be trusted."

"But aren't you getting—"

"That's completely different," he snapped. "I'm her boss, I know how to handle the boundaries. What the hell has it got to do with you anyway?"

"Nothing," I said meekly. "Only that she is obviously a good friend of yours and means something to you. If it's important to you, then it's important to me. Should I maybe—"

"No, I know what you're going to say and I don't want this – us – to become tangled up with my work.

"Aren't we tangled up already? After all, you said you've told Marjorie. And I work with you through the Council. I assumed that once we were together I'd be working full-time with you anyway."

"That's a discussion for another day. In the meantime, just stay away from Ellie. Okay?"

I could say the same to you. "Okay darling." *And you can bet your sweet, sexy arse that that is most definitely a discussion for another day. No matter how dark and smouldering your eyes become when I mention it.* I distracted him, as always, with sex. And when we'd finished there was only time to hurriedly get dressed and head back to our offices.

I knew I would get my way, I always did. And I wanted to live and work with Seth, whatever he said. I knew he loved me and he would come to realise that we would make a great working team as well.

I spent my spare time scouring the local property papers, fantasising about the house that we would live in and the lifestyle we would have. I knew how much he was paid, because they had to send their accounts to the Council, and with half the value of the house he shared with Roz as a deposit I knew we could afford the sort of house I'd always dreamt of.

*

"How much is your house worth, then?" He asked one day when I had phoned him at the office. It was the end of a long and dreary day and I had again been painting a picture of how wonderful our life would be together, with the boys.

"No idea."

"Haven't you had it valued?"

"Oh, we don't own it, it's rented."

"What? I thought you owned it? You always gave me the impression that you owned it."

"No, I wish. We're supposedly saving for a deposit. That's why Adrian is so mean with money."

He muttered something. It was barely audible but it sounded like, "Complete fucking waste of time."

I couldn't think what he was talking about but then I realised – someone must have come into the office. "Is there someone there? But it's good that we rent. It means it will be so easy to leave when we are finally together, doesn't it?"

"Hmm," he replied absently. "Imogen, I'll have to call you back. Something's just come up."

"Okay darling, love you," I said, but he had already gone. It must have been an emergency.

Looking back, that must have been when whatever happened, happened. It was that sudden. I didn't hear back from him that night and it was about then that he started being so busy at work and not able to meet up with me. I tried calling him at the office, but he never seemed to be in or else he was in a meeting.

Even Marjorie seemed to be under pressure. Seth had told me some time ago that she knew about us and that she approved, but she got quite snappy with me a couple of times when I tried to track him down. "Imogen, if he wants to speak to you I'm sure he'll be in touch," she said one time. "It's probably best if you don't call here again. I think you should just leave Seth alone."

"But how—"

"Goodbye Imogen." There was a click and then I heard the dial tone.

Which left me with no way to contact Seth, and no way to find out what was going on. I would have to think of something else.

*

A couple of days after being warned off by Marjorie, I was parked near Seth's house but far enough away not to be spotted. I could see his car parked in the drive and I hunched down in my seat until my eye line was just level with the bottom of the window. I rang his number but, as usual, it went straight to voicemail. "Hi, it's me," I said breezily. "I've got that game that Ben promised to lend Toby. As I'm passing by your house I thought maybe I could drop it in. Give me a buzz back." The boys had talked about the game some weeks ago but it was the best excuse I could come up with.

Some people would call this stalking, Imogen. You would call it stalking if somebody was doing it to you. Just because Seth hasn't been returning your calls, it doesn't give you the right to go spying on him. Are you crazy? Now, you've seen that he's not at Eleanor's. Give up and go this moment.

Just then, Seth came out of the house and got into his car. I ducked down even lower, praying that he wouldn't spot me. He didn't. I waited for ten minutes or so and then got out and walked across the road. When Roz answered the door she looked more of a mess than usual and had obviously been crying.

"Oh hi, Imogen," she said in a flat voice. "Seth's not here at the moment. Did he know you were coming? I don't know when he'll be back."

"No worries, I just have something for Toby from Ben." I put on a concerned expression. "Are you okay, Roz? You look awful."

"Thanks." She smiled weakly. "Way to make a girl feel good. Seriously, I'm fine. But I was about to have a glass of wine. Would you like one? Toby's also out at the moment, at a friend's, but he'll be back soon." She opened the door wider and gestured me through to the huge kitchen diner at the back of the house. A bottle of wine was already open on the kitchen table, half empty and with a glass beside it. She got another glass from the cupboard and split what was left in the bottle between the two, handing one to me. "Cheers. What is it that you've got for Toby?"

"It's just a game for the Nintendo thingy. But you don't look fine. Is it anything I can help with? I'm a pretty good listener." Actually, the last thing I wanted to do was listen to Roz drone on about her dreary life, but it might give me some insight into what was going on with Seth.

"Oh, it's nothing. I've just had a bit of a row with Seth, that's all."

This could be useful. "Do you want to talk about it?"

"Not really. How are you?"

By the time Toby came home an hour later, she had opened another bottle and drunk half of it – I was still on my first glass – and all I had managed to glean from her was that there was trouble at work and Seth was concerned about the future of the Project, particularly his own job. If she knew what the trouble was she was tight-lipped about it. I was expecting her to become more aggressive as she drank and I was surprised that in fact she was amiable and very funny, nothing like the harridan Seth had made her out to be. When Toby's friend's mother dropped him off she chatted to her briefly at the door and I doubt the woman had any clue that Roz had just polished off the best part of two bottles of wine.

With Toby home, I wasn't going to be able to get any more out of Roz and I was reminded that I ought to get back for my own son's bedtime routine. I said my goodbyes and headed out to the car, having extracted a reluctant promise from Roz to call me if she needed anything. I was determined to find out what was going on with Seth and if I had to become Roz's new best friend to do so then that's what I would do. It was a new concept for me to have a girlfriend. I didn't tend to get on with other women; I found them to be competitive and bitchy - usually stemming from jealousy – but I was prepared to make an exception if it meant staying involved in Seth's life.

As I drove home I reflected on my time with Roz. She had borne no resemblance to the image Seth had created but, I reasoned, like many drunks she was probably well-practised at putting on an act. No doubt she had started the row they'd had earlier and he had gone out to prevent it escalating. My heart ached for him as I imagined him driving around, or parked up somewhere, waiting out the hours until he judged that she would have gone to bed and passed out.

I figured that making friends with Roz would be just like pursuing a new man. I had to make her think that I cared, that I was looking out for her. That meant making all those little gestures that make a person feel that they're important to you. So the next morning, after I had dropped Ben, I rang Roz's house. I timed it so that she would be on the way back from her school run so I wouldn't actually have to talk to her. I also knew that Seth would be at work. As the answerphone clicked in I forced a smile. "Oh, hi Roz, it's Immy." I hated it when people shortened my name, but I wanted to appear approachable and friendly. "I just thought I'd give you a ring as I was quite worried about you last night. I meant it when I said that if you ever want to talk… Also, I have a brain like a sieve and completely forgot to leave that game with you. Perhaps we could get together for a coffee and I could give it to you then? Give me a ring and let me know." I gave her my mobile number and finished the call with, "Take care of yourself, won't you?" in my most caring and sympathetic voice.

She called back within the hour. God, talk about desperate! Did the woman have no pride? She was pathetically pleased to be asked to meet up and we arranged to do so the next day. I sat at my desk after the call finished and stared out of the window, considering my next move. I decided to give up on my attempts to speak to Seth until after I had got the full story from Roz. I pictured myself placing a soothing hand on his forearm while murmuring, "It's okay, I know what's going on and I can help," or other such supportive sentences. I smiled as I concocted a scenario in my head of Seth gratefully unburdening himself, while we lay in the afterglow of sweet reconciliation lovemaking.

I'd put a 'Grant Enquiry' my diary to cover meeting Roz and met her, as planned, in the Arts Centre Café. "You don't have to tell me what's going on," I said as we settled down into two of the armchairs. "But I might be able to help and you know what they say about a problem shared."

"Oh, it's the usual thing – money." Roz sighed and took a sip of her black Americano. "Seth has got into a bit of a muddle, financially, and he wanted to use our house to bail himself out. I said no." She shrugged like it was no big deal. Like she hadn't flat-out refused to help him. I made my face remain impassive, but inside I was burning. I could understand how Seth was feeling, as I was feeling it too. No wonder he was avoiding me – she hadn't just shot him down in flames, but our dream also.

"But surely you want to support him?" I struggled to keep my voice calm.

"Do I?" she said with a bitter laugh. "Why?" Then, noticing my face, "Oh, don't get me wrong, Immy, I do support him. But my half of that house is the only security Toby and I have. I'm not giving that away, not after everything else." She gave a little shiver. "But you don't want to hear about all of my woes. For God's sake, I don't even want to hear about them." She smiled. "How's Ben? We don't seem to have seen so much of him lately."

That's because your husband has been avoiding me. And now I know why. "Oh, you know," I said quickly. "Life gets in the way. He's fine. But what's the trouble with Seth's finances? Is it anything to do with work? Could I help, or the Council?"

"I honestly don't know, Immy, I don't really know enough about it. I could ask him, I suppose." She sounded reluctant and I wasn't sure that I thought it was a good idea. Anyway, if I did manage to help I wanted him to know the credit was all mine.

"No worries, he knows where we are if he wants to ask for help. Now, what about getting our boys together? Shall I bring Ben round after school tomorrow?" We made the arrangements and then I left, pleading that I had to get back to work. I'd booked out two hours and we'd only been here about twenty-five minutes but I needed to get back to my desk and start investigating what was going on with Seth's finances. I wanted to see if it was anything to do with work and whether there was anything I can

185

do to help. I even tried Seth's mobile a couple of times but he didn't answer and I didn't leave a message. I was just going to have to work on Roz.

*

I spent quite a lot of time hanging out with Roz over the next few months. I got a perverse pleasure in leaving little hints and clues for Seth, to let him know that I had been at the house. I would write notes on the whiteboard that Roz used for shopping lists and reminders, or I would 'accidentally' leave some personal item that he would know was mine. One time, I left a ring on the bathroom sink. It was one of a pair that I had bought for us when we had first talked about moving in together, as a sign of our commitment to each other. I wanted to keep reminding him that I was still around.

Increasingly, Eleanor would be at the house when I arrived or she would drop in unannounced while I was there. It grated on me that Roz couldn't see that she must have an ulterior motive and it crossed my mind that she might be befriending Roz for the same reasons I was. It was also galling that the two of them always seemed to be sharing some hilarious joke whenever I came in, but were unable to share it when I questioned them. Roz always seemed much more relaxed when Eleanor was around and didn't reach straight for the wine bottle whenever she arrived, as she did with me. More often than not they would be sitting drinking tea, or would be out in the garden weeding or pruning. I knew nothing about gardening and would sit and watch, feeling useless. I began to feel that Roz liked Eleanor more than me and I couldn't figure out why. It just made me resent Eleanor all the more.

Ben wasn't getting on any better with Toby and would sit inside playing on one of his computer games while Toby would be in the garden with his mum and one or another of his school friends, who seemed to be around all the time.

The tramps, Trev and Dolly, seemed to be there a lot as well, and any number of random hangers on. Seth would have had a blue fit if he'd known but Roz seemed to have a sixth sense as to when Seth was on his way home and everyone would melt away, including me. I didn't mind leaving my reminders, but I couldn't trust myself if I came face-to-face with him in his house with Roz there.

And Roz would never talk about Seth, no matter how gently I tried to steer the subject his way. "Oh, Immy," she would sigh when I mentioned him. "Daytimes are for me and Toby and I don't want to spoil them by talking about Seth. We have far more interesting things going on, don't we?" I would have to bite back a response in Seth's defence.

"Give it up, Imogen," Eleanor said to me one day. "Give her a break. Things are bad enough between her and Seth without you dragging his name into every conversation. Anyone would think that you had some sort of crush on him." She laughed as if this was a ridiculous notion.

"What do you mean, things are bad enough?" I demanded. "Do you mean with her drinking? I know he finds it hard when she gets drunk and starts picking fights—"

"What? You don't know what you're talking about! I thought you were supposed to be her friend? You don't have a clue, do you?"

"A clue about what? I only know what he's told me. She never talks about him. And I try to be a friend to both of them, as I thought you did." I tried to make this last remark as cutting as I could, but then realised it was lost on Eleanor.

Her tone though, when she replied, more than matched mine. "Oh for God's sake, Imogen, use your eyes. For a supposedly intelligent woman, you can be pretty stupid." She turned her back on me and walked away.

I left shortly after that and fumed all the way home. How dare she speak to me like that? And as for implying that it was Seth who was the problem and not Roz, with her violent, drunken rampages and her inappropriate friends, I couldn't believe that Eleanor could be so blind. I considered phoning Seth and telling him that one of his employees had been so incredibly disloyal, especially when she pretended to be a friend, but realised I would need some proof.

I spent that evening, and the next couple of days, plotting how to get the proof. I avoided going to the house while I thought things through. I considered phoning Eleanor and recording the conversation, but of course you can't phone a deaf person and I doubt it would work by text. She would probably get suspicious. I could arrange to meet her, but we'd never really been friends and, again, she would probably smell a rat. I would have to think very carefully about this.

I spent a few days trying to get hold of Roz but got only voicemail on her landline and her mobile. Usually, if she didn't pick up a call, she would phone back within a couple of hours, but I heard nothing. Eventually, while he was at school, I 'borrowed' Ben's phone and texted Toby.

Dude hows it goin

          who is this

Ben

          hi

do you wanna hang out

          can't. am away with my mum

no school? Cool
when u bak

          dunno. Think my mum & dad have split up.

**we might not come back. Ellie drove us
up here but she's gone home now**

what happened?
where r u?

gotta go

Ok c u

I didn't think I could push it any further. I knew that Ben would never ask for details, boys don't, and he and Toby had never really been friends anyway.

But my mind was reeling. What did this mean? Had Seth told Roz about us? Was he ready for us to be together now? But why hadn't he warned me? Should I now tell Adrian? I tried to call Seth but a recorded message told me that his phone was switched off.

I drove over to the house but it seemed to be locked up tight and there was no sign of anyone. I scribbled a note asking Roz to contact me as soon as possible and went home to brood over this sudden turn of events. I was snappy and irritable with Adrian and Ben while I tried to figure out what the hell was going on. I couldn't get hold of anyone and it was driving me crazy.

Eventually, after a week, Roz called me. "Sorry I haven't answered your messages. What did you want?"

"Where have you been?" I asked in my most caring voice. "I was worried about you."

"That's really sweet of you, but I'm fine now and I'll be back on Sunday."

She can't know anything about us if she thinks I'm being sweet. "Fine now? Which means you weren't fine before. What happened? Ben tells me that Toby thinks you and Seth have split up…" I let my voice trail away in the hope that she would fill in the gap.

"Oh Immy, I really don't want to talk about it right now. But yes we have."

"I'm coming over," I said firmly. "You shouldn't be alone."

"No!" It was almost a shout. "I'm not at home, Ellie drove me and Tobes to a friend's and we've been staying there." I heard her take a deep breath and then she continued in a calm tone. "Ellie is picking us up on Sunday."

Eleanor. Of course. "I see." I tried not to sound resentful

"She's been absolutely brilliant, I don't know what we would have done without her."

188

"I would have helped if you'd phoned me. I had no idea there was anything wrong."
Why do I care that you phoned her, not me? Except that I've been trying so hard to be your best friend and you just seem to prefer her over me.

"I know. Look, Immy, it's been a trying time and I'm exhausted. I'll try and ring you on Monday, okay? Thanks for calling, it's nice to know who my friends are."

I mumbled something reassuring and we hung up. My mind was in overdrive, trying to figure out what this meant for me and Seth. Had she kicked him out? Could she even do that if he owned half the house? I had come to love that house while I had been cultivating Roz, and had started to harbour hopes that he and I could live there with Toby and Ben once the dust had settled. Should I call him and warn him? No, I would be more useful to him at the moment if Roz trusted me, then I could pass info to him. This was obviously why he hadn't been contacting me recently, so she wouldn't have a chance to get suspicious.

*

I still couldn't get hold of Seth and a message on the office phone said that they had closed for two weeks. Clearly something was going on. I had considered trying to see Eleanor, but the thought of crawling to her for information left a bitter taste in my mouth.

I didn't hear from Roz on Monday, so on Tuesday I called round the house without phoning ahead. She answered the door and glanced behind her when she saw it was me. "Immy, I wasn't expecting you," she said in a loud voice. "Can you hold on a moment?" She continued, dropping the volume. "I've just got something... Er, I just need to... Oh shit, hang on..." She shut the door in my face.

Shocked, I stood on the doorstep with my mouth open. *What the...?* I raised my hand to bang loudly on the front door when it opened again.

"Sorry Immy, I just needed to check... It's okay, you can come in." She gave a weak smile and stood back to let me go past. Eleanor was in the kitchen and she looked dreadful. Her hair was lank and bundled up into an untidy bun, her face looked drawn and she had purple smudges under her eyes. She was wearing leggings, flat boots and a huge jumper with holes in it, which was also fraying at the wrists. Her hands were around a large cup of coffee which she was cradling against her chest.

"Eleanor, my God," I blurted without thinking. "What happened to you?" But she wasn't looking at me, she was staring down into her coffee.

Roz went over to her and laid a hand on her arm. She gave herself a little shake and looked up at me, her eyes bloodshot. "Oh, hello Imogen." Her voice was flat. "How are you?"

"I'm fine. But you're not, clearly. What's the matter?"

"Nothing I can't handle," she said, jutting out her chin. "What are you doing here?"

"I came to see that Roz is okay," I replied, glancing over at Roz as I did so. "And with the office being closed for a couple of weeks…"

They looked at each other and Roz rolled her eyes. "Only for a couple of weeks?" Eleanor said. "Is that all?"

Roz had been making me a cup of coffee and now she put it down in front of me. "If you really want to know what's going on, you'd better make sure you're sitting comfortably because it's a very long story."

Actually, it only took them about twenty minutes. Twenty minutes to send my world crashing down in pieces about me. Of course, they didn't know that's what they were doing when they told me about Seth's alleged attack on Eleanor and about the supposed years of abuse that Seth had subjected Roz to, not that either of those stories would have particularly bothered me – seeing as I didn't believe a word of them.

I started to feel quietly triumphant when Roz told me she had finally kicked Seth out, but that quickly changed to confusion when she laughed and said, "Turns out I could have done it ages ago. I should have known that Seth would always have a backup plan."

Oh shit, she knows. I opened my mouth to speak but she went on.

"Yes," she said in a falsely bright voice. "The head teacher of one of the schools they work with. An apparently wealthy divorcee named Audrey, who has a large house which she is more than happy to share with Seth, it seems. That's where he's been all those times I thought he was at meetings or with Marjorie. He moved out at the weekend."

"No!" I screamed before I realised what I was doing. I put my hands on my head and shook it furiously. "That's not right! He was with me! We're going to be together!" Too late, I managed to get a grip on myself. When I looked up, Roz and Eleanor were both staring at me.

∗

"That must have been awkward." I thought I could trace a hint of a smirk on the face of the Detective Sergeant. I decided to ignore it.

"The worst of it was that Roz wasn't angry. She didn't scream or shout at me, or throw me out of the house. She pitied me. I could have coped with almost anything, but not her pity."

"Pity?" The Detective Inspector asked quietly.

"Yes, as if I wasn't the first. Which, according to her, I wasn't."

"You didn't believe her?"

"I'm not naïve, I knew he'd had other women before me. But I also knew that he loved me, and I was the first one who he had truly loved and was prepared to leave Roz for. But she even tried to take that away from me…"

"How do you mean?"

*

"Oh Immy, I'm so sorry." I could see tears glistening in Roz's eyes. "He never said a word—"

"Why would he have said anything to you? He was going to leave you! We were going to live together! We were going to be a proper family, him and me and Ben and Toby!" I was shouting but I couldn't stop myself.

"That's not what he told me. At first, he told me he was going to leave me and live with Ellie—"

"Eleanor!" I wailed. "But she doesn't even like men!" I glared at Eleanor, whose eyes were wide, trying to follow the conversation.

"I know that," said Roz. "But Seth didn't. And when he told me his plans, I laughed in his face and told him the truth. I told him that it was all in his sad little head. And I wish I hadn't." She reached out and took Eleanor's hand. "Because that's when he… When he…" She broke off with a sob.

Eleanor placed her other hand on top of Roz's. "It's not your fault. The only person to blame is Seth. He made his choice, although what was going through his head God only knows. I certainly never gave him any indication that he would be welcome to live in my house, in any capacity."

"Are you sure this isn't just sour grapes on your part?" I was so angry. "That you didn't try to seduce him and when he turned you down you made up this ridiculous rape allegation—"

"That's enough, Imogen!" I'd never heard Roz be so forceful. "I'm sorry you've had a shock, I understand it's a lot to take in, but I won't have you speaking to Ellie like that." She glanced up at the kitchen clock. "I have to go and get Toby shortly, so I think it's time for you to leave. If you want to come back and talk to me another time, you're welcome, as long as you ring first to make sure it's okay." She took my arm and steered me to the front door, closing it firmly behind me.

*

"And did you go back?" asked the Sergeant.

"Yes, of course I did. It was the only way to find out what was going on in Seth's life. I had to go crawling back to Roz and Eleanor and pretend that I was sorry, that I overreacted and I had now seen the error of my ways. And I had to pretend to be their friend, which was really hard work."

"What about Seth? Did he contact you at all?"

"No, and I couldn't contact him at work because Marjorie must have issued instructions to blank me. I think she must have pulled some strings at the Council, as well, because I was moved to a different department which had no connection with them. She must have forced Seth to change his number, and I even had a solicitor's letter warning me not to attempt to make contact."

"Really?" The two officers exchanged glances. "Marjorie did that?"

"Well, Seth wouldn't have done it and Marjorie knew that I would have made him stand up to her, so she wanted to shut me out and keep him all to herself."

"But he was living with someone else? Someone who, before his death, he was planning to marry," the Detective Inspector said in a voice that was exaggeratedly calm and reasonable.

Patronising bitch. "Yes, but he didn't love her like he loved me. How could he? Probably, like me, he was biding his time until all the barriers and the people who would keep us apart, were out of the picture."

"People like…?"

"Marjorie, Adrian, Ben and Toby…"

"Ben and Toby?" The Detective Sergeant looked up from some notes she had been scribbling.

"Well, yes! If we waited until the boys were eighteen we wouldn't have to worry about getting custody and all that. We could just be a family together."

"And how old were the boys at this point?"

"Ben was ten, nearly 11, which was perfect as it meant I had a seven-year plan. I could stay with Adrian, build up my career, buy the house he was always on about and then I would have something to offer Seth when we finally got together."

"But you would have no contact with Seth in all this time?"

"No! Don't you see? We had to keep it all a secret so that no-one would know. But someone must have found out and that's why they killed him. There's no way that he would have committed suicide when we were so close to achieving the life we wanted. And that's why I had to get this investigation opened up—"

"It was you who got the investigation opened?" The inspector asked. "How?"

"For goodness sake! It doesn't matter how I got the investigation opened. Let's just say that Marjorie isn't the only one with contacts and I can be very persuasive when I put my mind to it. Everyone has skeletons, Inspector Nixon, even if they are ones that I helped to put in the closet in the first place. Men, even respectable, high-ranking policemen, can be so susceptible to a bit of female attention, don't you find? The real question is, are you any closer to finding out who did this?"

The Detective Inspector gathered up her notes from in front of her and stood up. "I think we'll leave it here for today. Detective Sergeant Wood will show you out." She held open the door, clearly waiting for me to leave.

I don't think so. "You have to tell me," I said, also standing. "I have to know who did this."

"We will be in contact if we need to speak to you again. DS Wood, my office, after you have shown Mrs Barnes-Colon out." She turned on her heel and strode away.

"Wait!" I hurried to the door and shouted after her. "I have to know! You have to tell me!" She disappeared through some double doors at the end of the corridor. I turned to the Detective Sergeant. "Seven years," I sobbed. "I waited seven years for him and now he's dead. What am I supposed to do?"

"Go home, Imogen. Go home to your husband." She didn't speak again as she showed me out, but handed me a tissue before closing the doors of the Police Station behind me.

* * *

Beatrice

Alex was grim faced when she returned to my office and threw herself onto my sofa. "She's gone and I can't decide whether to feel pity for her, or contempt."

"I think the one who deserves your pity is her husband. And I would like to know just how she had the pull to get us to investigate this."

"I don't think we should look under that particular rock," Alex said with a laugh that had no humour in it. "Who knows what's lurking down there?"

"We're still no clearer as to whether there is anything to investigate." I sighed and raked my fingers through my hair. "And for the first time in my career I'm not entirely sure whether I care. If you didn't do it himself, then whoever did deserves a bloody medal, as far as I'm concerned."

"To be honest, I've been wondering not so much who did it but why did they wait so long? And how did such a loathsome creep have so many women falling at his feet?"

"Because they didn't know just how loathsome he was until he had sucked them in and it was too late." I walked across and closed the door to my office. "So, are we agreed that we're going through the motions on this one? It has to be your decision, as I'll be skipping off into the sunset with my pension in a couple of weeks."

"No need to rub it in." Alex smiled ruefully. "Let's just see what the others have to say, but I think this one is ripe for the NFA file for sure. Although you never know, tomorrow is another day."

"Home time then, Scarlett O'Hara, and let's see what Marjorie brings us tomorrow."

*

After everything that had been said about Marjorie, I think I was expecting something of a mix between Margaret Thatcher and Joan Collins. The woman Alex showed into the interview room the next morning couldn't have been further from my expectations. Although expensively dressed – Jaeger, I think – her clothes hung loosely on her slight frame. There was the extraordinary hairdo that Eleanor had mentioned, but I couldn't be entirely sure that it wasn't a wig. Her face was expertly made up, if paler than I would have chosen, and her hands were old lady's hands, albeit beautifully manicured.

I knew her to be in her seventies, which wasn't terribly old these days, but she walked like an elderly lady as well – slowly, as if measuring every step. When she sat, however, her back was ramrod straight, her legs elegantly crossed at the ankles and her hands clasped gently on her lap. All the same, I found it hard to equate the woman sitting across the desk from me with the woman Roz, Eleanor and Imogen had found so imposing.

"Thank you for coming in, Mrs Evans," I said. "I am Detective Inspector Beatrice Nixon, and you have already met Detective Sergeant Alex Wood. May I call you Marjorie?"

* * *

MARJORIE

"I suppose if you must," I replied to Detective Inspector Nixon. "It seems to be the way nowadays that everyone addresses each other by their Christian names." She was quite attractive, although she could have made much more of herself. A regular haircut and colour treatment would have helped, instead of scraping it back into one of those grips they all seem to use these days. And more supportive underwear would have made all the difference. I really don't know why women don't realise that beyond a certain age proper corsetry is as essential as regular facials and a sensible diet and exercise.

"This really is a monstrous waste of your time," I went on. "I would have thought that once the funeral was over, we could all have put this behind us."

"That's as maybe, but questions have been asked and I am obliged to investigate them." Her voice was clear and authoritative, I noted. "Why don't you start by giving me some history, by way of putting all of this into perspective? How and when did you meet Seth Peterson?"

"It was fourteen years ago. We met at a fundraiser for a charity I was thinking of getting involved with. I was recently widowed and looking for something to fill my time. My late husband had also left me a considerable amount of money and, as I had no-one to pass it on to, I was looking for worthy causes that I could support."

"And was Mr Peterson involved in this charity?"

"No. Like me, he was looking for a project. He told me that he was thinking of leaving the music business as he found it too shallow, and had grown tired of the cynicism and dubious practices."

"And did either of you get involved with that particular charity?"

"We didn't, but we met up for lunch the next day to talk it through. I liked him. He was nearly twenty years younger than me but he had a good head on his shoulders and some interesting ideas. I very rarely act on impulse, but I decided at that lunch that I would like to work with him."

"Just work with him?" The Detective Sergeant interjected.

"Yes, Detective Sergeant… Wood, was it? Just work with him."

"Do you think Mr Peterson had other ideas?"

"No, I don't believe he did. And I find this line of questioning quite distasteful, to be frank. Some people have motives other than what's going on below the waist."

"My apologies." Now she did, at least, have the grace to look contrite. "Please go on."

"As I was saying, I decided at that lunch that Seth Peterson was someone I wanted to work with, so we started looking for a project with which we could both become involved."

"You say you rarely act on impulse, and yet this was only your second meeting." Inspector Nixon raised her eyebrows. "What was it about Seth that made you act out of character?"

"Good question." I paused while I considered my answer. "He was engaging, he came across as shrewd and professional – a man of integrity."

"All the same, that's quite an important decision to make on the strength of two meetings, particularly for someone who doesn't act on impulse. Don't you think?"

"Many people have less than that when interviewing for a job. Take this situation, for example: you are making a judgement on me based on this interview alone."

She nodded as if recognising my point. "But I'm not considering placing a large amount of money into your control."

"Neither was I. I had only made the decision that I would like to spend more time with Seth. He… reminded me of someone. Someone I used to know."

"You must have known them very well to base your judgement on that similarity."

"I did. And it was a striking similarity…"

*

The function room was crowded with Suniton's great and good. I sighed, collected my complimentary glass of mediocre warm white wine and looked around for Arthur. It was at his invitation, probably in the hope of a sizeable donation, that I'd come here this evening so I felt the least he could do was keep me company for the evening.

I couldn't see Arthur anywhere in the crowd, but it was then I saw a ghost. Standing at the bar, quietly observing the people around him with that same half smile – Drew! Of course, it couldn't be. Even though it was forty years since I'd last seen Drew, I could still remember that smile and the wayward auburn curls. But this man was the image of him, or at least how I would have imagined him as a mature man, and not the youngster to whom I had given my heart.

Arthur appeared at my side with another glass of warm wine. "Marjorie, you came, I'm so pleased. They'll be announcing the meal soon, I hope you're hungry."

"I'm on your table, is that right? Who else is with us?"

"Oh, the usual suspects. Plus a couple of waifs and strays who weren't seated anywhere else. Shall we go and find our places?"

"Okay, but before we do can you tell me who that man is over at the bar? The one standing on his own?"

"Yes, he's one of our waifs. Pearce, Parsonson, something like that. Do you recognise him from somewhere, then?"

Drew's surname had been Haskell. "No, no, he just reminded me of someone I used to know."

"Well, you should get a chance to chat to him over dinner. He's been put on our table."

Not only was he on our table, but he had been seated next to me. He introduced himself by telling me that he was the manager of the band who were supplying the music for the evening. We hit it off instantly and were firm friends by the time the auction started, over coffee.

After an hour, during which I paid over the odds for an item I didn't want and would no doubt be donating to the next cause that asked me and he bid on nothing, he leaned over and said, "I really do have to make a move now, I have to get my singer home. Do you have a card? I'd quite like to continue our conversation another time."

Is he coming on to me? I'm surely old enough to be his mother. I gasped as I realised the implications of that thought, then scribbled my number on one of the paper napkins left on the table. "I'd like that too. Perhaps you'd better give me your card as well."

After Arthur dropped me home I sat on my balcony for a long time, staring out over the sea. I hadn't thought about baby Drew for many years; I couldn't allow myself to do so. I hadn't even told my husband about the child I had been forced to give away. Unable to father children himself, it would have felt cruel. I had already discovered that my parents had made damned sure I would never be able to track the baby down.

Nevertheless, every year on his birthday I had sent up a silent prayer that he was healthy and happy and that his new parents had treated him well. Other than that one annual indulgence, I never allowed myself to think about him. Now, though, my thoughts were racing. He would be forty soon, was he married? Did he have children? The thought of grandchildren that I would never know caused a physical pain. More than that, the old anger against my parents began churning again inside me.

You're getting ahead of yourself, Marjorie. You were never able to find him before. The chances of doing so now are remote, as remote as you bumping into your long-lost son at some random function. You're being ridiculous.

By the time I finally went to bed I was completely exhausted but I had managed to put all my demons back in their box. Of course I would never find my son again. And of course Seth Peterson was not that son. But we had got on well and I had found him interesting, so there was no harm in meeting with him again.

*

I was, however, quite surprised when he phoned me the next morning and suggested lunch. As it was Sunday and I had nothing planned, I agreed. We met at a pub nestled at the foot of the Downs and picked up our conversation where we had left it the night before. While we waited for our food, he told me about his plans to give up the music business 'in search of something more worthwhile.'

"And what do you think that something will be?"

"I'm not sure, something to do with children probably. I have a son of my own and a daughter who lives with her mother. It breaks my heart that not all kids have the same advantages as mine: health, security, love…" He trailed off. I know how it feels to…" He took a sip of his drink. "And how about you, Marjorie? What's your story?"

"I'm also looking for something worthwhile and something to do with children would definitely suit me. I've been looking locally but can't find anything that seems quite the right fit." I told him about being widowed and having time on my hands. "I just don't want to turn into one of those women who fill their lives with the appearance of being busy when really it's all just frippery and nonsense."

"What about children and grandchildren? I bet you're a brilliant granny."

"Sadly, my husband and I didn't have children so that's not an option." I smiled to show that this was something I had come to terms with. "I'll never know what kind of granny I would be."

"Well, if you ever feel the need to borrow a grandchild, my son Toby has no grandparents and I'm sure he would be up for a bit of spoiling," Seth said lightly, as he leaned back to let the waitress put a plate of food in front of him. "It could be a match made in heaven."

I couldn't tell if this remark was really as flippant as it appeared, so I answered in a similar light-hearted manner. "I've always wanted an excuse to go to a pantomime and boo and hiss and shout 'He's behind you!', so I may take you up on that."

"Toby would be well up for that, the more noise he can make the better."

For a while we concentrated on our food, which was quite good considering it was a pub, and then Seth spoke. "You know, Marjorie, I'm thinking that we're both in the same position: we want to work in the voluntary sector, we want to work with children and neither of us can find the right fit for our talents. Maybe we should think about doing something together. I know we've only just met but I have a good feeling about you and I think we could work well together."

"It's an interesting thought, what do you have in mind?"

"Nothing at the moment, as it's only just occurred to me. But I would prefer to set something up than to go into someone else's project, and I think you probably feel the same."

"To be perfectly honest, I hadn't thought about it. I'm not even sure I'd know how to go about it, let alone what sort of area I would want to concentrate on." The girl came to clear our plates and I asked her for the bill.

"Setting it up wouldn't be a problem. I can handle that and, with the elections coming up next year, there's plenty of money available for grants if you know how to go about it. It's just a case of finding a gap in the… An area which is lacking in support."

"You've certainly given me a lot to think about." The bill arrived and I put my credit card down straightaway, waving away Seth's protestations. "Let's meet again in a couple of days. I'll call you."

"Sure. As I said, it's something I'd only just thought of and I need to think it through as well. It would be a big undertaking and I would have to think about the financial implications for my family as well."

We left it that I would call him in a few days. He offered me a lift but I had my own car. Back at home I thought of little else for the next couple of days. I invited Arthur round and quizzed him on what he knew about Seth and his background.

"Not much I'm afraid, Marjorie old thing. I'll ask around but I think he had something to do with show business or pop music, something like that. Not my area of expertise, I'm afraid." He guffawed, which rapidly turned into a cough. "Isn't he a bit young for you though, my dear?"

I gave him a withering look. "Get your mind out of the gutter please, Arthur. We are talking about working together and I wanted to reassure myself about his background."

Arthur looked suitably abashed. "Very well, I'll see what I can find out for you."

*

I let Seth take the lead on how often we met and where. I've been told I have a tendency to micromanage situations and people, and I didn't want to scare him off. But he seemed happy to meet two or three times a week for lunch. He was easy to talk to and one day I was surprised to find myself telling him my story. Obviously, not that I had felt – hoped? – that he was my long-lost son, but about Drew and the baby and how it had affected the rest of my life. I told him about the years of searching, but then finding a form of love with my husband. Not the deep passion I had felt for my baby's father, but a companionship and security that made us both happy.

"Some people would call that settling," Seth said gently when I'd finished.

"They might, but what is so wrong with being settled? We liked each other, we had a comfortable life and no dramas. I didn't miss having children as we filled our lives in so many other ways."

"And have you looked for Drew or the child since you've been on your own again?"

"No, it's been forty years and I don't think I have the right to drop such a bombshell into either of their lives."

He leaned forward and patted my hand. "I think that's very selfless of you, quite noble."

"Hardly noble. I've got used to living a life without dramas, so why would I want to start now?"

"I'm sure you're right." Seth tactfully changed the subject and we didn't speak about it again.

*

I paused to take a sip of water. "I had never told anyone that story, including my husband. It was one of Seth's talents, to get people to open up about themselves."

"You must have trusted him," Sergeant Wood said. "It's clearly quite a personal story."

"I did, I hadn't told anyone in forty years." I gave them a brief explanation of what had happened to me when I was young. It might have been my imagination but they didn't seem surprised. I suppose police officers are trained to show no reaction to anything they are told.

"So you weren't working together at this time?" Inspector Nixon asked. "You were just meeting up to talk about the possibility? Did you have any plans at all at this stage?"

"We didn't, it was all still very much up in the air."

"And had you met his wife or his son at all?"

"No, we always met at restaurants or pubs and always for lunch. I did suggest dinner a couple of times, but he seemed reluctant and I didn't want to push him."

*

"I like to be home for bath and bedtime," he explained one day after he had turned me down again for dinner. "I need to be around in the evening for Toby. His mother…" He cleared his throat and suddenly looked unhappy. "His mother had a hard time with postnatal depression," he went on. "Which, I know, was awful for her. But she developed a habit of self-medicating with alcohol. I'm not saying she's not a good mother, but she tends to start drinking towards evening and I worry that if something happened to our boy she wouldn't be able to deal with it."

I reached out and patted his hand sympathetically. "That's quite a burden for you to carry, especially while you're also trying to provide for them both."

"It's nothing I can't handle. Sorry, I shouldn't dump my worries on you. Let's change the subject."

I could see that he was putting on a brave face, so I leaned towards him and spoke quietly. "Seth, I want you to feel you can always come to me, and if I can help in any way I will."

"I'm sure it's exactly what you want in a business partner: a drunken wife who likes to shout the odds when she's in her cups."

"Is she violent?" I said, alarmed.

"No, no, no. She just likes to rant at me, and blame me for all the troubles of the world." His smile was grim. "I keep out of the way in my study. I have a kettle and my computer in there, so I'm quite happy."

"How dreadful for you. Can't she get help of some sort?"

"I've tried to talk to her about it but, ultimately, she can only be helped if she wants to be helped." He shrugged.

"But what about your son? It can't be good for him to have that going on around him."

"She waits until he's asleep and, if I keep out of the way, she usually drinks herself into a stupor and then goes to bed. It's really not that bad, as long as I can keep an eye on it."

"But what about his grandparents?" I asked, aware that I was fishing. "If he was my grandson, I would be very worried about him."

"Toby doesn't have any grandparents, they're all dead." Seth said, in a tone of voice that let me know the subject was finished. I decided to leave it until another time.

Although it was enjoyable meeting up for these lunches and talking in an abstract way about setting up our own project, we were no closer to having the big idea. I was happy to let things carry on as they were, if truth be told, but Seth was concerned.

"Marjorie, I can't keep taking lunches off you like this," he said one day. "And I really need to start earning some proper money. Toby will be starting school soon and the odds and sods I've got coming in won't be enough to keep the wolf from the door." He gave me a slightly embarrassed smile. "I think I'm going to have to bite the bullet and go and get a proper job."

I felt my insides give a jolt. We'd become so close over the past few months. "That's such a shame." I kept my voice as calm as I could. "I do think we could work well together."

"So do I, but I really need to get a decent salary coming in. In an ideal world..." He closed his eyes and shook his head.

"In an ideal world?" I prompted gently.

"It doesn't matter," he said quickly. "Forget I said anything."

"I thought you and I were friends. I'd like to think you could tell me anything that's worrying you."

"It's not worrying me exactly, it's more a promise that I made to myself and it doesn't look like I'm going to be able to keep it."

"What sort of promise?"

"I told you, it doesn't matter." Seth had never snapped at me before and the shock and hurt must have shown in my face. "I'm sorry, Marjorie. It's just..." He took a deep breath. "It's just that when Toby was born, I made a promise to myself that he would have all the things that I never had, like a stable home and a good education. At the time, the band I was managing was just taking off and it looked like I would be able to do that. But, as I told you before, that all went pear-shaped and now he's nearly school age and he's going to have to go into the state education system." His voice broke and he paused for a moment before continuing.

"And I just wanted better for him. My own time at school was so miserable. I was bullied and I can't bear the thought of my little man going through what I had to go through. It's bad enough, the situation with his mother, but what if he has the same sort of experience as I did?"

"Oh Seth," I said. "I'm sure he won't. I think schools are much more aware of that sort of thing these days."

"Yeah, they say they are. But I don't think the teachers really care. And I've seen the OFSTED reports on our local schools. They're not good. I'm even thinking of selling up and moving over here to Suniton, where the schools do seem to be marginally better. Anyway, it's not your problem and I'm sure I'll sort it out." He signalled for the bill. "It's on me today, by the way. I can't keep letting you pay for everything, and I'm not totally destitute yet." He smiled to show that this little joke marked the end of the conversation.

*

I spent the next couple of days doing some research on my laptop at home, and when I was done I rang him and asked him to a meeting at my apartment.

"I am going to set up a charitable Foundation in my husband's name," I told him. "I'm going to use the money my parents left to me, which I always refused to touch before. It's been sitting in a high interest account, doing nothing, since they died. After what they did to me, I wanted nothing to do with their money but now I think this would be an excellent way to use it. There's enough capital to provide a substantial salary for you, to run it for me, which would cover Toby's fees for a private prep school. But I would be honoured if you would allow me to pay the first year in any case. There is an excellent school within walking distance here, but I do appreciate you would probably prefer to choose the school yourself."

Seth looked stunned, as I had expected he would. He raised a hand and opened his mouth to speak, but I got in first. "Do not think of turning this down, Seth. Quite apart from offending me by refusing, I have already instructed my solicitor to start the process and I do hate wasting his time."

"But I couldn't accept this, Marjorie. How can I run a Foundation when we don't even have a project? And as for the school fees, well, I wish I'd never said anything now. You've never even met Toby."

"True, but I've met you and it's clear that you are a decent and honest man who wants to do the best for his son. Please allow this old lady the indulgence of helping you to do that."

There were tears in his eyes as he took my hand. "I don't know what to say. This is so incredibly kind of you, but—"

"No buts, just say yes. I want to help you and I can afford to do so. And it's not entirely altruistic – I don't want you going off and getting another job before we've even had the time to get a project together. Of course, it does mean that we'll have to think of something quite soon." I smiled. "But I'm sure we can do that if we really put our thinking caps on."

"I'm sure we can, but you'd better tell me about this school."

That afternoon proved to me that my instincts were right and that we could work extremely well together. By the time he left to go home we had booked an appointment to see the school, and had found a couple of properties to look at that seemed promising. He had also phoned a couple of his local estate agents and made arrangements for them to value his apartment.

"Shouldn't you talk to Roz about this first? It's a big decision."

"Oh, she'll go along with anything I decide," he assured me. "She'll see that it's a fantastic opportunity. I can't tell you how grateful I am, Marjorie."

"Well, I suppose I ought to meet her soon and particularly Toby. I am so looking forward to meeting him." We made arrangements to meet for Sunday lunch at the pub where he and I had first had lunch.

*

"I don't like to interrupt—" Sergeant Wood began.

"And yet you're going to."

"I'm finding it hard to understand how you could make such a monumental financial commitment to this family, before you had even met Seth's wife and his son? And when you had only known Seth himself for a matter of weeks?"

"Months. But it's a valid point. And if I were on the outside of this situation looking in, I would be wondering the same thing. It's not something I can easily explain. Looking at it from the distance of time, I can see that it was a decision based on emotions. I was vulnerable after the death of my husband, and Seth had stirred up all the feelings I had repressed since losing my baby so many years before."

"So it's not a decision you would make today?"

"That's hard to say. Seth was very charming, very plausible, and I believed in the work we went on to do. But I did have a fear of being lonely, and it was almost like Fate had dropped a whole little family into my life. It makes no sense to you, Detective Sergeant, you probably have a family as well as a career and friends. I had none of those – my life had been devoted to my husband and his career. I had many acquaintances, but if I had dropped off the face of the planet very few people would have paid it more than just passing attention. I was in my late fifties and my future was looking quite bleak."

"So Seth Peterson took advantage of you?"

"Let's just say that our situations coincided to our mutual benefit."

"You were about to tell us about your first meeting with Mrs Peterson – Roz," Inspector Nixon said. "How did that go?"

"Actually, despite my expectations from what Seth had told me about her, I liked her. She seemed quite quiet, and appeared to be a very good mother although I was aware, of course, that appearances can often be deceptive. And Toby was just an absolute delight…"

*

Seth was very nervous about the meeting between Roz, Toby and myself which I found quite endearing. It was obviously important to him that we all get along well. Roz also seemed quite nervous, but she could have just been shy.

I tried to set her at her ease by telling her how pleased I was to be working with Seth. "I've been looking about for a project to give some meaning to my life and when I met Seth, and heard about his ideas, it seemed like the perfect match. Now that you two are planning to move over near me for Toby's school—"

"Sorry?" Roz didn't seem to have heard me and Seth took her hand and gave it a squeeze.

"We haven't finalised the details yet, have we darling?" He smiled at her.

"Er, no."

Oh dear, perhaps she doesn't want to move? "I think it's a lovely idea, and it would be such fun for us to be living closer together. I would love to see more of Toby."

"We'll see." She picked up her wine glass and Seth held the bottle towards her to pour some more. I had been surprised when he had ordered wine, bearing in mind what he had told me about her problems with alcohol, and I was concerned to see that he seemed to be encouraging her to drink. He glanced at me, and I raised an eyebrow. *Are you sure you should be doing that?*

I turned to Toby, who had behaved perfectly all the way through lunch. It was a long time for a small boy to sit and listen to grown-ups talking, I would have thought he would have been happier running around in the garden. "You'd like that, wouldn't you Toby?" Seth had been nervous about Toby's behaviour, and had been quick to squash any potential trouble, and I felt I hadn't really made a proper connection with him as I would have liked. I was longing to touch him, to give him a cuddle or play with him, but I contented myself with ruffling his hair. "He's so lovely." I smiled at Roz. "And the image of you."

"Perhaps we should let him outside for a while," Roz said. "This is a long time for four-year-old legs to be keeping still. I'll take him out for a run around that garden." She stood, picked up Toby and carried him out before I had a chance to ask if I could join them.

"I'm sorry she's being so moody," Seth said as soon as she was out of earshot. "She's hung over from last night. I tried to tell her about our plans, but as she had already started drinking it degenerated into a rant. I'll talk to her about it again tonight."

"I must say, I was surprised that you seemed to be okay with her drinking wine."

"Believe me, it's best to get her on the hair of the dog. Otherwise, there would be no talking to her."

I sighed, shaking my head. "It seems such a shame. She strikes me as quite a sweet person, and clearly Toby loves her."

"Sweet? Huh." Seth's laugh was cynical. "You wouldn't say that if you'd seen her last night. Shall we go and settle up?"

*

By the time I'd finished paying the bill, Roz and Toby had come in from the garden and we all said our goodbyes, then went our separate ways. But I had already fallen in love with Toby, and I told Seth so when I met him the next day.

He nodded, clearly pleased the meeting had gone so well. "He liked you too. In fact, it was so sweet..." He chuckled nervously. "... he asked if he should call you Granny Marjorie. I told him I would ask you, but I understand if you think it's too much. It's just that, of course, he's never had a granny like all his little friends. I thought we could make you an honorary Granny."

I felt a pang at the thought of the little boy with no grandparents, but also for Seth and for whatever had happened with his parents. I had tried to bring it up a couple of times but it was clear it was not something he was prepared to talk about. "To be an honorary Granny would be an honour," I said lightly. "Please tell Toby I accept. That is, as long as it's okay with Roz?"

"Oh, she's fine with it," he said carelessly. "I also managed to talk to her last night about the other stuff, and she's on board with that too. I thought you and I could pick Toby up from nursery one day this week and take a look at that school near you, if that's okay. I've also got a couple of houses to look at and I thought you might want to look at them with me tomorrow."

"I'd love to, but doesn't Roz want to do that with you?"

"It seems not. She's made friends with a couple of tramps who hang around the beach, drinking, and apparently she would prefer to spend her time with them, rather than looking after her son's future." He made a face and then looked away.

"Oh dear, Seth. I'm so sorry. I really hoped we'd made a connection yesterday, I was looking forward to getting to know both of them better."

"If you want to get to know Roz better then I suggest you stop washing for about a fortnight, pour as much cider down your neck as you possibly can and then go and sleep on the beach, preferably in a pool of your own urine," he said bitterly. "And she thinks these are appropriate people for my son to be spending time with."

"She lets Toby see these people? Surely not!"

"It's another reason for us to move away, I can't have my son thinking that sort of behaviour is acceptable. And God knows what kind of creeps and perverts these people hang out with. I've banned her from taking Toby along now, I need to get them both away from that environment. For their own good." His face was a picture of misery. "Sometimes it feels like I'm the parent to both of them and I have no-one to turn to."

"You do now. You have me."

"I know, and it means so much to me."

*

The school was charming, and felt warm and welcoming. The children were very smart in their uniforms and seemed happy. I would tell Roz all of this when I saw her. Toby also appeared to like it, particularly that it was opposite a swimming pool. I wrote a cheque for the deposit there and then, and we all went to celebrate at Pizza Express.

"I've never been to a Pizza Express before," I whispered to Toby as we sat down. "Do you know, I don't even think I've ever eaten a pizza before. You'll have to help me choose."

He stared at me with huge, round eyes. "Never?" he said in amazement, and then went on solemnly. "You have to go careful, because if you eat too much pizza you won't have room for ice cream afterwards."

"Thank you for telling me," I replied, matching his serious tone. "I'll bear that in mind."

"Stop bothering Granny Marjorie now," Seth said. "You get on with your colouring and let the grown-ups talk."

"But he wasn't…" I broke off as Toby snatched up the crayons that the waitress had provided and became absorbed in colouring in the back of his menu.

Seth was full of the news that he had put in an offer on one of the houses that we had viewed at the beginning of the week, and it had been accepted. It was a sweet little house, not far from the beach and about fifteen minutes' walk from the school, with my apartment in between.

"How lovely, we'll all be so close together. But when did Roz see it? I'm glad she liked it too."

"She hasn't." He glanced at Toby who was paying us no attention at all. "She said she's happy to leave it all up to me."

"Did she?" I couldn't believe how this woman could be so casual with her family's future. "Well, I suppose it will all still be there when she finally gets around to seeing it."

My heart was breaking for Seth and his little boy so I tried to make up for it by ordering a whole pizza for Toby, even though Seth said he would be happy with a couple of slices from ours, and a big bowl of chocolate ice cream.

*

Seth put their own place on the market and within days had an offer for the full asking price.

"Those agents have obviously stitched me up," he complained. "No-one gets the asking price that quickly. They've probably arranged for it to go cheap to one of their mates, and then they'll sell it again for a higher price."

"I don't think so." I tried to pacify him. "It's a good offer from people with no chain, so you can move as quickly as the solicitors can get it through."

"I was going to talk to you about that. Roz used this decrepit old solicitor when we sold the place in London, but I don't think he's up to the job now. With all the help you're giving us it would probably be easier to use your guy, if that's okay with you."

Arthur used to handle all my affairs and, since his retirement, I had continued to use his firm. There was a slight blip when Roz's sister – a brash American woman – arrived, wanting to deal on Roz's behalf. She changed some of the terms of the purchase but it was quickly sorted out.

"It works better for me," Seth told me. "Obviously, her own sister doesn't trust her. Basically, it boils down to Roz not being able to drunkenly sign away my half of the house. So at least Toby and I are safe."

"I think that's very wise."

*

They were in their new place by the middle of August and seemed to be settling in very well. I offered help with decorating but Seth said that Roz preferred to do it on her own. "And it does at least keep her occupied," he said. "Although God knows what it's going to look like when she's finished. She won't even let me help with the gardening and insists she's going to start growing her own veg, like some sort of hippie. I shouldn't think it will last, but it does mean I can bring Toby round for some 'Granny Marjorie time'."

He had started a routine of bringing Toby to see me at weekends, which I loved. Toby had started at a local nursery, just for the summer, to make some local friends. Judging by the number of times Seth had to cancel our days out together so Toby could go on a play date, the plan was working and he was making friends. I was pleased, because he seemed such a shy little boy whenever his father brought him to visit.

I had hoped to go with them on Toby's first day at his new school, but unfortunately Seth had an unavoidable appointment and even he couldn't go. Roz took a couple of pictures of Toby in his smart new uniform and Seth had one framed for me. I put it in pride of place in my apartment and showed it off to everyone who visited.

*

Toby had been at the school for a few months, and Seth and I were on our way back from visiting a children's project in London one afternoon, when my mobile rang as we were on the train on the way home. It was Judith, one of my neighbours.

"I'm so sorry to disturb you, Marjorie," she purred into the phone. "But I thought you ought to know, that little boy Toby – your grandson, is it? I'm sure I just saw him down on the beach, opposite the apartments. I recognised him because that uniform is so distinctive, isn't it?"

"Well, it's a lovely afternoon," I replied, puzzled as to why she felt the need to ring me. "I expect his mother's taken him down to let him run off some energy." Seth's head came up and he stared at me.

"That's what I thought, but then I realised who he was down there with." Her voice had a slight, excited edge to it.

"Who was he with?"

"As far as I could tell, a couple of those awful street drinkers who hang around in the town centre. The man was down at the water's edge with him, throwing pebbles. I was going to go down, I didn't want to approach them on my own so I waited for Michael to come home. By the time we got down there, Toby had gone."

"You must be mistaken, Toby is with his mother."

"There were a couple of women there, sitting by one of the breakwaters, but they seemed to be drinking as well."

"Thank you for letting me know, but I'm with Toby's father now and I can assure you it wasn't him. Give my regards to Michael and I'll talk to you soon. Goodbye Judith." I ended the call.

"Who was that?" Seth's voice was very calm.

"I'm sure it was nothing, just an interfering busybody with the wrong end of the stick." Briefly, I told him what Judith had said.

"Bitch, she's back to her old tricks." He picked up his phone.

"Don't go jumping to conclusions." I put my hand out to stop him dialling. "And don't go rushing in without establishing the facts first. We don't even know if it is Toby."

"Yes we do, it's just what she used to do before."

"That's as maybe, but don't you think it would be better to confront her face-to-face? When you've had a chance to calm down? We're nearly back now, you can be home in half an hour. Why not wait and ask her for the full story?"

He took a deep breath and then let it out slowly. "You're right, if he's not there now it can wait until I'm at home. We'll have to do our debrief tomorrow. If she's been drinking, I won't be able to go out again tonight. I'll pick Toby up from school tomorrow and bring him round to you, if that's okay? Then we can run through our thoughts from today. I thought it was an interesting project, very much along the lines of what I was envisaging for us."

"Of course that's okay, you know I love seeing Toby. But right now you need to calm yourself down and focus. I'm sure there's a simple explanation."

"Oh, I'm sure there is," he said with a bitter laugh. "But I am calm, don't worry. I don't lose my temper very easily."

"No, one of the things I admire about you is your even temper. I imagine you're very calm under pressure."

*

I'm not sure that Saturday School is a good thing for the little ones, even if it is only for a couple of hours. Toby was very tired the next day, and therefore very quiet. Seth had taken him home to change after school, and reported that Roz was still out when they'd got there. When I asked him how things had been the previous evening he just shrugged and I felt it politic not to ask more.

He did, however, want to talk about the meeting he had had that morning. "Fergus was in one of the bands I managed," he told me proudly. "They had some success but switched management after the first album and it all fizzled out after that. He's been on at me to work with him again, but I told him I'm not interested in music management anymore. I told him we were thinking of setting up this project and he's really keen to be on board."

"But we don't actually have a project yet."

"No, but we will. We're getting closer all the time."

"Granny Marjorie, do you like Doctor Who?" Toby piped up from the floor of my sitting room, where he was sprawled on the rug quietly doing some drawing.

"I don't really know much about him—" I started, pleased that Toby was trying to make conversation with me.

"Not now, chap. Granny Marjorie and I are trying to talk," Seth interrupted, glancing over at him.

"Oh, okay." Toby bent his head over his drawing again.

My disappointment must have shown in my face, as Seth said hurriedly, "Maybe later, and I'm sure Granny Marjorie would like to hear all about school as well."

"Yes I would. Perhaps we could go for a walk on the beach later on, and you could tell me all about it." I smiled warmly at Toby, but he was engrossed with his drawing.

"I'm not sure the beach is a good idea," Seth said quietly. "Bearing in mind what happened yesterday. I wouldn't want to run into Roz's alchy friends." Speaking a little louder, he went on. "Let's take him to the laser place. You'd like that, wouldn't you, chap?"

"Yeah, I suppose." Toby still didn't look up.

"It seems such a shame not to be outside on a lovely day like this," I said brightly. Toby didn't seem so keen on the idea of the laser place and I wasn't sure that it would be my idea of fun either. "Let's go to the park instead, and then we could have a cup of tea in the little café afterwards."

That's what we did in the end although, after giving Toby a perfunctory push on the swings, Seth was quite happy to stroll over to the café, leaving Toby in the playground. "He doesn't want us cramping his style and he's more likely to make friends if he hasn't got his dad and his granny hanging around. We can see him from here, so he's quite safe."

Watching from the café, it didn't seem to me that Toby was making many friends, but Seth was his father and knew him best. What did I know about raising children?

After a while, Toby came and joined us in the café. "What time are we going back, Daddy?" he asked as he drank his orange juice. "Only don't forget about Doctor Who."

"No, I won't forget about Doctor Who," Seth said, carefully. "Now, why don't you tell Granny Marjorie all about school? What's your favourite lesson?"

"I like Golden Time, that's my favourite. That's when we talk about Doctor Who. We—"

"I haven't forgotten about Doctor Who!" Seth snapped. "What about Maths? And English? Surely they teach you something useful? We're paying them enough money."

Toby's voice was very quiet. "Yes, we do sums and we do our times tables. And I'm in the top band for reading."

"That's really good, Toby," I said, trying to encourage him. "You must be a very good reader. What are you reading at the moment?"

Toby's lip wobbled and he looked like he was about to cry. "Doctor Who and —"

I'd never seen Seth lose his temper before. He banged the table with his fists, making Toby and I both jump. "That's it! I'm sick to death of Doctor Bloody Who! You can't have a conversation without mentioning him. You've been incredibly rude to Granny Marjorie, when she is kindly paying for you to go to that school, and all she wants to know is how you're getting on there."

"Seth, it's fine," I said. "If Toby wants to talk about Doctor Who—"

"No! It's not bloody fine!" Seth was almost shouting. "It's all I've heard since this morning! His mother was on about it as well! For God's sake, it's only a TV show."

Toby's face was a picture of misery. "I'm sorry, Daddy," he said in a tiny voice. "Only Granny Marjorie asked me what I was reading at the moment…"

"You're quite right, Toby, I did," I said briskly. "So it's my fault that Daddy's cross. Why don't you and I go and have another play on the swings and let Daddy finish his coffee? Then we can all walk back to my house. Go on, I'll see you over there." Toby scuttled off and I turned to Seth. "I suggest you calm down. You've upset Toby and embarrassed me. I'll see you over there when you can control yourself." As I turned to walk away, I heard him start to apologise but I ignored him and went to join Toby all the same.

Toby was sitting on the swing when I reached him, but not moving. "But it's not a house, is it?" he said as I approached.

"Sorry?"

"Where you live. It's not a house, it's an apartment. Like we used to live in. We live in a house now, it's got an upstairs and a downstairs and a garden. You don't have upstairs and downstairs, and you don't have a garden."

"Oh, I see. No, I don't have a garden but I live right next to the beach, so if I want to go outside, I can go there. It's like a great, enormous garden and I don't have to worry about weeding or mowing the lawn, do I?"

"But I like weeding. And Mummy could mow the lawn for you. She likes mowing and doing gardening, and making things grow. We want to grow all our own food."

"That's very admirable. But I bet you like going to the beach as well, don't you? I heard you went there after school yesterday, I bet that was fun."

216

His face closed immediately. "Yeah," he said in a flat voice.

I hadn't been consciously fishing, but it was clear he wasn't going to tell me any more and I felt a twinge of guilt that he thought I had been.

Just then, Seth came over and joined us and he crouched down in front of Toby. "I'm really sorry, Tobes. It's just that we don't get to spend much time together on our own and I want it to be really special when we do. And it's hard for me to compete with Doctor Who – you know, not being a Time Lord and everything." He gave a little laugh and Toby nodded slowly. "Now, a true lord will always look after his lady. What do you say, we escort the Lady Marjorie safely back to her ivory tower and then we direct our horses homewards?"

Toby sniffed and nodded solemnly. "Sorry, Daddy."

Seth also nodded and then ruffled Toby's hair. "Good boy." He turned to me. "I do apologise, Marjorie. It just means so much to me that we all get along, and I guess I overreacted."

"No harm done. But I ought to give Toby some tea before you go home, he hasn't eaten since lunchtime."

"He'll be fine until we get home, don't worry about that."

Toby was very quiet on the walk back and I made a mental note to learn about Doctor Who so that the next time I saw him I would be able to talk to him about it.

*

I didn't see him the following week, as Roz had arranged a play date with one of his friends from school. Seth was not happy about it.

"She's done it on purpose," he grumbled. "It's her revenge for me shouting at him about Doctor Who, he must have told her. She knows I don't get to see him much all week because I'm working, so she's decided to spoil my Saturday afternoon with him and you."

"But you see him every evening for bath and bedtime," I pointed out. "And I suppose that weekends are better for some of the other parents. Not everyone is as lucky as you, to have such flexible working hours, and able to leave in time to be home for things like that."

He glanced at me quickly and then nodded. "You're right, I'm lucky to have such an understanding boss."

"It's nice to be appreciated." I smiled. "Do you think that sometimes you misread Roz's motives? I only ask because sometimes it seems you immediately think the worst of her, and I wonder if that's fair?"

He scowled. "You don't know her like I do. Anything she can do to disrupt my plans, she will. Don't be fooled by her sweetness and light act. She's an addict, and like all addicts she's manipulative."

"Well, obviously you know her better than I do. I just wondered if it might make your life easier if you didn't always automatically think the worst."

"Marjorie," he said with a sigh. "I know what you're trying to do, and bless you for always thinking the best of people, but I've tried everything and I promise you: nothing could make my life easier with her."

I left it at that and, after Seth had gone home, I spent some time thinking about this conversation, particularly Seth's attitude to Roz. I felt that if I really was going to have a granny-type role in this family, then surely I should do my best to heal the rifts in it? But then again Seth had been struggling on his own for so long, maybe it was time for him to have someone completely in his corner.

*

I was still pondering this dilemma when Seth phoned me later that evening, clearly very excited. "I've got it!"

"Got what?"

"What our Charity can do, I've got it." He went on to explain about the friend that Toby had had over and how he had got so involved when they were making music together. "Not that you could really call it music, more like a cacophony, but they thought it was music. I haven't worked out all the details yet, but I'm going to set up a meeting with this kid's parents for next weekend and we can talk it through then. Which gives me this week to put a project proposal together."

"Don't you mean us? Gives us a week?"

"Oh!" He sounded startled. "I wasn't sure that you would want to be involved with all the minor details. I thought you wanted more of a figurehead sort of role."

"Whatever gave you that idea? I want to be in on everything, that's the whole point. Did you honestly think I would just want to be floating in and out and signing cheques occasionally?"

"Sorry, my bad," he said sheepishly. "I clearly wasn't thinking straight. Of course you want to be involved in all of it, I wouldn't have it any other way. And it would be great to have your support."

"So we'll meet this boy and his parents next weekend? What's his name?"

"Billy, or is it Bobby? Something beginning with B anyway. I got so excited I completely forgot. So I'll see you on Monday and we can brainstorm some ideas, yes?"

"I'll see you then." I was so happy to hear his excited enthusiasm.

*

By the time we met up with Benji's parents, Alice and Paul, the following weekend, Seth had already drawn up a proposal and a business plan and had applied to several sources for funding. He had also sounded out local schools and groups who might be interested. He certainly didn't let the grass grow under his feet and I felt a glow of satisfaction that my confidence in him wasn't misplaced.

Benji was a sweetie. "You'd never know there was anything wrong with him," I remarked to Seth as we stood watching him and Toby running around the garden.

"There isn't," Alice said sharply and Seth raised his hand in a calming gesture.

"That's the whole point of our Project, Marjorie." His voice was gentle as he explained. "It's to show that no child is 'wrong', just different. And that there's nothing wrong with being different."

I turned to Alice. "I'm so sorry, I didn't mean to offend."

She smiled, a tight little smile. "I just get so fed up with him being labelled."

"And I think that's just proved why there's a need for a project like ours," Seth said smoothly. "Shall I show you our ideas so far? Paul, Alice, why don't you come over to the table and we'll go through them on my laptop? I'd really appreciate your input. Roz, can you go outside with the boys and make sure they don't interrupt us?"

"Oh," she said, sounding surprised. "I was hoping to see for myself what you've been up to." She gave a little nervous laugh.

"But I can show it to you anytime," Seth said. "And it's important that we get Paul and Alice's input without the boys bouncing around."

"Okay then." She headed out to the garden.

"I think I'll go and keep her company," Paul said. "Benji can be a bit of a handful and those two boys are very excited. Alice, you can fill me in later, right?" She nodded, already distracted by Seth firing up the programme on his laptop.

"Marjorie, what do you want to do?" Seth asked.

"I think I'll stay and watch the presentation. I haven't seen it all the way through yet." I wasn't sure if I saw irritation flash across Seth's face, but I told myself not to be ridiculous.

The presentation was very good,. And it wasn't surprising that he'd got a lot of interest already. Alice was very enthusiastic and made some suggestions as it went along, which Seth noted down. He was clearly very knowledgeable about the subject and I was impressed that he had all the information – not to mention the jargon – at his fingertips.

After about half an hour it became apparent that I had nothing useful to contribute. Seth and Alice had their heads together working intently on the laptop – barely acknowledging my presence – so, feeling uncomfortable, I decided to go out and give Roz a hand with the boys. That way, Paul could come and join the discussion with his wife and Seth.

The boys were having a great time, 'digging over' one of the flowerbeds. This apparently involved pulling up every plant they could see and throwing it at each other, before piling most of the uprooted plants into a wheelbarrow. Then taking it in turns to push each other down to the bottom of the garden, dumping the contents of the wheelbarrow, rider included, in a heap.

Roz and Paul were sitting on a bench nearby, smoking and chatting. They hadn't noticed me approach and both started when I spoke. "I hope you were intending to dig over that bed. Otherwise they've just made the most unholy mess of your garden." I meant it as a light-hearted comment but even to my ear it sounded harsh, cutting across the relative peace.

Roz visibly bristled. "They're doing exactly what we asked them to do. Toby and I want to plant vegetables in that bed," she said icily.

The way she spoke made me feel like I was the Wicked Witch of the West, come to spoil the fun. Feeling defensive, I explained that I had come to give Paul the opportunity to go and join his wife.

"Thanks, but she's much better at that sort of thing than me." He nodded towards the boys. "And I'd prefer to be out here keeping an eye on Benji."

I didn't want to explain to these two that I had an uncomfortable feeling about Alice and Seth. I wasn't even sure I could explain it to myself, as I certainly hadn't witnessed anything that would give rise to any suspicion. I just felt that it would be a good idea for Paul to be inside, keeping an eye on his wife.

"I think you should go inside, I'm sure you have valid ideas to put forward." My voice clanged inside my head, again sounding harsh. I made an effort to lighten it. "Actually, why don't we all go inside? I'm sure the boys would be up for a drink and some biscuits."

Both boys' heads went up at the mention of biscuits and they ran into the house, with the three of us trooping behind.

*

"What do you mean by uncomfortable?" DI Nixon interrupted. "What were you concerned about?"

"I didn't really know, it was something about the way Seth was behaving around Alice but I couldn't put my finger on it."

"I felt he was overfamiliar. Detective Inspector Nixon, are you going to allow me to tell my own story?"

"I apologise, Mrs Evans. Of course. But we have been going for some time now and I'm aware that we might all need a break. Why don't we all go and get a cup of tea and some fresh air and we'll see you back here in half an hour."

"I'm perfectly able to proceed, Detective Inspector."

"I'm sure you are, Mrs Evans, but we have rules about how long you can be questioned without a break. DS Wood will escort you to the main entrance and will see you back there in half an hour."

I had no choice. Sergeant Wood escorted me to the door and pointed out a sandwich bar across the road. "You can get a tea or a coffee in there and then take it to the park if you like."

There was no point in explaining to her that a properly brought up lady would never be seen eating or drinking in the street, as it were, but the park did have the little café – the same one that Seth and I had taken Toby to all those years ago – so I decided to go there. It wasn't far to walk, which I suppose was a blessing, and although I knew I wouldn't be able to eat anything I could at least get a herbal tea. I was feeling dehydrated and I needed to gather my strength to continue with my story.

I hadn't expected it to take so long; I hadn't realised how much I wanted to get my full story out. And it was important to get all the details right. I briefly wondered if I could ask the policewomen to come to my home to take the rest of my statement but dismissed the idea. It was better to do this in the formal surroundings of the Police Station.

I bought a chilled bottle of water from the café and, when I returned to the Police station, I asked the Detective Sergeant to bring me a clean glass. "I don't hold with all this slurping out of bottles. To my mind it's not only uncouth, but also unhygienic."

"Now, Mrs Evans," DI Nixon said, once we were all settled. "You were telling us how Seth's behaviour towards Benji's mother had made you feel uncomfortable. Did you ever mention it to Seth himself?"

"Not on that occasion, no."

"On that occasion?"

"I spoke to him the next time I saw him, but he reassured me that I had nothing to worry about."

*

"I'm so sorry if I made you feel uncomfortable," Seth said when I raised it with him. We were reviewing the presentation back at the office after Seth had made some of the changes he and Alice had discussed. "Alice and I just got on very well and she's a very tactile person. I used to be but I get so little affection at home I guess I've got out of the habit. Then, when I meet someone like that, I suppose I overreact."

"I probably shouldn't have said anything. It was just that with her husband and child being there, as well as Roz and Toby, it seemed inappropriate."

"No, I'm glad you did. I would hate to offend anyone so I'll keep an eye on it in future. Never be afraid to talk to me about anything, Marjorie. I've never had someone older and wiser looking out for me before." He smiled and I could see tears glistening in his eyes.

I wanted to give him a hug but my own upbringing meant that any sort of physical contact made me feel uncomfortable and, as a consequence, I always came across as stiff and awkward.

*

"So you turned a blind eye to his cheating on Roz?" DI Nixon didn't sound accusatory, more sympathetic.

"No! I wasn't aware that he was. I knew he had the odd crush, and he liked to flirt, but in general these were harmless, like it had been with Alice. It was the same with Eleanor and with Imogen. The problem was when they read more into it – that's when it could get tricky."

"What do you mean by tricky?"

"Like with Imogen, for example. She got all sorts of ideas into her head, no matter how much Seth tried to discourage her, and we had to get very firm with her in the end. I just tried to make him feel loved and supported, so he wouldn't feel he was lacking in affection and go looking for it in the wrong places."

"How would you do that?"

"I instigated car sharing to work, and I insisted that we attended meetings and, later, schools together. I made his lunch for him, and we ate in the office, or we went out to lunch together. He never felt alone, I made sure of that. I used to feel dreadful when I dropped him home in the evenings, knowing that he would have to deal with Roz and her drinking, but I hoped his time with Toby would help to ease it."

"I see. But surely it crossed your mind that you could have helped him and Toby leave that terrible domestic situation?"

"I tried. I offered to rent him somewhere to live, but he said he didn't want to take Toby away from his mother. He insisted that, despite everything, she was a good mother. I admired him for sticking it out with Roz for Toby's sake. What I didn't realise was how few evenings he really was spending at home, and that Roz's drinking was nothing like he chose to portray it. I didn't find that out until much later. Like a lot of things."

"Such as?"

Such as the tens of thousands of pounds he embezzled from the Foundation, money that should have gone to the children; the women he had, despite my best efforts; the lies upon lies that he told me… Not now, Marjorie, unless you want to break down in front of these women. Deep breath and continue with your story…

"Let's not get ahead of ourselves, Inspector Nixon. The Foundation and the WE CAN Project were great successes and for a few years we went from strength to strength. We were doing good work and I was proud of Seth, of all of it. And when it was threatened—"

"Threatened?" DS Wood interrupted.

"Yes, when Eleanor Chandler made that horrid rape allegation. I'm sure she must have told you about it. Anyway, I shut that down straight away, although I'm ashamed of it now."

"I think you'll find Roz shut that down…" DS Wood started, but came to an abrupt halt at a look from her superior officer.

"Why are you ashamed of it now?" DI Nixon had abandoned her notes.

"Because now I think it was probably true, although I didn't at the time. I believed Seth over her and I deeply regret that now. I hope she can forgive me but, somehow, I don't think she will."

"You'd need to talk to her about that." Inspector Nixon was brisk. "What I'd like you to explain is how you came to this complete reversal of your opinion, and when."

"That would be three months ago…"

*

I was on my own in the office, going over the accounts and a rather disturbing report that had accompanied them from the accountant. He had requested a meeting with me 'in confidence and at your earliest opportunity'. Seth was away from the office. One of the Sunday supplements had run an article about our work a couple of weeks before and we had had a lot of enquiries that he was busy following up.

"It's getting hard to keep up with all the work," he'd said to me on the phone last night. "Have you had any more thoughts about bringing someone else in? That girl I met last week is very keen."

"I'm not sure we can afford it, but even if we could I would insist on a proper application procedure. We'd have to advertise and hold interviews."

"That seems like a waste of time and money to me, when we have someone keen who's ready to go."

"Seth, we have to be seen to be above board and professional. Let me think about it and I'll let you know my decision." By now, I knew the signs when Seth had a new infatuation and I certainly wasn't going to take someone on just because Seth fancied her. The last time that happened was with Eleanor, although I hadn't realised it at the time, and I certainly didn't want another situation like that.

"I think you'll find, Marjorie, that it should be our decision – not yours alone – but we can discuss it when I'm next in the office." His tone was quite frosty as we said our goodbyes.

I put this conversation out of my mind as I went over the report from the accountants. Although we were a not-for-profit organisation, it seemed to me that our finances were not nearly as healthy as they should be, considering the amount of work we were generating. I didn't know what the accountants were going to tell me but I had an idea, and I certainly didn't want to believe that anyone who worked with us would cheat the Project we had worked so hard to achieve.

It was as I was mulling these thoughts over in my head that the door opened and a woman entered the office. At a guess she was about my own age, but she certainly hadn't aged as well. She had long, frizzy, grey hair and no make-up and it looked as though she had thrown her outfit together from every colourful item of clothing she could find. She had a large, cloth shoulder-bag which looked as if it had been made from sewing scraps of material together, and I also noted lots of costume jewellery – if brightly coloured glass beads, bangles, dangly earrings and rings on almost every finger could be called jewels. At first glance, it was almost as if Eleanor had aged about thirty years and come back to visit and I did a double take. "Oh!"

"I'm sorry to disturb you," the woman said. "A young man outside let me in. I believe I have the right place, I'm looking for Seth Peterson?"

"He's not here, but maybe I can help? I'm Marjorie Evans."

"It's a pleasure to meet you, Marjorie, but I'm afraid you can't. I'm Annie Peterson." She came forward with her hand outstretched to shake mine. "I'm Seth's mother."

I had stood to greet her but now sat down abruptly. I spoke without thinking, "But I thought you were dead."

She looked shocked. "No, I'm very much alive, as you can see. Did Seth tell you I was dead?" she asked, incredulous.

"Not in so many words, but he always said that Toby had no grandparents…"

"I have a grandchild?" She grabbed a chair and sat down as abruptly as I had. "I did wonder, over the years," she murmured, more to herself than to me. "But I'd always hoped that would be a reason to get in touch. Obviously not." She shook herself quickly, coming back to the present. "Toby, you say? That's a great name. How old is he?"

I shook my head, remembering the snippets that Seth had told me about his childhood. "I don't think it's my place to give you any information, you clearly haven't been in contact with your son for many years. If you leave me your details, I'll make sure Seth gets them. It will then be up to him to get in touch if he wants to." I stood up again, intending to show her to the door.

To my surprise, she wailed. "My details are exactly the same as they were when he walked out thirty-five years ago. I've never moved; I wanted to be sure that he could find me if he ever needed or wanted to but he never has. Then, when I saw the article in the magazine, saw the picture of him and he looked so much like his father, I thought I would come to find him." She burst into tears, which she angrily tried to shake off as she grabbed her bag and started scrabbling about inside it, presumably looking for tissues. In her frustration she tipped the bag upside down, emptying the contents onto the floor, and began putting things back until she came to a handkerchief.

I decided to give her a couple of minutes to collect herself, noting with surprise that although the bag looked handmade, it had been beautifully lined and that the handkerchief appeared to be embroidered.

"I'm sorry," she sniffed as she pulled herself together. "I promised myself that I wouldn't make a scene. That if Seth didn't want to see me, I would be content to know that he was well and happy. But then you told me you thought I was dead, and that I have a grandchild, and it just seems so cruel of him to keep that from me. For years, I wondered if he were dead – my husband died convinced that he was – but I thought I would know, that a mother would know. Are you a mother yourself, Marjorie? Do you know what I mean?"

This woman's pain brought back all of my own and I felt tears springing to my eyes. "Yes," I said. "I know what you mean, more than most. Let me make you a cup of tea, and we can talk. Seth won't be back today, but you can tell me your story and we can work out where to go from here."

*

The two detectives were looking stunned.

"At no point in this investigation has anyone mentioned Seth's mother being in his life," DS Wood said. "Not even Roz."

"I imagine, like everyone else, she thought Seth's parents were dead."

"Isn't that what he'd told you?"

"He had never specifically told me that his parents were dead, but certainly he had implied it. I imagine the same went for Roz, and anyone else. From what Annie had just said, I doubted he even knew that his father had actually died."

"But—"

"Detective Sergeant, I really think that we will get through this a lot quicker if you just let me tell my story. You can ask questions when I've finished, but in the meantime please refrain from interrupting me again. There is a lot to get through and I wish to spend as little time in this room as possible, so if you wouldn't mind?"

She looked as if she were about to speak, but DI Nixon placed a hand on her arm and nodded at me. "Before you go ahead, Marjorie, I want to make sure that you still don't want a solicitor here?"

"I'm quite sure, thank you." *If I get my solicitor in here, he will only advise me not to talk and Annie's story deserves to be told…*

*

I closed the office for the afternoon. This only involved switching on the answering machine, closing the outer office and telling Fergus he could go home. Seth wasn't due back and everyone else was out doing school visits. I made Annie a cup of tea and we sat on the sofas. She had pulled herself together somewhat, although she still looked dreadful.

"Please don't feel you have to tell me anything," I spoke as gently as I could. "I know I'm a complete stranger, but if you want to talk I'm happy to listen."

"You're very kind." She took a tissue from the box I had placed in front of her. "But I'm not sure where to begin, my head is still full of the news that I have a grandchild."

I hesitated for a moment. "Actually Annie, you have two grandchildren. Seth had a daughter from a previous marriage, although he rarely keeps in touch with her now. She's working in the States."

"In America? But how old is she?"

"She's twenty-four and a lovely girl. I have photos on my phone of both of them. Let me fetch them up."

"Oh my word." She swiped back and forth through the photos, enlarging them so she could take in every detail. "Toby is the image of Seth when he was young. And she is beautiful, she looks a lot like my mother. What's her name?"

"Donna. She got her degree at Stanford University in California and stayed on there. Roz's sister lives out there and helped her get her place. Roz is Toby's mother."

"Do you have a picture of Roz?" She was still poring over the photos hungrily.

"Sadly, no. Roz and I don't keep in touch. I think she felt I sided against her in the divorce – well, long before that really – which wasn't true. But Seth had no-one on his side, and I felt I should support him. I just wanted what was best for Toby…" I fell silent as I realised the implications behind what I had just said. "Actually, I have always admired Roz. She's had her problems, but she's been a fantastic mother and stepmother. I think Seth would have lost touch with Donna when she was just a little girl if it hadn't been for Roz encouraging visits and contact. I should have told her that long ago, but we always had a difficult relationship. It's probably my fault, and it's such a shame." I leaned forward to pour more tea. "You said Toby looks like his father did. Tell me about Seth when he was young."

"He was a beautiful little boy." She sniffed, and then smiled at the recollection. "So loving. And clever – he got a scholarship to a local private school. It was when he started at that school that everything began to change. We weren't wealthy – my husband was a mechanic – but Seth had everything he needed. The problems began when I couldn't seem to get him to appreciate the difference between needing and wanting. Do you know what I mean?"

My own childhood had been privileged, my parents had been rich and I had always had everything I wanted. Everything except their love and attention. But I nodded and let her go on with her story.

"It started with a bike. Apparently, all the other boys had these racing bikes and so Seth wanted one. They were so expensive and we couldn't afford one, but someone gave my husband an old second-hand one. He worked on that bike for hours down in his shed, in the evenings after he got home, and he did a really good job. To me, it looked brand-new and Bill was really proud of it. We gave it to Seth for Christmas, but he never rode it to school or if he was meeting his friends. When I asked him why, he said it was the wrong make, that it was obviously second-hand and his friends would laugh at him. I never told my husband, I just said he wasn't allowed to ride it to school. Bill would have been so hurt if he'd known." She paused to take a sip of tea and to dab at her eyes with another tissue.

"He never brought his friends home from school, but he would always go to their houses. He said it was easier to do his homework with them, or in the library, so he wouldn't have to do it at the kitchen table while I was cooking tea, or working."

"You worked at home? What did you do?"

"Yes, I'm a dressmaker. Many of my clients were the mothers of the boys he was at school with. They would bring me magazine pictures of dresses they wanted copied, and I would make them up. Then they could pass them off as having been bought from some fancy designer." She smiled and I nodded, remembering my mother had a similar 'lady from the village' who did the same thing.

"Of course, that was another thing he hated – that it was his friends' mothers who were employing me – and that I made most of our clothes as well. I'm good at what I do, Marjorie, no-one would look at them and think they were home-made. Other than they were better quality than anything you could usually buy in a shop. But Seth hated feeling different, hated feeling 'inferior' to the other boys at school. It didn't help, either, that most of their fathers used the garage where Bill worked. It probably wouldn't have been as bad if he'd owned the garage, but he was just a lowly grease monkey as far as Seth was concerned."

Her voice had begun to wobble and she stopped to take another sip of tea and then some deep breaths before continuing. "He was a good man, my Bill. He worked hard and he was honest as the day is long. He looked after us and he was always ready to help anyone out if they needed it. Seth was a late baby – we were getting on a bit when he was born – and Bill loved him. It broke his heart when Seth left and he was never the same again…"

"When did he die?"

"Ten years after Seth left. It was cancer, officially, but I think he just gave up the will to live. All the spark had gone out of him, you know? He'd lost his beloved boy, believed he was dead, and couldn't see the point in going on."

"But you could?"

"I didn't believe Seth was dead. I told you, I thought I'd know if he was. I always hoped he'd come back."

"When did Seth leave? How old was he?"

"He was seventeen. He had been doing so well at school, on track for really good A-level results the following year, and we were hoping he would go to university. He would have been the first person in our family to do that and we were so proud. Then it all started to go wrong…

"He told us he'd got a summer job working at the Golf Club, caddying and generally helping out. Bill had hoped he'd work at the garage, but he told us he had no intention of dirtying his hands with manual labour. And he did seem to be doing really well, he was buying new clothes and records, you know the sort of thing boys like to spend their money on." I nodded. I didn't know but I could guess.

"Anyway, he wanted to learn to drive so Bill took him out a few times in our car and we got him some lessons for his birthday. He passed the test first time and then he wanted us to buy him a car. Bill said he'd look around for a reliable old banger that they could do up together, but of course that wasn't good enough. It was the Christmas bike all over again. He told us that all his friends at school were getting cars, as their mothers had saved the Family Allowance from when they were babies, and he demanded to know what I had done with 'his' Family Allowance. I told him that we had used it as the government intended – to provide for him – and that perhaps if those other mothers hadn't needed it, they shouldn't have claimed it. He lost his temper and shouted that he knew I'd probably spent it on 'fags and gin'." She paused, taking a deep breath and looking at me. "I don't smoke, Marjorie, I never have. I have a couple of glasses of wine on special occasions, but I'm not a drinker. I didn't know where he was getting this from."

Seth had occasionally made comments to me about his parents' drinking and neglect during his childhood, but I decided not to say anything to Annie about this. I would let her tell her story and, if I felt it didn't ring true, then I would talk to Seth about it later. I was already feeling, however, that this woman was genuine and Seth had been lying to me. And if he'd been lying about this, what else was there?

Although he wasn't due back that day, I felt it was important to get Annie out of the office in case he changed his mind. But she looked uncertain when I invited her to stay with me.

"I couldn't impose. I'm sure I could book into a Travelodge or something, although I haven't booked anything."

I had the impression that she hadn't thought this trip through, much beyond getting down here and seeing her long-lost son. "You look like you could do with some fresh air and then a shower and a change of clothes. If you've driven down from Gateshead this morning then you've already had six hours in the car." She nodded. "With the shock and all the emotion this afternoon, you must be exhausted." I scribbled down my address and postcode on a piece of paper and handed it to her. "I'll ring ahead and tell Mrs Wheeler – she's my part-time housekeeper – that you're coming and she will let you in and show you where everything is. Make yourself at home. I have a few things to finish up here, but I won't be far behind you."

She took a little more convincing but eventually agreed and left. I made myself a chamomile tea and, while it was steeping, ran through various conversations with Seth over the years. The more I thought about it, the more I came to the conclusion that, while he hadn't actually lied, he hadn't been truthful either.

Along with this thought, I was beginning to have a nagging suspicion that my accountant's request for a meeting 'in confidence' might have more than a little to do with Seth. A couple of incidents recently had caused a small alarm bell in my mind. Previously, he had always been amenable and had let me lead the Foundation and the Project as I saw fit. But lately he had been argumentative, almost disruptive, and didn't bother to hide his irritation with me. A couple of times he had come close to losing his temper, as he had that day in the café with Toby. I had wondered if he was planning to leave the Foundation, and what sort of position that would place me in, but then I had dismissed the thought as being ridiculous. Seth loved me like a mother, I had told myself, he wouldn't hurt me. But, after what Annie had told me, that clearly meant nothing.

I checked the office diary. I had a doctor's appointment scheduled for the following morning. It was only to get the results of some tests I had had last week, so I rearranged it for the day after and arranged to meet the accountant straight after that. That way, I didn't have to put the accountant into the diary and, as far as Seth was concerned, it would just be an extended doctor's appointment.

*

When I got home, Annie had showered and changed into another eclectic, yet beautifully made, outfit. She insisted on helping me to make dinner and as we cooked we chatted about inconsequential things. She was an interesting and vibrant woman, and I suspected she would have a lively sense of humour under different circumstances. I was reminded of my days as a student nurse at The London Hospital and realised, with a pang, how much I had missed friendships with women of my own age. My husband being a professional man and much older than me, meant that our social circle had consisted of his colleagues, friends and their wives. Since his death, the only new connection I had made had been Seth.

We ate our dinner on the balcony, overlooking the sea, and afterwards we drank a glass of wine while Annie continued with her story.

"Seth had thrown the offer of a car back in Bill's face and had said all those horrid things about me, so there was a huge row and he stormed out. He didn't come back that night and we had no idea where he was. I was worried sick, but Bill said we had to give him time to calm down. He said he was probably staying over at some friend's house and would be back with his tail between his legs the next day." She produced another handkerchief and dabbed at her eyes. "When he didn't come back the next day, Bill phoned the Golf Club to see if he could speak to him and persuade him to come home and talk to us. They told him that Seth had never worked there."

"So what had he been doing all that time? Where was he getting all that money from?"

"That's exactly what we were asking ourselves. So we rang around his friends to see whether he was staying with one of them. No-one knew where he was. Well, you can imagine how worried we were."

"Of course."

"Eventually one of my clients phoned me. She was a lovely lady and the mother of one of Seth's friends, and she told me that her son had said that Seth had got involved with some rock band in Newcastle. That's where he had been all the evenings he'd said he was working at the Golf Club. He'd been roadying for them."

"Why did he tell you he'd been at the Golf Club?" I was puzzled.

"Maybe because he was underage and he thought we would disapprove of him hanging out in the pubs and clubs in the city centre. We wouldn't have liked it, not with his exams coming up, but we'd have tried to work something out if the band was so important to him. But that wasn't the worst of it, not by a long chalk." She shook her head as if trying to dislodge the memory. "My lady came round to see us the next day, and brought her son with her. He told us that Seth had been showing off to everyone at school that he had this connection with the band, and how much money he was making, and that he had been selling drugs to the other boys at school." She choked and stopped speaking.

"Oh Annie, how dreadful."

"Bill jumped straight in the car and drove to Newcastle to try and find him. The Police were sympathetic and gave as much help as they could but he was seventeen, and had left of his own accord, so he wasn't a priority. Bill went to all the music venues he could find, but if they knew anything they weren't telling. Most of them claimed not to have heard of the band, and those that had said they had no contact details.

"Bill's boss at the garage helped us make up some posters and he gave Bill loads of time off to go and search. We put the posters up everywhere and went to all the homeless shelters we could find, but we didn't really think we'd find him in one of those… If I knew nothing else about my son, I knew that he would always land on his feet. He wouldn't be sleeping rough."

She had a point there. I had got to know Seth quite well over the past few years, albeit not as well as I had previously thought, and I knew that he would always find a way to provide himself with a bed for the night, or at the very least someone's sofa.

"Anyway," she continued, heaving a deep sigh. "Eventually we heard that the band had changed their name and moved to London. No-one knew if Seth had gone with them or not. Bill was all for going down to London and resuming the search, but we had no idea if Seth was actually there. With all the time off, Bill wasn't getting paid and the bills were mounting up. We decided that it would be better to make sure that Seth had a home to come back to. We honestly thought he would, we never thought that row would be the last time we would see him."

"He never came back at all? Never tried to contact you?"

"Never. I became an avid reader of music magazines, hoping that one day I might see a mention of him. It was the only clue I could think of. And the irony is that I don't even take the newspaper that carried the article about your work. It was pure chance that I picked up the supplement in my dentist's waiting room a couple of days ago. That's why it's taken me so long to get here."

"Well, I am very glad that you did." I took her hand. "We need to plan what you're going to do next. I'm sure you'd like to meet Toby."

"I would, but I think I should meet up with Seth first. I think I should let him introduce me to his son."

"I think that's very wise. Let's make a plan."

*

Seth was not happy when I telephoned him, the next morning, and told him to clear his appointments for that afternoon and meet me at my apartment. I said I had something important to discuss with him.

"Can't it wait?" he grumbled. "What could be so important?"

"Please just do as I ask, Seth. I will see you here at 2.30." As I replaced the receiver it occurred to me, momentarily, that he would not be in the best frame of mind when he arrived here. But, I reasoned, surely reuniting with his mother would overcome any bad mood?

Annie was visibly nervous as we waited for him to arrive. She paced up and down my sitting room, went out onto the balcony and paced some more out there. Finally, the buzzer sounded and I pressed the entryphone to let him in.

It was a disaster. I opened the door and he strode angrily past me. "What's all this about? I had important meetings this afternoon... Oh, for fuck's sake!" He had seen Annie, who had cried out at the sight of him and was standing by the window, one hand to her mouth and the other fumbling for a chair to sit down. "What the fuck is she doing here?"

"Seth, my boy, it's been—"

"I have nothing to say to you. You have no right to be here." His voice was cold and his face thunderous as he turned to me. "What the hell do you think you are doing? Has she been filling your head with lies?"

"Your mother came to me. She saw the article—"

"She's not my mother. She's dead to me, and that man she's married to."

"Seth, you should talk to her. You should—"

"I don't have to do anything, and you shouldn't have got involved. It's nothing to do with you and she is nothing to do with me."

"Please, Seth..." Annie took a couple of steps towards him. "... I don't know what happened, but I've missed you so much. Can't we talk about it?"

"I've told you, I have nothing to say to you. Get the fuck out of here and don't come back." He grabbed her arm and propelled her towards the door.

"No, Seth." I swallowed hard and spoke more calmly than I felt. "Annie is my guest, she is staying here, and I won't have you speaking like that to a guest in my home. If anyone is leaving, it will be you. Although I think you should stay and we can all talk this through together."

"There's nothing to talk about. If you won't throw her out, then I will leave. I have work to do. Call me when she's gone and we will talk about your monstrous betrayal of trust." Before I could think of a response he had gone, slamming the door so hard a vase of flowers fell off the table in the hall and shattered.

For a few long moments there was silence. Then Annie, still crying, grabbed her bag and pushed past me. She ran into the guest room where she snatched up her overnight bag. As she passed me again, stumbling and heading for the door, I put my arms out to try and stop her.

"Annie, please, don't go anywhere. You can't drive in this state, and we need to sort out what we're going to do next—"

"No! You heard him, he wants nothing to do with me. He hates me! I should never have come here!"

"It was just the shock. The shock of seeing you after all these years. He'll calm down. Please stay, I don't think you should be driving anywhere like this—"

"No! I'm so sorry, Marjorie. Thank you for everything, thank you for trying. I have to go, I can't stay here after that." She got the door open and turned to give me a weak smile. "I'll be fine, I promise. I just need to be on my own for a little while."

"At least promise me that you'll not try to drive back to Gateshead now, you shouldn't drive when you're upset like this. I'd like you to stay tonight, but if you won't stay here at least get a hotel room and call me later to let me know you're okay." I didn't want to let her go but she was already through the door.

"I will. Really, I'll be fine." She'd pressed the button for the lift, but turned and headed for the stairs and I heard her running down them, sobbing.

I went back into the apartment and fetched the dustpan and brush to clear up the broken vase. I would give her five minutes to get to her car and gather herself, then I would call her and see if I could talk her into coming back.

*

You hear people talk about the worst day of their lives, usually as a melodramatic overstatement, but believe me when I tell you that the next day truly was the worst of my life.

I had barely slept at all, for a start. I had been trying to ring Annie but her phone just went straight to voicemail. I left countless messages and hoped that she hadn't tried to drive back to Gateshead after she left me, but had got a room at a hotel as I had begged her to do. I couldn't stop thinking about how badly I had handled the situation and Seth's callous cruelty to his mother. I couldn't imagine what she was going through and I desperately wanted to try and help her work through it.

So, if anything, the appointment with Doctor Bailey was an inconvenience I didn't need. I would have cancelled but his receptionist had been most insistent, when I had telephoned on the day of Annie's visit, that it was very important that I came in. Consequently, I wasn't completely focused during the meeting and initially didn't take in what he had been saying about the results of my tests.

"I'm sorry," I said as a couple of the words registered in my head. "That's ridiculous. I can't have lung cancer, I've never smoked."

"But your husband did, didn't he? Quite heavily, as I remember."

"You know he did, you treated him. He had lung cancer, I can't have it. Are you sure you haven't got our notes muddled up?"

"No, Marjorie, I haven't. You need to listen to me, this is serious."

238

My head was reeling as I left his office. I seemed to have stepped into a parallel universe, one with a whole new language: stage IV, metastases, brachytherapy, pain management… I almost couldn't take it seriously. I wasn't feeling any pain, I had only gone to see him because I wanted a tonic to help me with the chronic tiredness I had been feeling recently, following an odd virus that had laid me out for a week or so. I nearly hadn't told him about the specks of blood I had seen a few times, after a particularly bad coughing fit, as they had seemed so insignificant.

My doctor's offices were in a beautiful Georgian crescent opposite a park and I went over and sat on one of the benches, forcing my thoughts into order. I had half an hour before I was due at the accountants, which looked like being another stressful meeting. I resolved not to think about the news I had just been given, in order that I could focus on what the accountant had to say.

Once again I found myself sitting opposite a professional man using terms I couldn't fully comprehend: forensic audit, Charity Commission violations, possible HMRC investigations and sums of money that would buy a small house.

"How can you be sure that it's Seth?" Although I knew in my heart that it was. "And what do you suggest should be our next step?"

"It couldn't be anybody else, Marjorie, I'm sorry. And, at the moment, all we have is a suspicion, albeit a very strong one. I think our best course of action would be to gather as much evidence as we can and then go to the authorities ourselves before they get wind of it."

"How do we do that?"

"I have spoken to a colleague who specialises in this area. He and his partner are former Fraud Squad detectives. He would like to plant someone in your office who could then have access to all your files and suchlike."

"That seems rather underhand," I remarked.

"Not as underhand as embezzling thousands of pounds from a charitable organisation. We need to get ahead of this before Mr Peterson realises we suspect him and starts covering his tracks, better than he already has. Would it be possible to put someone like that into the organisation without tipping him off?"

I thought about the conversation that Seth and I had had the night before Annie's visit, about taking someone on for office admin. "Yes, I think so."

By the time I left their offices we had a plan. I had met the two fraud detectives and was pleased to see that the woman who would be planted in the office was attractive and in her early 40s. It would be easier to get Seth to accept her if he could think of her as a potential conquest. We arranged that she should start the following Monday morning and I telephoned Seth to tell him that I would meet him back at the office that afternoon.

"We have things we need to discuss," I told him. "I made a mistake and I don't want this hanging over us. Please, let's talk about it and I'm sure we can sort it out."

*

Seth's manner was cold when I arrived back in the office. I had decided that my best approach was to be contrite and apologetic. Although it stuck in my craw to betray her, I made out that I had realised that Annie had deceived me and I had now seen the error of my ways. He let me grovel for some time before he magnanimously consented to forgive me.

"Oh, and I thought about what you were saying about the workload the other night," I said as casually as I could. "I think you're right, we do need someone. So I've been onto an agency and we have a temp starting on Monday."

"But I had someone in mind, and temp agency fees—"

"Don't worry about the fees, I'll cover them from my personal account. It will be better to get a professional admin officer who can hit the ground running, don't you think?"

He had no answer to that and I pleaded a headache and went home. I wasn't sure I could tolerate being in the office with him just then, and I needed time to process my thoughts alone.

*

I had barely got in the door when the entryphone buzzed. I checked the video display and could see two uniformed police officers standing at the entrance to the building. My first thought was that the accountant had changed his mind and called in the Police after all, but I knew that he would have notified me first. It occurred to me that the Police had got the wrong apartment, but then they asked for me by name.

"Yes, what is it?" I could hardly keep the irritation out of my voice.

"Mrs Evans, will you let us in please? It's extremely important and not something we can discuss over an entryphone."

I sighed, buzzed them in and was waiting for them as they emerged from the lift. "I hope this really is important, officers. I have had a very exhausting day."

"Mrs Evans, do you know a Mrs Annie Peterson?" The younger officer couldn't have been more than about twenty years of age and he looked extremely nervous. His prominent Adam's apple was bobbing about as he spoke.

"Yes I do. In fact she was here yesterday."

He glanced at his older colleague who said, "if we could come in, please, Mrs Evans. It would be better to talk inside."

I had an uneasy feeling as I led them both through to my sitting room and indicated that they should each take a seat on the sofa. I chose to sit on one of the dining chairs – the same chair, I realised, that Annie had used for support the day before. "What is this all about?"

"Mrs Evans, how do you know Mrs Peterson?"

"She's a friend." I wasn't about to start airing Annie's dirty laundry in front of these two.

"And how long has she been a friend?" The young officer kept glancing nervously at his notebook.

"Actually, I only met her the day before yesterday. She came to visit my office and then stayed over here. What is this all about?"

"Oh! Are you…? I mean, were you…?" He cast a stricken look at his colleague, who cleared his throat.

"Was your friendship a romantic one?"

"No, it most certainly was not. For goodness sake! If you must know, she's the mother of my employee – Seth Peterson."

"Oh, so that would make him her next of kin!" The young one burst out as his colleague put a restraining hand on his arm.

Next of kin. The vague feeling of disquiet that had been hovering at the back of my mind since they arrived now came to the forefront. "I think you had better just come out and tell me what this is all about, officers."

In gentle, professional tones the older officer explained to me about the accident on the M1, stressing that Annie would have died immediately and wouldn't have felt anything. It appeared that she had fallen asleep at the wheel, he explained, and drifted into the path of an HGV in the next lane. Unfortunately, there was nothing the driver could do and it was unlikely she had known anything about it. But their enquiries hadn't been able to turn up any family, or anyone with any information, at her address. On checking the satnav in her car they established that the last two destinations, other than her home, had been the WE office and my apartment block. A quick check on the electoral register had established that I was the only link between the two addresses and that is what had led them to my door.

I am not a person who cries. It has been said that I'm a cold fish and have no feelings. Not being given to public displays of emotion does not equate to having no feelings; it's simply that my upbringing taught me to keep a very tight rein on them. And I am particularly good at it. But all I could think about was how I had begged her not to drive back straightaway and to get some sleep. She hadn't, and it had caused her death. She would never have been on that road if Seth hadn't rejected her out of hand and so coldly. I could have done more, but ultimately there was one person who was really responsible for Annie's death.

I squared my shoulders and arranged with the two officers to travel back to my office, where we would tell Seth what had happened to his mother. I wasn't sure how he would take the news and explained to the policemen that Seth had been estranged from his mother for a long time.

I was ashamed of Seth's reaction to the news, more ashamed than I had been the day before when he had utterly rejected Annie's attempts at reconciliation. He showed no remorse, no feelings at all, at the news that the woman who had given him life, nurtured and cared for him for seventeen years, was dead.

He listened impassively while they told him the details. "This has nothing to do with me. You're surely not expecting me to travel to Gateshead to sort out the affairs of a woman who has been dead to me for many years?"

"In the absence of any other next of kin, we will need someone to identify her," the older of the two Police officers said, maintaining a composed expression while the younger one was visibly shocked.

"I saw her briefly yesterday, for less than five minutes. I couldn't tell you for sure if that was my mother or not. Now, if you don't mind I have work to do." He turned away and left the office, leaving the officers and me staring at each other in horrified amazement.

*

I took care of everything: I arranged with the Police that I would travel to Gateshead to identify her; I organised Fergus to show the 'new girl' the ropes when she started on Monday and I let everyone know that I would be out of the office for at least four weeks while I took care of Annie's affairs. I told them all that a distant cousin, with no other relatives, had died. I said nothing to Seth about her – I didn't trust myself.

I moved into her home while I sorted through the remnants of her life. It felt strange to be in the house where Seth had grown up, and where he had clearly been very much loved still. There were photos everywhere of him as a boy, and his bedroom appeared to have been untouched since the day he walked out of it.

In the evenings I sat in Annie's quiet, comfortable, colourful sitting room with her cat asleep on my lap. I tried to imagine how life had been for her over the past thirty-five years, without her beloved son. I packed up her belongings, putting obvious

242

treasures in boxes for Toby and Donna and arranging with the solicitors to sell everything else. She had left a will naming Seth as her sole beneficiary and I burned with resentment that he would benefit from her death when he had already taken so much from her.

My health started to deteriorate rapidly, almost as if having been told that I was ill my body felt free to manifest it. I began to need a stick to help me walk and I grew tired very easily. I contacted my doctor and asked him to refer me to a private practitioner in the local area. The new doctor organised a full body MRI scan for me which showed how the cancer had spread through my body – even to my brain. He tried to persuade me to consider treatments, but we both knew that they would be invasive and, ultimately, they would only prolong the inevitable. He agreed instead to help me 'manage my pain' with some extremely strong medications.

It was while I was researching these drugs that I began to formulate a plan. I accepted every pain med he offered me and went back for more whenever I could. I wasn't in as much pain as I made out to him that I was, but I laid it on thick and persuaded him to prescribe the strongest possible drugs. I took as few of them as I could, knowing that any pain I was feeling was fuelling my anger and my resolve to make Seth pay for what he had done to Annie, and to me.

I contacted Seth and arranged that my four week 'sabbatical' would be extended to eight. He seemed relieved that he wouldn't have to see me and reassured me frequently that I could leave everything in his capable hands, especially now we had the new girl who, he assured me enthusiastically, was fantastic. The irony made me smile.

I kept in touch with the accountant and – as my eight weeks were drawing to a close – was vastly relieved to learn that, although Seth's fraud was serious, the Foundation couldn't be held responsible in any way. "We do need to talk about next steps though, Marjorie," he said. "We need you back down here as soon as possible."

"I'll be there next week. Don't do anything until after we've discussed it."

*

Mindful of what had happened to Annie, I took it slowly on the drive back down south and stopped overnight at a Travelodge just north of London. Ordinarily I hated such places but this time its bland anonymity suited me perfectly.

I had arranged to meet with my accountant and his fraud colleagues the day after my return. They came to my apartment and we spread their papers over my dining table while Alison, who had been planted in my office, went over the details of Seth's betrayal.

"Does he suspect you at all?" I asked her.

"No," she said with a wry smile. "I think he believes he's so clever that he will never be detected. He has a very high opinion of himself, doesn't he?"

This young woman had known Seth for eight weeks and had got the measure of him. It had taken me fourteen years. I swallowed down the bile building at the back of my throat. "For now, I want you to hold fire on any further action—"

"Marjorie, we have to report this to the authorities as a matter of urgency," my accountant said. "At the moment, the Foundation is not in any legal peril, but now that we are aware—"

"Charles, it's just to give me a couple of weeks. It will all be sorted out then, I just have a couple of things I need to see to beforehand." They weren't happy but agreed to give me until the end of the following week. I reckoned that would just about give me enough time.

After I had seen them out I telephoned Arthur and arranged for him to come over that afternoon. I needed his help with some of the things I wanted to do and, as he had been my trusted legal adviser – and friend – for so many years, I wanted to seek his counsel on the situation. If I had been in any doubt about the effect the cancer had taken on me it disappeared when I saw his face as I opened the door.

We sat and talked as the sun went down and by the time he left I felt more at peace than I had done in a long time. I sat on my balcony and gazed at the sea, taking comfort from the gentle sounds of the waves.

*

"Marjorie." This time it was the Inspector's voice that broke in, firm but gentle. "I am going to stop this interview right now. I want you to go home and get a good night's sleep and think very carefully before you continue with your statement. We will call on you tomorrow at 11 a.m., which will give you time to consider whether you wish to continue or not." She stood up and nodded to the Sergeant. "Please show Mrs Evans out and arrange transport home for her. Not in a Police car, get her a taxi." With that she left the room, leaving the Sergeant looking as nonplussed as I felt.

"But I hadn't finished," I said to her as she began bustling about gathering files together.

She shrugged. "I'll show you out to Reception. You can wait for the taxi there."

*

Inspector Nixon arrived promptly at eleven the next morning, without her Detective Sergeant. I showed her into my sitting room and made her tea, while I myself had juice.

"Marjorie, having had some time to think, please tell me what you've decided."

"I'd like to continue with my statement."

"Are you absolutely sure?" Her expression was one of concern. "And you don't want anyone else here with you?"

"I am absolutely sure and no, I don't want anyone here." I sipped my juice. "Now, I believe we had got to last month…"

*

I didn't tell anyone else I was back and I spent the days resting and sitting on my balcony, writing letters and reading. It was a peaceful, happy time and I relished it. Arthur visited me once or twice and we chatted about old times.

On his final visit he brought some papers for me to sign and I got my housekeeper, Mrs Wheeler, and her son to witness them. After Arthur had gone, and while his mother busied herself around the apartment, I sat on the balcony and talked to Zach. I had known him since he was a small boy and his mother had been housekeeper in the house my husband and I shared. He had been more than happy to oblige when I had telephoned him the day before to say that I had a couple of favours to ask, and it was such a pleasure to see him. We talked about the troubles he had had with heroin addiction, how pleased I was that he seemed to have come through it and was sorting out his life, and I made him promise that he would do everything he could to make his mother proud.

When I was alone again I telephoned Seth. "I'm travelling back tomorrow, but there are some things I need to discuss with you away from the office. I'm stopping overnight to catch up with a friend, so why don't we meet there?" I gave him the address of the Travelodge I had stayed in on my way back from Annie's and arranged to meet him there the following afternoon.

*

Seth was on full charm offensive when he came to my room, enquiring solicitously after my health and managing not to show his shock at my appearance. I had brought champagne and greeted him at the door with a glass which he downed quickly, enquiring what we were celebrating.

"Well, for one thing, your money worries are over. You are the sole beneficiary of your mother's will." I handed him the buff folder containing a copy of Annie's will and watched for his reaction, but he was cleverer than to appear pleased. He glanced at it, then shrugged noncommittally. "But let's not talk about that now. First, catch me up on all the news from WE CAN."

"It's going tremendously well…" Greedily, he gulped another glass of champagne. "And you were right about the temp, she's terrific." He chattered on, telling me about the new leads he was cultivating, his plans for expansion and how well the office was running, the underlying implication being how much better everything was going without me. After about twenty minutes he was on his third glass and I noticed his voice starting to slur. "I'm sorry, Marjorie, I think I may have downed that champagne too quickly. I'm feeling a little woozy."

"Oh dear," my voice was full of concern. "Let me make you some coffee. Perhaps you'd feel better lying on the bed?" I got up and crossed over to the kettle, taking it into the bathroom to fill it. I took my time and when I returned to the room I fussed about with teacups and coffee sachets. When I looked across at him he was lying on the bed, shaking his head as if trying to clear it.

"I don't understand it," he slurred. "Champagne doesn't usually affect me like this."

"That's probably the Rohypnol. I wasn't sure how much to put in, so I put it all."

He struggled to raise himself on the bed. "What the fuck, Marjorie?"

"I really wouldn't try to fight it, Seth. You're not going to be able to and the more you struggle the quicker it pumps the drug around your body. I have quite a lot on the agenda for this meeting, and I need you conscious while we go through it.

"We could start with the tens of thousands of pounds you have embezzled from the Foundation. Or how your tomcatting around has nearly brought everything I have worked for crashing to the ground more than once. We could talk about the shameful way you have manipulated and abused the mother of your child, or even how you have neglected that child – both your children – except when it suited your own selfish purposes. But I think I would like to start with Annie, particularly as she is no longer here to speak for herself."

All the while I had been speaking his mouth had been opening and closing like a newly landed fish, but he was beyond speech now.

"You have manipulated me from the beginning. As soon as you wheedled the story of Drew out of me, you played me. And yes, perhaps at first I did look on you as some sort of surrogate son, but now I thank God that you are nothing to do with me. The way you treated your mother was appalling and inhuman and for that – if nothing else – I hope you burn in Hell. You didn't just abandon her, you humiliated her when she tried to reach out to you. And that was on top of trashing her reputation – everyone thought that she and your father were drunks who abused you – when nothing could have been further from the truth. So for that reason, I'm not just going to kill you, I'm going to make sure that you die in such a humiliating way that everyone will know about it and remember it whenever your name is mentioned."

I turned and opened my overnight case, taking out a length of rope. I tied one end to the bedpost and as I uncoiled it he could see that the other end was tied in a hangman's noose, which I looped over his head and arranged around his neck. His eyes were pleading but I ignored them and carried on.

"Some might say I should hand you over to the Police and let justice be done, but I don't have that kind of time and I have no doubt that you would lie and manipulate your way out of it. And I can't risk my name, my Foundation and my husband's good name being forever tainted. You have poisoned the people around you for too long and I am not prepared to leave that as my legacy."

I took some surgical gloves out of my bag and put them on. "You see, I watched a documentary while I was away. It was about some popstar who had died and no-one

247

knew if it was suicide or misadventure. But then they interviewed his girlfriend and she said that it wouldn't have been suicide, because he was found naked. She said he would never have wanted to have been found like that, it was humiliating. And I sat in your mother's house, surrounded by all her mementos of you, and I knew it was a sign."

I scattered the contents of the buff folder across the bed, dropping the folder itself into my bag. "In the end, they concluded that he had been having some kind of private little party which had gone wrong. And it's going to look like you had quite some party in here, Seth. Celebrating your mother's death and your inheritance all by yourself." I took the things that Zach had acquired for me – a mirror and a rolled up £20 note, together with a small bag of cocaine – out of my bag. I dipped the note in the powder and brushed it around his nostrils, then smeared the mirror with traces of the remaining cocaine before scattering it all over him and the bed. "Some champagne, some cocaine, and then your own special way of celebrating…"

I stripped him of his clothes and retrieved some magazines from the bag which I placed around him. "Hard core porn," I explained. "Really, quite revolting and quite specialised. I had to go to some dark places on the Internet to obtain these." Adjusting the rope around his neck, I remarked, "Who knew my nursing training would come in so handy? It means I know the location of your vagus nerve. The compression of that is what will kill you… eventually."

I collected my champagne glass. "Right!" I said brightly as I put it in my overnight case and cast a last appraising look around the room. "I'm going to leave you now. It's only fitting that you should die alone, don't you think? I'll put the 'Do Not Disturb' sign up. We don't want anyone wandering in by accident, do we now? By my reckoning, it's going to be at least eighteen hours before the chambermaids come round." I pulled him into a sitting position on the edge of the bed and then pushed him forward so he was on his knees on the floor, his body weight pulling the rope taut.

I left the room, putting up the 'Do Not Disturb' sign as I had promised Seth I would. I felt lighter and brighter than I had done for weeks and I managed to walk to the railway station without needing to stop for a rest.

*

"And to be quite honest with you, Inspector, that's how I've felt ever since." I smiled and took another sip of my juice. "And now I suppose you're going to arrest me."

"No Marjorie, I don't think I am. I really can't see the point."

I hadn't expected this. I gazed at her, unable to process my thoughts. "But I have just confessed to murder."

"What I heard was a terminally ill lady, with a tumour on her brain and possibly befuddled with meds… No, let me finish," she continued as I started to protest. "… confess to causing a death which has already been classified as misadventure. I can see no useful purpose in instigating a long and drawn out case, costing the taxpayer thousands of pounds, which you – forgive me – are unlikely to see the end of. I thank you for your candour, Marjorie, but I feel this would be better if it remained between you and me." She stood up to leave but then, seemingly on an impulse, crossed the room and bent down to kiss my cheek. "You are quite some lady, Marjorie Evans. Look after yourself." She left the apartment, quietly closing the door behind her.

I drained my juice, reached into the pharmacy bag beside my chair and drew out a bottle. There were enough opioids in there to down a horse and, although I had calculated there had been enough in the juice I had been sipping during my confession, just to be sure I refilled the glass straight from the bottle. I drank the whole glass. I had positioned my chair so I could see the sea beyond the balcony and I settled back in the calm quiet, closed my eyes and waited for sleep.

* * *

EPILOGUE

My dearest Roz,

I hope that you are reading this, in accordance with the instructions I left my solicitor, on the balcony of my apartment looking out over the sea. For that is where I'm sitting while I write it.. Although, of course, if you're reading this it's your apartment now.

Look at that view, Roz, at the infinite possibilities beyond the horizon. That is what I want to give to you - a future with infinite possibilities.

I know that money can't make up for all the times I misjudged you, believed the lies that Seth told about you, or for the shameful way he treated you and Toby and Eleanor, and God knows how many others, but I hope it can help you to start creating a new, happier life.

I have left the Foundation to be run by you, Toby and Eleanor. I know it is in safe hands I imagine you will want to do something to support the homeless - those people have been more of a family to you than I ever was, for all that I tried. If I could beg one favour, there's a young man called Zach - my housekeeper's son - who has had his own brushes with homelessness and addiction and who stuck his neck out for me recently to help with a tricky problem. He needs a job with prospects and people who believe in him.

There are some boxes on my bed with mementos from a remarkable woman, Annie, together with another letter that explains her story to the best of my ability. It is such a sadness that you and Toby never got to meet her, I feel sure that you would have loved her.

I am so sorry that we never got to know each other properly and were deliberately misled, and encouraged in our mutual misunderstanding. I want you to know that I admire you and wish that we could have been friends.

Be happy and take good care of yourself,

Marjorie

Acknowledgements

Sarah (S.J.) Higbee, Paula Glenister, and all the past and present members of the Northbrook College Tuesday afternoon Creative Writing class, for their support, advice and encouragement.

My patient, long-suffering friends for listening to me whingeing on about my characters not behaving themselves, making suggestions and generally being a little bit brilliant: Jan and Sally.

To all the people who read the drafts and offered me advice, none of which was to go and lie down until the urge to write had passed … and proofreading!: Jacqui, Gill, Kate, Rosie, Kate and Shelley.

Love and thanks to my niece, Steph, for never batting an eyelid at my numerous questions about the best ways to drug and/or kill people. And still letting me see Will and The Ginger One! Happy **th birthday!!!!!

And finally to my adults, Georgia, Sylas and Hector, for being awesome human beings. Every day you make me proud and I love you guys so much xxx

Caron Garrod, April 2020

Printed in Great Britain
by Amazon

51667940R00151